rage

INHERITED SIN, BOOK 1

ROSE VOHS

First edition, 2026

Editing by: The Golden Editorial, LLC

Cover design by: Nicole Berger of NKB Art + Illustration, LLC

Published by: Rose Vohs

For information, contact Rose Vohs via www.rosevohs.com

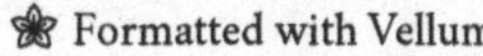

This is a work of fiction. Names, characters, places, and incidents are either the products of the author's imagination or used fictitiously. Any resemblance to actual persons, living or dead, events, or locales is entirely coincidental.

First edition, 2026

Editing by: The Golden [illegible] LLC

Cover design by: Nicole Berger, [illegible] Art & Illustration, LLC

Published by Rose Vohs

For information, contact Rose Vohs at www.rosevohs.com

Formatted with Vellum

content and trigger warnings

RAGE addresses themes of sexual assault (referenced), human trafficking, violence, misogyny, abuse of power, and trauma. This is a story about survival, anger, and justice, but it does not shy away from the realities that create them.

Reader discretion is advised.

dedication

For those who were blamed instead of believed.

For those taught to survive quietly
while predators thrived loudly.

May the rage you inherited
finally be unleashed.

May those who profited from our pain
finally learn what it costs.

PROLOGUE

Catherine, Age 15

17 years ago

Is that the sound of a helicopter? Are they here to take me?

I've never left the island, but I've always wanted to leave this hellish place. Of course, the first time I might get a chance, I'm barely able to keep my eyes open.

I don't know how much time has passed since I was last awake. Muted voices argue around me, but I can't tell what is going on.

Ow, ouch, fuck, I'm in so much pain. *Why does it hurt so bad?*

Sophie is yelling but I can't make out what she's saying. Something about my dad overreacting—"too big of a risk."

Of course, that woman can't be bothered to care. She's the actual worst. Why is Dad still with her? I hate her. We all hate her. Can't he see that she is horrible?

I can't stop shivering.

Where am I? Who's crying? Is that Elizabeth? Victoria needs

to take her away; she's too young to see this. I'm bleeding so much, it's going to freak her out.

I chuckle in delirium at our stupid names. "We named you after royalty, now act like it," Dad and Sophie always say. As if my sisters and I care about being proper young ladies.

For who? Them? The Volkovs? We never get to see anyone out here. People come and go, but we get hidden away in the bunker, never to be seen.

Well, not always.

Sophie made me think it was such an honor. I remember being so excited when she told me I got to spend time with someone besides my sisters, like a playdate.

I tilt my head side to side, watching the blonde catch the light. It doesn't look like me. That's the point.

Elizabeth and Victoria burst in without knocking, a familiar hurricane of limbs and laughter.

Elizabeth freezes first. "Oh my gosh. Catherine. Your hair."

I smile at my reflection. "I know. Isn't it great?"

My voice sounds steadier than I feel.

Victoria's expression doesn't change. It never really does. "Dad's going to hate it."

"So?" I say, sharper than intended.

That gets them both. Elizabeth bites her lip, like she's trying to decide whether this is exciting or a mistake.

Victoria crosses her arms. "You can't trust Sophie," she says. "If she let you do this, there's a reason."

I roll my eyes. "I know. I'm using her. I wanted a change." I flick a strand of blonde between my fingers. "You know I hate the red."

Elizabeth blinks. "You do?"

I shrug. "It's too much."

Silence stretches, thin and strange.

"I'm fifteen," I add. "Dad will just have to get over it."

Victoria doesn't argue. She just watches me in the mirror, like she's already counting the cost.

I'm so stupid. I should have known better.

A stabbing pain emanates from my core.

Someone enters the room. I nearly don't catch the word "surgery."

Surgery? Where?

I'm trying to say that I don't want surgery when someone grabs my hand.

"Catherine, darling, we have a surgeon on the way, okay?" It's Dad. "You're going to be okay. Who did this to you? Tell me, honey. Was it Junior?"

He thinks Junior did this to me?

I knew Sophie hadn't told him, but surely now she'd have to admit what she did. Right? What *they* did…

I try to find my voice. It's so hard.

"Troy. Magnus Troy. He and Sophie…"

My dad's eyes go wide, his face pales, but he doesn't speak.

Dad, did you hear me?

As he looks at me, I know he doesn't want to believe me. I know he's ready to tell me I'm lying. He's battling what he knows to be true against what he wishes was not true. He's never been overly affectionate with us. Not like dads we see on TV, but he's always cared, been kind—not at all what you'd expect from a monster.

I've come to learn he's dangerous in other ways. Quiet, dark ways that shouldn't exist.

"The blonde hair," he says with a menacing expression.

My chin wobbles as I tilt it to confirm.

He stands and paces the room, before leaving altogether without a word.

Drained of energy, my eyes fall shut as my world fades to black.

ONE

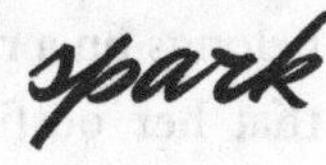

Enzo

Present, Thursday Evening, Day 1

I hate this side of town—too clean, too smug—but if you want to make real money in DC, you drink with the politicians who sell their souls by the glass. And if you want to control and launder all the illegal money that gets funneled to their pockets, you own the bar where those politicians like to let loose.

I step out from the back room of The Vault, the bar my family has owned for generations, just two blocks from 1600 Pennsylvania Avenue. I lock eyes with Niko, my head of security, and give him a nod to let him know I'm ready. He'll radio my driver, Luca.

I navigate the polished chaos of the main room with purpose, weaving between booths, clinking crystal, and whispered conversations. I stride past women and men who pretend not to notice me, but the low light on the dark mahogany tables doesn't hide the eyes that follow as I pass. At six feet and three inches tall, I'm hard to miss.

I catch sight of bright red hair and stop in my tracks.

All the senses on my body ignite. I turn slowly to face the stunning redhead sitting at the bar.

Who is she? I've never seen her here. She certainly looks like a DC type. She's wearing a jade green jumpsuit that looks like it belongs on a red carpet, not a bar stool. Even from here, I can see that her outfit makes her eyes pop. She exudes power, confidence, and sex appeal.

Is that Speaker Max McCarter she's sitting with? That piques my interest.

I've clearly been staring too long, because her head turns, and she makes eye contact with me. It lasts only a moment before she turns back to McCarter.

Well, that won't do. I need her eyes back on me. I need to know her name. I need...*more.*

I should not walk over there. McCarter would not like it known that we know each other, but I seem to be walking over there against my will.

McCarter turns to see what or who caught his guest's eye—his expression easy, eyes bright with mischief—until they land on me. His eyes widen, the mask faltering for the briefest moment.

"Good evening. Speaker Max McCarter, right?" I ask, pretending we don't know each other. I surprise even myself. I wish I could explain it. I can't. I just know I need to find out who this woman is.

"Yes, hi." McCarter's confusion is apparent as he shakes my hand.

"I'm Enzo Luciano. My family and I own this fine establishment."

They both look at me like I have three heads.

It's official, I've lost my damn mind. The Luciano family

owning The Vault is one of those horribly kept secrets. Everyone knows, but no one talks about it. We can't have Washington elites frequenting a mafia-owned bar "knowingly." Even if it is where they all come to get money laundered, unregistered weapons, extra protection, and various other illegal needs met.

Standing next to her, every part of my body feels chaotic and out of control. It feels like a spike of adrenaline has caused my pulse to race and my nerves to light on fire. I've never had a physical reaction like this to another person.

"I wanted to introduce myself and ensure you are both being taken care of." I motion to the bartender to get them another round. It's clear I'm grasping at straws.

The redhead barely acknowledges my existence.

I turn to shake her hand next, fooling no one as I ask, "And who is this lovely woman joining you tonight?"

She doesn't extend her hand to shake mine; she tilts her head in challenge. "And why would you want to know that, Mr. Luciano?" Her raspy voice is intoxicating.

I offer a slow, charming grin. "Enzo. Please, call me Enzo. Mr. Luciano was my father." I wait for the softening—the smile that usually comes when I try to endear people with this line.

It doesn't come. She remains unaffected.

"I don't think I've ever seen you at my bar, and I make a point of knowing our VIPs. I assume if you're here with the Speaker, I need to ensure my staff knows to take care of you."

I'm just taking care of a VIP in my bar, that makes sense. I tell myself this isn't simply about attraction—something is off. My instincts are screaming, and they've never been wrong. I need to know who she is and what she's doing here with McCarter. Yes, that's it. It has nothing to do with the fact that my pulse hasn't slowed since I saw her from across the room.

She finally smiles and extends her hand. "Well, I am certainly not the VIP that the Speaker is, just a lowly overworked and underpaid Washington staffer." She pretends to defer to McCarter, but anyone who knows anything sees exactly who is in charge in their dynamic. And it's not him.

At her touch, my skin sparks. Every neuron in my body wants more contact in more places. But too soon, she pulls her hand away.

"Yes, we are here on business." McCarter interrupts, with a very clear undertone that it's time for me to leave. Normally, I'd take his lead and be on my way, but I can't leave yet. I don't have her name.

"Of course. Have the two of you eaten? Can I send out any food?" I ask as the bartender delivers their next round. "Caleb, send me the bill for the Speaker and his guest, please."

"Thank you so much, Mr. Luciano—" McCarter says with a curt politeness.

"Enzo. Call me Enzo, I insist."

He continues, "Of course. No need for food, though, Miss Saint James and I are almost done here. We'll finish this round and get out of your hair."

Miss Saint James. Her name floats like poetry in my mind as I commit it to memory. And it tells me several things I need to know right now. He said "Miss," not "Mrs." Very important. And Saint James is not likely to be a common name on the Hill, so she will be easily identified by my team.

Lastly, the name is charming, regal, graceful, even.

Which makes it a lie. No one this composed—this precise and calculating—is just a demure staffer in DC.

No. She's not *just* anything. She's strategy in stilettos.

I know danger when I see it. And Miss Saint James is the epitome of danger.

"Take your time," I respond. "It was a pleasure. Caleb will see to you." I step back, mask back in place.

The way she returns to McCarter without another glance my way tells me we are both wearing masks tonight.

I dial my sister as I step outside.

Niko follows me out the door, where Luca is waiting by the car.

Eva picks up on the third ring, as I settle inside the backseat. "Hey bro, heading home?"

"Yeah, I finished up with the governor and I'm heading home now. I need you to do your magic and get me a file on someone."

"Of course. What's the name?" she asks.

"Last name Saint James. She was here tonight with Speaker McCarter. She said she was a DC staffer."

The clicking of Eva typing at a keyboard filters through the other end of the line. "Have anything else for me to go on?"

"I don't know if she works in the Speaker's office, or somewhere else. She's either late twenties or early thirties. Tall, bright red hair, green eyes."

"Wait... Is this for work? Or is this some woman you're trying to pick up?" Eva teases.

"Oh, come on. When have I ever had to do such a thing?"

Eva laughs. "Oh right, I forgot, women just *throw* themselves at you."

My sister likes to tease me about how little I date. I try to play it off like I'm just a typical thirty-something billionaire, not looking for anything serious. The truth is a little more complicated than that.

Eva is right that women do throw themselves at me. And I have taken some to bed, but in the decade since my parents died, I've carried an anvil-sized weight on my chest that rarely goes away. The anxiety and stress make it hard for me to let go and sex has never been the release I need it to be. It has never been as pleasurable for me as everyone else claims. The truth is, after a few years of trying to feel "normal," it stopped being worth the hassle. I have too much to do anyway.

Maybe if women made my body spark like Miss Saint James just did, I'd feel differently. Is this what attraction feels like? Is it lust? No doubt about that. She's easily the most beautiful woman I've ever seen in real life.

"No, this isn't for personal reasons, E. Let's just call it a hunch. Think you can find out who she is?"

"Don't insult me. I'll see you when you get home." Eva hangs up.

I immediately call Hudson. My best friend answers on the first ring. "Hey. I just left The Vault. I'm heading home. I'm calling because I may need FBI eyes on someone I asked Eva to track."

"Big fish?" he asks.

"Hard to tell. Could be nothing, but seems like something."

"Sounds vague and illegal. I like it. Have E send me what she finds."

"Of course. Thanks. What are you up to tonight?"

Hudson and I catch up on my drive home. He plans to go to one of my underground casinos. I accuse him of only going there in hopes of running into this woman he's been hooking up with, a "smoke show" he's been talking about for the better part of a year now. He admits I'm right.

He's always asking me to join him, but it's not my idea of a good time. I'm in the casino business for the money, and it's my house that always wins.

Hudson and I have been best friends since we were kids. He's more like a brother to Eva and me than a friend. He had a single mom who wasn't around a lot. My parents took him under their wing when it became clear he and I were attached at the hip. He fit into our family seamlessly.

It was my dad's idea for him to go into the FBI. Hudson

wanted to work for our family's business, but Dad decided that he wanted a man inside the Bureau. Hudson was honored my dad wanted it to be him, and that was that.

Dad wasn't wrong—having an inside man with family loyalty has kept us out of a lot of trouble. It just means Hudson has to live a double life and I'm constantly worried about his safety. It also means Hudson and I can never be seen together in public. That didn't seem like a big deal at the time, but it sucks that a simple invite to meet him out gambling is never a real offer; just an ongoing inside joke in a life that isn't really all that funny.

When Hudson and I end our call, my mind immediately returns to the redhead. The beauty at my bar was correct: She's not a DC VIP. If she were, I'd already have a file on her. Knowing the major players in this town is my business. But sitting at my bar with the Speaker of the House? That's not a nobody.

The true power players in DC don't make headlines. No, they make deals in the shadows. And something tells me she's playing chess while everyone else is stuck on checkers.

TWO

verdict

Pippa

Thursday Evening, Day 1

The moment Enzo Luciano disappears into the swirl of bodies and bourbon, my pulse spikes like a warning flare. That wasn't a casual introduction. That was a power play—smooth, deliberate, dangerous. And for one dizzy second, it worked.

It wasn't his muscular frame, the sharp suit, the chiseled jaw, or the way his voice dragged over my name like soulful jazz. No, of course not—I don't let men affect me like that. The issue was his presence. He wanted me to know I was on his radar. And *fuck*, that is a problem.

I knew who he was before his little introduction. Of course I did. We've got files on every mafia boss in the Americas and Eastern Europe, and Enzo Luciano's file is as thick as they come. But nothing could have prepared me for the reality of him. Too tall, too close, too encompassing, and way too focused on me.

We've made it a point to not cross paths with men like him.

Staying off the radar of the mafia bosses is half the job, but McCarter insisted on coming here tonight. In a place this size, I assumed I could go unnoticed. So why the hell did it feel like he just zeroed in on me like I was his mark?

I excuse myself with a polite smile and some throwaway line about "freshening up." The Speaker barely notices. I could tell him I'm stepping out to join his wife for an orgy, and he'd just smile and adjust his cufflinks. The man is basically deaf and still recovering from a recent stroke. How men of his age and health are allowed to run this country, I'll never understand.

The second I hit the hallway, I ditch the smile. My heels echo against the marble tiles on my way to the private bathroom tucked behind the wine walls on display. As soon as the door closes, I press two fingers to the tiny mic tucked under my hairline, ensuring it's still in place. I then move my fingers further down my hairline, feeling the faint ridge where the tracker sits. Small as a grain of rice, big enough to find a sister in trouble.

"Code Janice," I whisper.

The crackle of the device fills my ear briefly.

"Talk to me," Jules cuts in, voice low and steady.

I lean over the sink, staring down at my trembling fingers. "What do you make of that interaction with Luciano?"

"Okay, yeah. That was unexpected," Luna says, voice light but laced with concern. "Enzo Luciano isn't known for making small talk with strangers. Especially not when they're sitting with the Speaker of the House, who is *definitely* on his client roster. I can't imagine they are supposed to be seen together in public."

Luna verbally processes. Usually, it's helpful. Right now, I feel like she's pointing out all the reasons for me to be worried, spiking my anxiety.

"But," Luna continues, "he didn't challenge you or make a scene. He pretended not to know McCarter. To be honest, he seemed a bit strained. Probably flustered by your swagger."

"I told you that jumpsuit was a power move," Jules jokes. "The man looked like he forgot how to breathe."

The air feels heavier when I exhale, like it now carries everything I've been holding in. Enzo Luciano unnerved me and I can't pinpoint why. "You think I should abort?"

"No," Jules says sharply. "He's got your last name and a gut feeling. That's not enough. And Luna has eyes on him; he's already left. I've got eyes on McCarter. Everything is going as planned."

"And the tox panel will be clean—you made the compound yourself," Luna reminds me. "We've run every angle. McCarter's heart failure won't happen for a week, and it will look textbook."

"This is our best shot. Getting back on McCarter's calendar will be suspicious." Jules is firmer. "It's taken almost a year to get this kind of unfettered access to him. Plus, the gala is only a month away."

Fuck, she's right. I know she's right. It's not like me to second-guess a plan, especially not mid-op like this. I take a few deep breaths. Slow. Measured. I run cold water over my wrists to cool my temperature. Collected, I look up into the mirror and square my shoulders. I'm not letting some GQ mobster shake me with a lingering handshake and eye contact. *I'm Pippa fucking Saint James.*

"Copy that," I whisper. "Going back in."

A pep talk from my sisters was exactly what I needed. My center of gravity snaps back in place. Nothing about tonight will trace back to us. It never does. We're too careful about that.

He just got under my skin. That's all it is—too much intensity in those dark eyes, too much heat in that look. Probably just his damn dangerous bad-boy look wrapped in a well-tailored suit. Every woman's wet dream, mine included.

I return to the bar, calm disguise firmly back in place. "Ready to get out of here?" I ask. I slip my hand onto McCarter's arm with a level of comfort that makes us look way more intimate than we really are.

He downs the last of his drink and stands. "I thought you'd never ask."

"Hotel's just around the corner," I say, practiced and effortless.

"Convenient," he mutters with a smirk, following my lead.

I just smile demurely, selling the desire.

He believes young women want him for his power, his connections, his money. I am well-rehearsed in selling men like him that illusion. But I know most of the women in his orbit aren't choosing him; they are trying to survive him. Tonight is only "convenient" for the girls and boys who'll never find themselves locked in his basement ever again.

Because after tonight, Speaker Max McCarter's reign of secret terror ends.

Moments later, we arrive at the hotel. My jade green jumpsuit now unzipped halfway in the front to tease. His eyes are glued to my chest like I'm a prize he already believes he owns.

Inside the hotel suite, I slide out of the jumpsuit in one smooth motion, revealing a matching green lace bra and panty set. "Sit," I command, pointing to the edge of the bed.

McCarter obeys.

I trail my fingers up his chest as I lean down to whisper, "No touching. Not yet."

His breath stutters.

Good. I pull a deep-green silk tie from my clutch, one that matches the jumpsuit and lingerie. I tie his wrists to the headboard, slow and deliberate.

He chuckles, clearly turned on by the charade of losing control.

I take my time being seductive and distracting as I pour him a drink. Can't let him see what I'm really doing. He's too distracted by my heels, lingerie, and sensual movements to notice much. Plus, he must be almost blind at this point.

This man is old enough to be my grandfather and is still convinced he's irresistible. Pathetic, really. But the delusion works in my favor because men like him never see the predator in their midst—only the prey they mistake me to be.

"Drink," I say, as I tip the glass of dark liquor laced with a potent paralytic down his throat. Tasteless. Fast-acting. Perfected in my own lab.

The Speaker gulps it greedily, high on the power he thinks he has. Within minutes, the muscles in his arms go slack. His smile fades. Confusion flickers in his eyes. "What the hell is this?" he slurs.

I slide onto the bed beside him; all warmth drained from my smile. "I know you don't know who I am. That's okay, you don't need to. But Jared Whiteman made sure I knew who you were. Every *dirty* little detail."

Thank you, Daddy Dearest.

McCarter's eyes widen. He panics, but he's trapped behind a body that won't respond.

"Do you even remember your trips to Maribel Island? It must seem so long ago now. I'm sure you thought all your secrets died with him in that jail cell, didn't you?" I ask, brushing a hand down his arm like a lover.

"You and Jared were such good friends. Living that party life, never worried about any consequences, right? Untouchable. So many powerful men coming and going. Did you ever stop to wonder about the girls funneled in and out of the island?" I lean in, my voice tightening. "Did you care what you were stealing from them?"

I see it hit, the moment he understands. I pause for dramatic effect. Letting the words sink in. I avoid flashbacks to the island, faintly touching my abdomen where the physical scar has long faded. The touch anchors my mission, reminds me to stay grounded in the present.

McCarter isn't my first mark from Maribel Island. But he's the move that forces Magnus Troy into play.

"Of course not. You were owed it, weren't you? That's what Jared and Sophie made you believe. That men like you deserve anything they want." I laugh.

If only those naïve, powerful men understood the game Jared and Sophie were *really* playing. They were so evil, but *fuck*, they were smart. When you hold the dirtiest secrets of the most powerful men in the world, *you're* the one with all the power.

McCarter can't move, can't speak, but his eyes are frantic now, pleading.

I retrieve the syringe from my purse and gently lift his leg. The needle slides under the crease at the base of his toes, into a patch of thin, wrinkled, forgotten skin. The dose is precise. The effect untraceable. His end has already begun.

He'll wake up in a few hours, groggy, feeling slightly hungover. He won't remember anything that happened after we left the bar. But his heart? It's already on the countdown.

He won't remember what I said, but my words weren't really for him—they were for me.

I despise Dad and Sophie for all the pain and suffering they caused. I wasn't surprised—or even all that sad—when he died in that jail cell fifteen years ago. Hundreds of powerful men were terrified he would reveal their secrets. And they believed killing him would bury the horrors of their actions.

There's a quiet poetry in knowing those secrets were never theirs to destroy.

My sisters and I have spent the last eight years dismantling the men who used their money and power to abuse children on a private island under Jared Whiteman's protection. We've hidden in plain sight, and they don't even know we exist. Dad's only true gift to us was our anonymity.

I untie McCarter's wrists, smooth his shirt, and straighten the covers like a hotel maid. It'll look like he passed out. It'll feel like a wild night he can't quite remember, but in a week, he'll be dead.

And in that week, Luna will expose his dirtiest secrets to the public. If the media catches the trend again, headlines will credit a secret, dark-web group they've nicknamed TruthDrop. Some of the media and law enforcement have caught on enough to know these leaks happen intentionally but somehow keep missing that the men always die of natural causes soon after.

Which means our plan is still effective.

I redress, gather my belongings, and wipe my fingerprints. I confirm my extraction with my sisters. We sign off.

We are never seen in public together. No one can know our connection.

As I walk down the sidewalk, a few blocks from the hotel now, my adrenaline is still high, blood pumping loudly in my ears. I need something to take the edge off and I know just the place.

Should I go to another Luciano establishment tonight? Probably not. But I'm always a little reckless after working my marks. I've been increasingly reckless as the gala approaches, come to think of it. My biggest target mere weeks away.

Playing cards at the underground casino at Club14 has a way of calming my nerves. Besides, I've never seen Enzo there.

I can't seem to talk myself out of going. Something about the lies people tell when money's on the table makes me feel right at home. Because no one bluffs better than a girl raised in silence and motivated by vengeance.

THREE

kismet

Hudson

Thursday Evening, Day 1

The only thing worse than the cards in my damned hand right now is my shit luck tonight—and that's saying something. I'd be more annoyed about losing my money if I didn't know it was lining my best friend's pockets and would eventually find its way back to me. Technically, I'm in his employ, as well as the government's.

If anyone from law enforcement recognized me here, they'd assume I was on a case. Heading the organized crime unit at the FBI has that effect. It's my actual job to have a pulse on the illegal establishments of men like Enzo Luciano. That must be why I'm always in a good mood at this underground casino—I can't fucking lose. I always have fun blowing off steam at the tables and I never go home alone. Plenty of DC's finest women and men frequent this establishment, and most are willing to warm my bed.

I scan the room to see who piques my interest for the evening, and as if on cue, in walks the woman who's occupied my dirty thoughts for the past year. Wild, bright red hair, legs for days, a walk like she owns the room, the floor, and the air we all breathe.

Suddenly, I'm all in again, because my luck just turned around.

The woman calls herself *Jane*. We both know that's bullshit, but I don't care. My name isn't John, either, and she knows that, too. After the nights we've shared, I'd let her tell me sweet lies forever.

When we make eye contact, she smiles and heads my way.

I pick up my burner phone and shoot a quick text to Enzo, letting the fucker know he didn't jinx me and my Jane just arrived.

My Jane? Where the fuck did that come from?

Enzo and Eva have teased me relentlessly about my obsession with this damned woman, but I enjoy letting them. Because it means I get to talk about her, think about her, dream about her.

"Hey, John. How's the table treating you tonight?" Jane asks as she sits across from me.

All the men stop and stare. I don't blame them. She's a stunner, impossible to overlook. And Christ, tonight she's wearing black, painted-on jeans, a sheer black top that allows her red-lace bra to peek through, and matching red heels that look like sin on stilts.

"I've been losing all night, Jane, but you always have a way of turning my luck around," I say with a seductive smile as I look her up and down, unapologetically.

She winks at me. "Good, I was hoping you weren't leaving just yet."

"No chance of that now."

We share a knowing smile while the dealer deals her in.

She's got that edge tonight, like she often does. Jane shows up here once a month or so ready for danger. High-limit poker only being the start of what she needs to let loose. I may not know her real name, what she does for a living, or a damned personal detail about her…but I can read her body like a well-loved book.

And she's amped tonight.

Fuck yeah. I'm here to help, beautiful.

She's one of the first people in a long time who makes me want to ask more questions. To get to know the *real* her. Given my life as an FBI agent on the inside for the Italian mob, I don't let anyone get close. Evidently, neither does she, because after a dozen or so hookups that live rent-free in my brain, I know nothing about her. *Nothing*. And I work for the FBI *and* the mob, for Christ's sake.

It's not that I haven't tried, but she has never once given me any information—not a single tell. Which means whatever she is hiding is more interesting than I can probably imagine. And my imagination is very fucking vivid.

Jane wins the first few hands. While I'm still losing, my improved mood is worth the ante. Her poker game reflects her persona: calculated, risky, and impossible to ignore. The table grumbles, guys cash out, but me? My ass is staying right here.

"Well, look at you, Jane. Walking in and bleeding these poor bastards dry. Where's your sense of mercy?" I grin, leaning back casually, as if I'm not wildly turned on.

"You know I don't do mercy," she says, licking her thumb before spreading her cards to see what she was dealt. "Especially not for men."

"No, gorgeous, mercy definitely isn't in your DNA. It's one of my favorite things about you." I wink. "So how long do I have to sit here losing my money before you're ready for your next release?"

That gets me a small smile. Damn if that tilt of her lips doesn't send a jolt right to my crotch. *Fuck*.

"Depends. I'm staying right here until I see a better offer on the table." Her voice deepens to show she definitely wants me to give her that reason.

"I mean, I can offer alcohol, bad decisions, and a solid seven out of ten performance. Eight if you do most of the work."

She graces me with a real deal laugh.

Victory.

"You're lucky I have a thing for hot men with a sense of humor."

"And you're lucky I have no fucking shame. So, what do you say? Cash out while you're ahead, and we take this party somewhere with fewer clothes?"

She quirks a brow. "Just us tonight? Or do we want to find a third? Not that guy from last time!" she demands with a stern look in my direction.

"Hey, don't knock Eric. He made waffles after. Very thoughtful," I joke.

She laughs. "The waffles weren't *that* good. He was way more into you than me." She pushes her chips in to cash out. "Let's go, John. Before I start feeling generous and let these guys win one."

"Too late, sweetheart. You already let us all win just by showing up." I'm nothing if not a shameless flirt.

"Stop while you're ahead. And don't call me 'sweetheart' again," she feigns annoyance.

I grin as we step into the hallway. "Fine. What should I call you when you're moaning my name in twenty minutes?"

She tosses a smirk over her shoulder. "Lucky."

Jane takes me to her sleek Logan Circle condo just five minutes from the casino. Exposed brick, modern fixtures, just enough charm to sell the lie that she lives here. I know very little about this woman, but I know this is more of a crash pad than a primary residence.

We've used this apartment a few times to hook up—when we aren't going to someone else's place or a hotel. I know there isn't one personal detail behind these walls. If there were, I sure as hell would have found them by now.

As she punches in the code to the building's front door, my mouth finds her neck and my hands move to her hips. My brain is already short-circuiting.

Once the elevator doors close, I have her against the back wall. We are surrounded by mirrors as we ascend, and the 360-degree view of our bodies only increases my desire.

"I don't know how to keep my damned hands to myself when you're wearing a red lacy bra as a top, Jane." I groan as I move my mouth to her cleavage over her shirt.

"I have a blouse over the bra," she says as she nips my ear in return.

"This see-through number sure as shit doesn't count."

"Mm, good point. We should probably take it off." She moans. "Think you can hold off 'til we're in the privacy of my apartment? Or should we just get started right here in the elevator?"

Ping!

"Saved by the bell. Not sure I'm in the mood for anyone else to see these perfect tits tonight, so hurry up and open that fucking door." I slap her ass playfully as she unlocks the door. Inside, I turn us so her back is against the now-closed door. My mouth crashes into her, all tongue and tension. I pull off her top, then my own, roaming her body with my hands and mouth in between.

She pushes me down the hall to the bedroom and shoves me onto the bed. She climbs on top, but I flip us.

"As much as I fucking love to watch you take control, gorgeous, tonight I want to hear how many different ways I can make you say my name."

"I don't even know your real name." Her laugh is soft and gravelly.

I look up, a wicked grin already forming. "John has never

disappointed and he won't start tonight," I say as I pull her jeans down. "Jesus, I knew it'd be a matching set, but what are these sexy panties? Are you trying to kill me?" I groan at the sight of her. I strip her jeans the rest of the way off, but I slide her heels back on.

Fuck. I have a thing for heels. "As much as I need to be inside you, I've been dreaming about the taste of your pussy," I tell her as I slide her red lace panties aside, letting my hands linger, teasing her inner thighs.

"You dream of me, John? That sounds wildly inappropriate," she whispers, already breathless.

"Mm, my dreams *are* wildly inappropriate," I murmur. My tongue darts out, lapping up her arousal mid-sentence.

She moans loudly, and the sound alone nearly undoes me.

"Jane, baby, all this wetness for me?"

She mumbles her agreement, then gasps. "John! Fuck, that feels so good. Your mouth is fucking magic."

I don't slow. I work her right to the edge, then slide two fingers inside, pumping steadily.

Her noises are pure music. "Yes. I'm so close. Keep doing that. *Fuck*," she moans.

I add my thumb to her back entrance, pressing just enough. Exactly the way I know sends her over every time.

She cries out, letting me know she's coming.

I stay right there, holding her through it.

"Damn, gorgeous," I say when she finally comes down, "I've missed the sounds you make when you're coming on my tongue." I grab my wallet, kick my pants down, and roll on a condom. "Now get those sexy-as-fuck legs in the air like you know I like."

She lifts them like a good girl.

I push her thong aside, driving into her in one hard, fast thrust. I'm just as desperate to be inside her as she is to have me there. I know I'm a bigger guy, and between my size and the

Jacob's ladder piercings lining my shaft, there's an edge of pain I know she craves. I grip her thighs and thrust harder, watching her take every inch. I kiss up her legs, licking and nibbling as I go.

"God, look at you in this red lingerie set and these matching fucking heels." I pick up speed. "Did you wear this hoping you might see me tonight, Jane?"

"Mm…maybe," she whispers. She starts massaging her breasts over her bra. "Remind me," she says innocently, "do you like heels?"

I lean down, pull her bra cups down with one hand, and pinch her nipples, one at a time, watching the pleasure ripple through her. "My exact words the first night we met," I say slowly, humming, "were, 'Damn, gorgeous, tall women in heels are my kryptonite. Are you trying to kill me?'"

"Oh, yeah," she says, pressing one heel into my chest just enough to sting, "that does sound familiar." She drags her heel down my chest, then does the same with the other before wrapping her legs around my hips.

I gasp, the pain only fueling the pleasure. She leans up, kissing my stomach and chest. "And I remember telling you I'd only try to kill you if you deserved it."

"Turn over and put that sexy ass up for me. Now," I command.

She obeys. I slap her ass a few times playfully, on the edge of pain—exactly how she likes it. I knead her ass roughly, then thrust back into her.

"Fuck, Jane," I growl, picking up speed.

"Yes. Fuck. Yes. I'm close again," she mumbles.

"Good," I say. "Rub that greedy clit of yours and come on my cock, Jane. Now." My voice is rough, my pace relentless.

She does exactly what I tell her. When I add pressure to her back entrance again, she comes even harder.

I follow moments later, chasing my own release.

We collapse into each other, both of us sweaty, breathless, and spent.

I finally pull away. "I'll get us some water. We can rest for a few minutes, then I'll be ready again. If you're going to make me wait this damned long between nights together, I'm just getting started, Jane."

After very little sleep last night—thank you, Jane—I'm downing a second cup of coffee. I have a huge smile on my face as I say hellos and good mornings to my colleagues at FBI headquarters and make my way to my desk.

"That smile is very telling," Stone says as he approaches my desk. Marcus Stone and I are both Assistant Directors. He leads the anti-trafficking unit. We often work together on cases and share resources and agents, given that anti-trafficking and organized crime often overlap. He's a good guy—a little square, but easy to work with. A real Bureau guy through and through.

"I have no idea what you're talking about, Stone," I respond with a smirk.

"Oh, to be single again, my friend," he says wryly. "Don't misunderstand me, I don't need to be single, but to be kid-free? That smile on your face is a smile of a guy who wasn't cockblocked by his kids last night."

We both chuckle.

"I will neither confirm nor deny."

"That's all the confirmation I need." He laughs. "Listen, quick question: is Steele almost wrapped on your laundering case with the Donovan clan?"

Ten years have passed since Ciara Donovan chose Konstantin Volkov Junior over her fiancé, Enzo Luciano. That single decision ignited a war between the Russian, Irish, and Italian mob families, leading to the deaths of the heads of each family—including Enzo and Eva's parents, the only real parents I ever knew.

Micky Donovan is dead now. Ciara escaped back to Ireland. She never married that asshole, Junior, after all. But the Donovan and Volkov names still crawl under my skin, making my blood boil.

"Yup, the Donovan case goes to the prosecutor's office tomorrow. I believe Steele is almost done. I was about to find her, actually, so I can confirm. You need our best hacker?"

"Yeah, something landed on my desk last night I want her eyes on."

"No problem, man. I'll send her your way."

"Appreciate it. And when you're ready to let a married father of three live vicariously through your exploits, you know where to find me."

"You know I don't kiss and tell, Stone."

"I know you don't and it drives me *crazy*. A guy that looks like you…I can't even imagine, man."

I laugh and stand as he walks away. I need to speak to the woman in question. Luna Steele is indeed the FBI's best hacker. We recruited her about nine years ago when she was only nineteen. I've been lucky enough to work with her the past five years. To describe her as a hacker isn't even fair—she's a literal magician.

When I approach her desk, she's typing away, zoned in. I always get a kick out of seeing her work. She's chaos in action. Her wild, curly hair is always pulled into a messy bun. She wears oversized, bright-pink glasses and is always sporting some sort of 90s pop-culture tee or neon top. Her personality can only be described as sunshine incarnate.

"Whatcha working on, kid?"

She startles and her eyes snap up to me. "Hey, Cross. Wrapping the last reports for the Donovan case while I run some backend queries on some outstanding dark-web cases we've been looking into."

I lean a hip against the edge of her desk. "All in a day's work for you. How ya been?"

"Good. Busy. Late night. You?"

"Same," I answer, hiding a small smile thinking of my night with Jane. "It's about time I get you and your team out for another night at the bowling alley. I need my damned dignity back."

"That was all them, I'm as hopeless as you and Stone. I much prefer darts or pool."

"Oh, trust me, I remember! I've yet to win a single game against you."

We both laugh.

"Let me guess: You're here because the mob stopped returning your calls?"

I snort. "Exactly. I figured I'd send our best after them instead. And spoiler alert, that's you."

She gestures for me to continue, faux-humble. "Flattery will get you everywhere, please continue."

"Looks like Stone has something he needs your help on. As soon as you're wrapped on Donovan, go ahead and check in with him. Also, I've got someone I need you to look into—something politics-adjacent. Could be nothing, but a name landed on my desk that I need more info on. Should be a quick file pull."

Her brow quirks. Politics and organized crime have a long, intimate history in this city. "Go on," she says. "You have effectively piqued my curiosity."

"Pippa Saint James. She's an executive assistant in Senator Lowell Cramden's office."

For a fraction of a second, she looks blindsided. All the color drains from her face, and she's slow to respond. Luna Steele doesn't get flustered—her mind moves too fast to pause on anything as inconvenient as nerves.

"Pippa Saint James," I say again, casually. "Is that a name you recognize? I'm tracking a lead. She or Cramden might have some overlap on a case I'm working."

There it is again, just a flicker. Too quick for anyone else to notice.

I tilt my head. "You okay?"

Her expression smooths back into place. She looks up at me. "Yeah—I mean—that name! Pippa?" She forces a laugh. "Just has me picturing royalty, someone with pearls and a clipboard. Like she was born in a tiara, sipping tea while delegating world peace. Probably with a swan as a pet."

I hold her gaze a beat longer than necessary. Five years working together has taught me Luna's tells, and she was definitely caught off guard by my request and I clocked it.

I chuckle to put her back at ease. I'm not pursuing this right now. "Something tells me pearls aren't your thing."

"Never! Opal is too neutral of a color for me, you know that."

"Good point. Besides, I like your bright wardrobe, brings some life to this place! Text me if you find anything. I owe you a coffee."

"More than a coffee! Talk to Hale about getting me a raise, Cross." An ongoing bit.

"If anyone deserves it, it's you, Steele," I say as I leave her desk.

I file her reaction where I keep things I don't yet understand but know better than to ignore. Luna Steele is fast, composed, and careful. So, when something slips, it matters. She's definitely heard of—or even knows—Pippa Saint James.

I'll see what lands on my desk later today. And I'll be paying attention to what doesn't.

FOUR

Pippa

Friday Afternoon, Day 2

Senator Cramden's office smells like burnt coffee and desperate ambition. The lights are too bright, the air too cold, and the carpet too old to ever look clean. His staff calls it "the heart of conservative leadership." I call it a holding pen for people who like the sound of their own voices.

I'm on my third latte—I didn't get any sleep last night. *John* did exactly what I needed, helping me clear my mind after McCarter. And he managed to quell the flame Enzo Luciano sparked. I feel sated and calmer. I've barely thought about him today.

Or so I'm telling myself.

As I sit in this office, my thoughts wander. I'm bored and tired. My desk sits in the open area outside the senator's office, where junior staffers like me answer calls, schedule meetings, and pretend we don't hear what's said behind closed doors.

I'm finishing the energy brief that's been sitting on my desk since last week, trying to make the senator sound informed without giving him too much credit. It's a delicate balance. I keep my government clearance and access to politicians by staying useful and unremarkable. The quiet aide who always has the right file, the right answer, the right smile.

My guise is a function of just that: trust-fund baby who isn't ambitious enough to get ahead but is wealthy enough to get paid scraps and still sport designer labels. I make sure most people think I'm a pretty face, a silly woman who is simply excited to be around powerful people. The useful diversity hire.

My diversity being that I don't have a penis.

The elevator dings, and a staffer from Senator Weller's office passes my desk. I've seen him before—Jason, I think. *Or maybe Jake?*

He leans on the partition with that practiced Hill charm. "Hey, Pippa. You ever let a guy buy you a drink after saving democracy all day?"

I tilt my head, perfectly pleasant. A lie. "Depends on the guy," I say demurely. *Let him think I'm flirting back, let him believe he has a shot. He could be useful someday.*

He laughs, quite happy with himself. I tell him I can't tonight but would love a raincheck. Jason-Jake leaves with a promise to "circle back," telling me he knows a great new bar down the road that I just *have* to check out. I keep the smile on my face until he's gone.

It's always the same here; they're all entitled pricks who expect you to be flattered by their attention.

Bvvvt. Bvvvt. Bvvvt.

My burner phone vibrates in my bag. I confirm no one is looking my way before opening the flip phone in my bag.

Luna sent a message to our group thread.

Log into the chat room, asap.

She wouldn't send a message during a workday unless it was urgent.

Luna set up a secure chat room the three of us can log into safely from any device, to use when texts won't do. I type the URL I have memorized into the web browser, enter my login and password, and find Luna is already there.

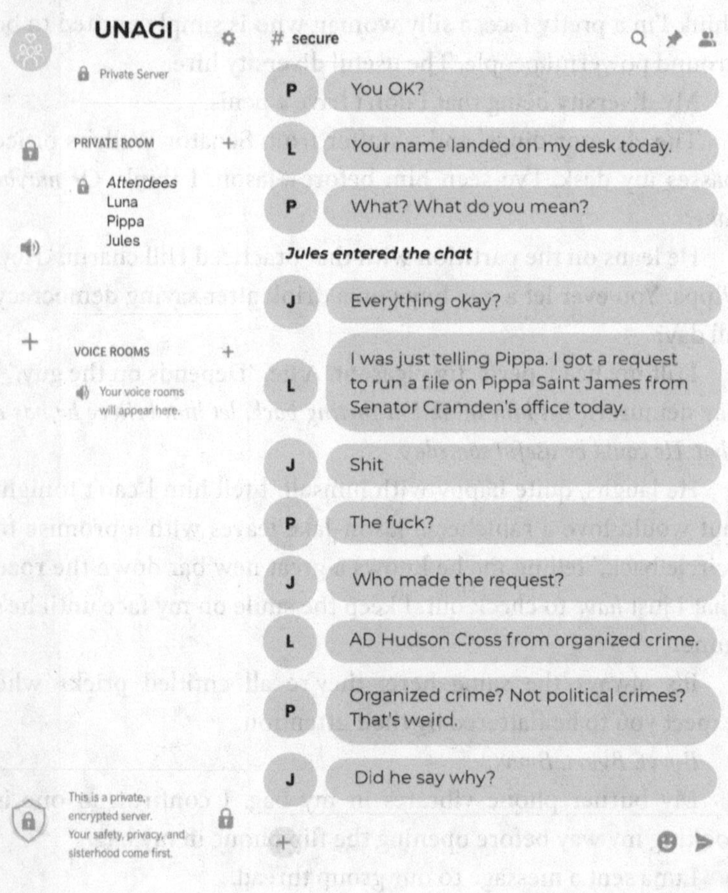

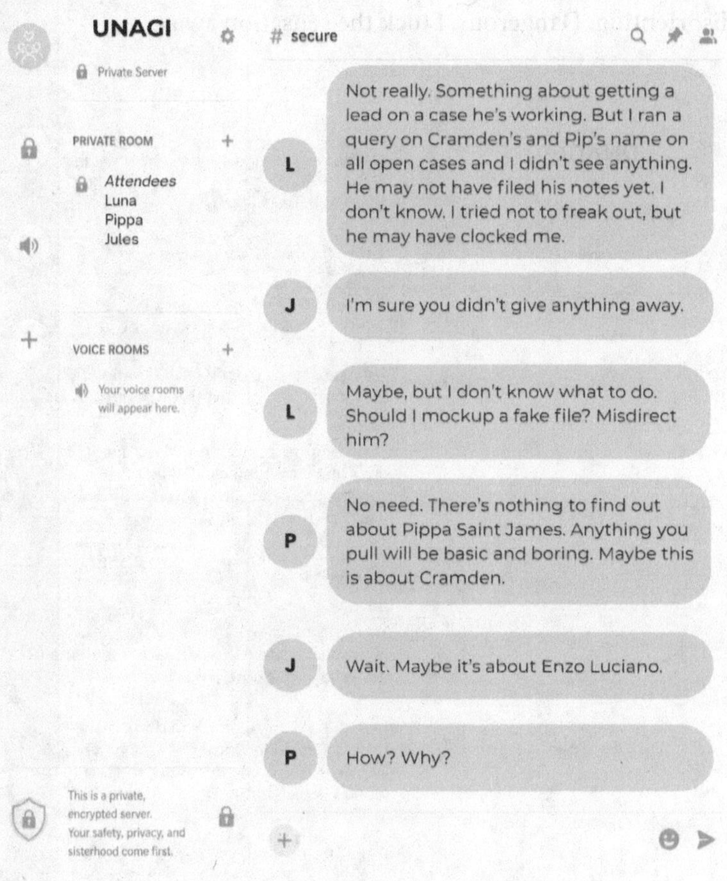

Just the mention of Enzo has my skin warming—a reaction I don't give myself permission to feel. I try to push the memory of our encounter out of my mind, but it presses back anyway. The way his attention found me, the way something tight and unfamiliar stirred in response. I've never experienced that kind of immediate physical awareness before, never felt my body react so sharply to a man I didn't know. It was… disorienting. Dangerous. I tuck the sensation away.

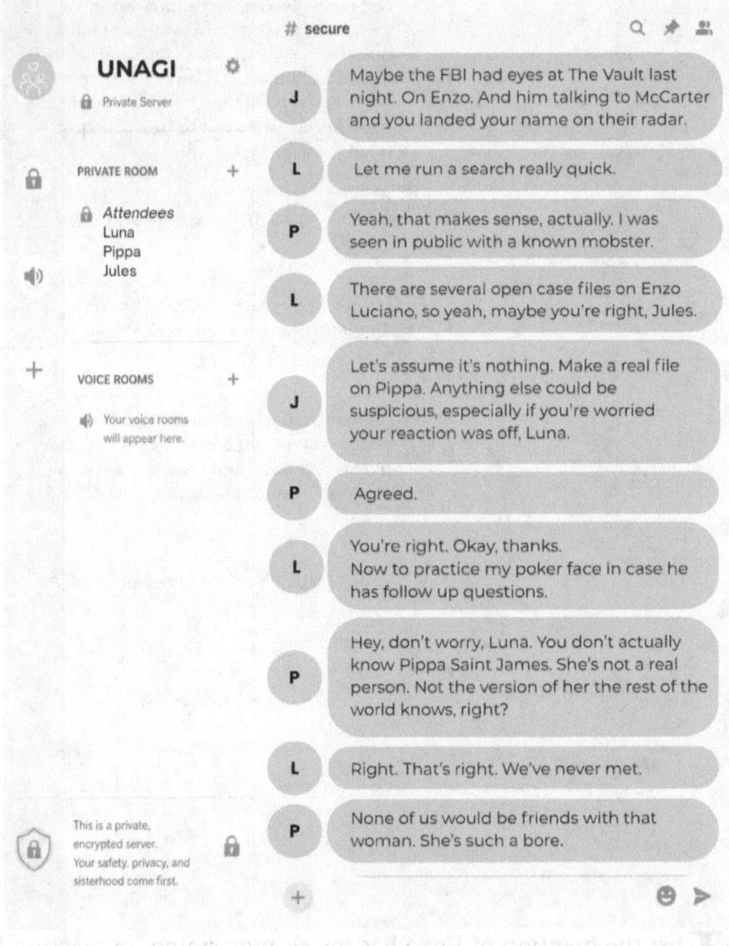

I laugh out loud at my desk, then glance around to ensure no one noticed. There are only two other staffers at their desks right now, and neither turned my way. What Jules said is true, though. This DC persona of mine truly is the worst. Playing her all day is rote at this point. I've been doing it for so long, it doesn't really bother me.

But the real me would never be friends with Pippa Saint James. Nor would my sisters.

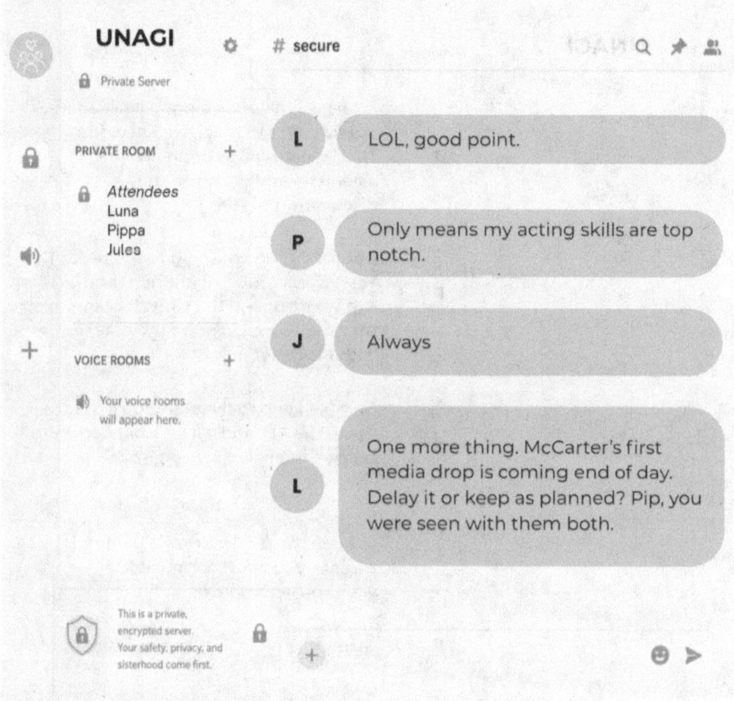

I guess I did such a great job putting the McCarter hit out of my mind, I didn't think of that myself. The closer we get to our end goal, the more I find myself disassociating again. I need to stay focused.

We must take Magnus Troy out. That's been the goal since we started this a decade ago. Longer, really. Probably since I was fifteen. Before we even knew any of this was possible.

And certainly before the predator who abused me as a child, and so many others, became President of the fucking United States. We've finally identified the best shot at taking him down, and we are only a month away. McCarter was the first step. Now, we have to stick with the plan.

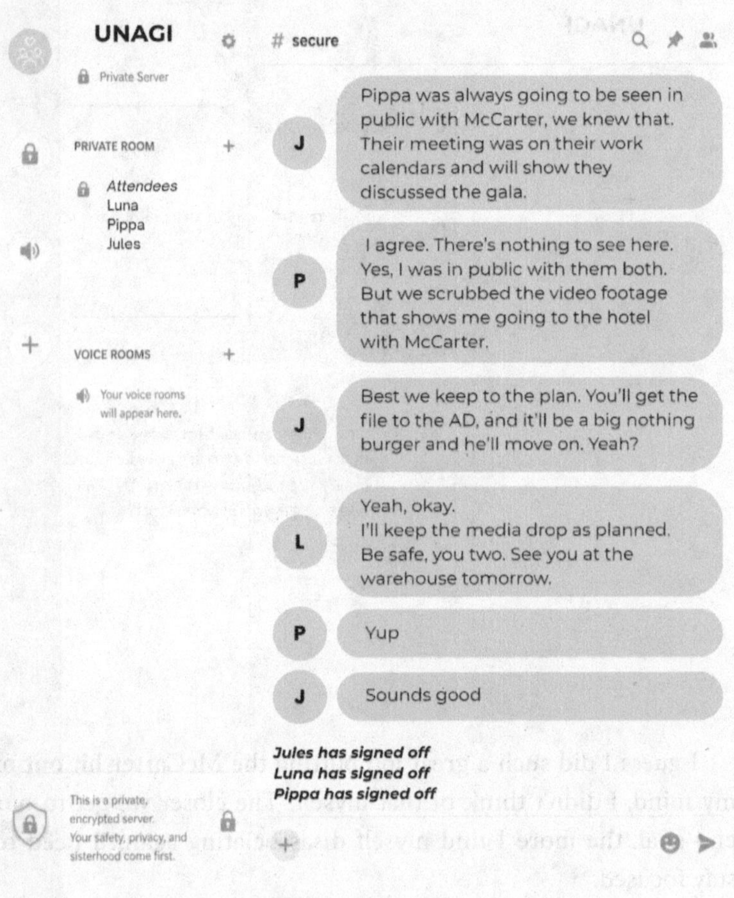

Well, that is an interesting turn of events. The stupid, handsome mobster got me on the FBI's radar. Another reason to forget all about his stupid, perfect face. Leave it to a friggin' man to cause a blip in our perfectly-laid plans. But Jules is right. There's nothing to see here. My sisters and I have crafted pristine public personas. Close enough to the major players but not involved in anything that could get us on the radar of the men we are taking down. Our extracurricular vigilante justice activities are untraceable.

We certainly won't be uncovered by some FBI agent.

This is exactly why we have Luna there. Everything is fine.

The closer we get to the gala, the harder it is for me to compartmentalize all my personas. I feel the edges blurring—I'm running out of places to put the things I don't want to feel. I spend so many hours as prim and perfect Pippa, that my nights are getting increasingly wild and reckless.

Last night was healthy; it was exactly what I needed. A release. Jules and Luna know I go to the underground casinos. They know I have a very active sex life. They know it's how I forget, but I haven't told them about the motorcycle club houses I started frequenting again. Or the illegal street races I've attended recently. Or the less-than-reputable sex clubs I have checked out a few times.

I had a similar reaction when Magnus Troy was elected president two and a half years ago.

He wasn't supposed to win.

We worked *so hard* to spill all his dirty secrets.

We had footage and images, victims who came forward. The news cycles were constant on both sides. It was obvious this man was a liar, a con artist, and a predator.

We really thought it was enough.

We couldn't imagine a world where millions of people would still want him in the White House.

I went on a bender that week. I couldn't help it. I didn't show up to work—I drank myself to oblivion, slept with several faceless men that I don't quite remember. I stopped returning calls or texts to my sisters.

They only found me because of my tracker. We all had rice-sized GPS trackers implanted in our hairlines when Jules joined the CIA. She was working in Russia and Ukraine and we needed to always be able to find each other, especially when we couldn't call or text.

They found me face down in my own vomit, naked, at some motorcycle club house on H Street, surrounded by a group of equally naked men. They took me back to our warehouse, which I barely remember. And when I woke up…seeing the fear and sadness in their faces, I promised I would never do it again.

I've kept that promise for over two years now. And I really want to keep it now.

My hand hovers on my abdomen. The scar from the unlicensed surgery I had at fifteen is mostly gone. But the real scars were never visible.

I close my eyes and shake the memories that threaten to send me into a spiral. We have a plan. Troy will be gone next month. I'll be able to move on. His other victims will be able to move on. I can keep my head on straight for another few weeks.

The phone at my desk rings—a staffer from another senator's office. I pick it up and put my mask back on. Pippa Saint James can push the past down, contain the signs of unraveling, and keep with the plan.

We've worked too hard to get here. I won't mess this up.

Magnus Troy must pay for his crimes.

And since he's evidently above the law, we will be the consequence he never saw coming.

FIVE

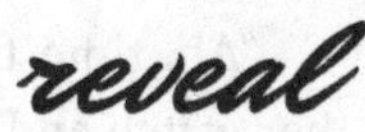

Enzo

Friday Evening, Day 2

The glow from six monitors paints the room in shades of electric blue as I enter Eva's office. Hudson will arrive soon and we're going to compare what he and Eva could find on Pippa Saint James—the redhead I've known for less than twenty-four hours but obsessed over for twenty-three of them.

Neither Eva nor I wanted to sleep in our parents' room after they died, so we turned it into her hacker paradise. The high-end monitors and tech help her run our operation from the safety of our mansion. Keeping her safe is my top priority.

She's locked in, zooming in on a grainy parking lot camera feed, flagging plates, tracking patterns. Right now, Eva is supporting an operation for our Virginia crew. She holds up a hand without looking in my direction. "I'm mid-op and two keystrokes away from making someone disappear. Don't make it you."

I chuckle but stay otherwise quiet. I'm a smart brother, I know when to let my sister work her magic.

Two minutes later, the deal on-screen wraps.

She swivels to face me. "You owe me a quiet entrance next time," she says dryly. "Crew just landed facial recon on the target. They'll finish it tonight."

"Great work, thanks. Hudson should be here any minute."

"Ah, time flies when you're having fun, I guess." She checks her watch and turns back to her desk. "I pulled what I could find on Pippa Saint James, which wasn't much. Here, sending it to you both now. Hopefully Hudson found more."

"He said he put Luna on it." My sister's cheeks flush.

Hudson and I like to tease her about her not-so-secret-crush on Luna. She claims it's a professional crush only, "hacker respecting hacker vibes," but we like to tease that it's more.

"Well, if anyone can get the real dirt on this woman, it'll be her," she replies wistfully.

"Mhm. Well, you're as good of a hacker as she is, so…"

She scoffs. "You know that's not remotely true but thank you for believing in me."

"E, you're single-handedly keeping the Luciano crew *in* business and *out* of trouble. The way technology has changed in recent years, I would never have been able to keep up."

"Well that much is obvious." She's always been snarky and I love that about her. She stands and we head for the den.

Hudson always enters the property through our back entrance to remain undetected. Few know Hudson is part of the Luciano crime family. Besides Eva and me, only my head of security, Niko, my driver, Luca, and our family chef, Marco, know the truth. They are my most-trusted men. And they are trained to keep my family alive. Hudson is family.

As we settle into the large couch, the back door opens. Hudson strides in with a huge smile on his face.

"Wow, someone had a good day," Eva teases.

"Shit, how did you two do it? How did you finally find the real name of my girl, Jane?"

Wait. What?

"What do you mean?" I ask.

"Pippa Saint James. The name you asked me to run. My Jane Doe from the club! I'm so fucking pumped! Thank you for finding her real name. Seriously! How did you do it?"

Eva bursts out laughing. "Well, this is entertaining," she chokes out through laughter.

My brain is still trying to compute. Hudson has been waxing poetic about this woman from the club for almost a year—a sexy redhead.

There is no fucking way.

Eva's continuous laughter breaks me from my thoughts. I look up to see Hudson's smile has sobered.

"Shit. What's going on?" he asks.

"Pippa is the woman from The Vault who was with McCarter last night," Eva explains. She's a little too giddy at this revelation.

Hudson and I stare at each other, blinking. I'm trying to remember what I said to him last night after I met her.

"Huh," Hudson starts. "Okay, well yeah, shit. Okay." He mumbles a few curses, as is his way. "Well, based on what we found out about her, that makes sense. She is a DC staffer. Must have been there for work."

I clear my throat. "Yeah, let's compare notes. Like I said, I had this hunch when I saw her last night that something was off."

"Off how?" Hudson asks.

"When I saw her with McCarter, everything about that scene screamed that she was working a mark. She was baiting him. And he was eating out of her hand," I explain.

"Yeah, that sounds like my Jane," Hudson says. He doesn't attempt to keep the adoration from his voice.

I close my eyes and take a deep breath.

Hudson has been sleeping with Pippa. Pippa and Hudson... Well, fuck!

This is complicated. Not just because I think she may be up to something, but because she's the first woman who's truly captured my interest in a long time. Maybe ever, if I'm being honest with myself. The way my body came to life just being in her presence. And my best friend found her first? *Fucking hell.*

"Hudson, Enz said you had Luna run her file. What did she find?"

"I'll send over what she found. It wasn't much." Hudson pulls out his phone.

"Same," Eva admits. "Which is kind of odd in itself, right? We have her employer, alma mater, the usual résumé fluff—Yale, PoliSci major, Chem minor—but zero social media, which in DC, is basically a felony. She's either allergic to cameras or hiding something."

"You're right about that. Looking at these files, it seems you and Luna found the same information." He pauses. "Hm...I guess my hunch about Luna was off then," he says almost absent-mindedly.

"What hunch?" Eva asks.

"She was caught off guard when I mentioned Pippa's name. Or at least I thought she was. It wasn't anything obvious, I've just worked with her long enough to know her reaction seemed off, but maybe it was nothing."

"Interesting." Eva types a few things into her device. "Well, I certainly don't see any overlap between Luna or Pippa. Unless you count the fact there is almost no information to be found about either of them. *Much* to my disappointment."

Hudson clears his throat. "We don't really have much to go on here, but I am curious what a staffer for Cramden is doing meeting with the Speaker of the House?"

We all agree it is odd. Eva takes a quick look at McCarter's calendar. We have phone-mirroring and tracking apps installed on the devices of all of our clients. They don't know that, but they do know we are an organized crime ring, so it's really on them for not considering the means we utilize to keep them under our thumb.

"The Speaker's calendar says he was meeting with Pippa about an upcoming gala. Oh, this is the opening of the new presidential ballroom. The Speaker is the official host, so maybe there's nothing to see here," Eva says.

"Yeah maybe," I say.

We fall into silence as we run more searches on our devices.

I'm also distracting myself from this Hudson development.

Eva interrupts my thoughts. "Shit, guys, files just dropped on McCarter."

"What do you mean?" I ask.

"I have Google Alerts on all our clients for media article mentions and such. I just got a notification about McCarter. I'm skimming some headlines now, but it looks like a bunch of files were dropped linking him to child sex trafficking, child abduction, and child pornography."

This is the third client of ours in the last twelve months who has been exposed as a predator. *How do we keep missing this?*

My eyes meet Hudson's. Both of us likely thinking of his mom.

My family has never touched trafficking. My grandfather despised it and my father did, too. They allowed sex work, though, something I never fully agreed with. Hudson, Eva, and I decided those operations ended when our parents died ten years ago.

Hudson's mom was a high-end escort. Got into it young as a runaway, had Hudson in her teens. The likelihood his father was a sleazy politician is high, but his mom never revealed his identity. She was a good mom, raised him the best she could on her own.

Unfortunately, she believed the lies those men sold her. Once or twice a year, she'd meet a client who promised her the world. He "loved" her and would take care of her and Hudson. They always promised to set her up in a nice home, with a new car. She'd tell Hudson their luck was going to turn around, promise him the world.

Hudson caught on far sooner than his mother. He was a junior in high school when he discovered what his mom did for work. We didn't know it when we became friends at such a young age, but his mom was part of my father's business. I was so angry at my dad when I found out. He eventually convinced me it was the reason he and my mom took Hudson under their wing. He promised he'd take good care of Hudson's mom, too.

When we were in college, she committed suicide.

For that reason—and many others—I ensure all our clients know that we don't tolerate abuse against women or children. If we find out any of them are involved in trafficking or exploitation of any kind, especially against children, we take care of them ourselves.

Which is why I don't understand how McCarter could have been doing this right under our nose. As I look through the pictures, emails, and texts, it's clear to see the depravity he has been up to.

"How does this keep happening?" Eva whispers, echoing my own thoughts.

Silence stretches between us, thick with the shared realization that we missed something big. *Again.*

Hudson finally speaks. "Are they crediting TruthDrop again?"

"Not yet, not that I'm seeing, but it seems to be the same blueprint. Anonymous photos delivered to all major media outlets,"

Eva answers. "No one has ever claimed credit for the leaks, though, so who knows?"

"Wait a second. Could Pippa be part of this online group?" I ask. Details click together in my mind. "I mean, she was with him just last night. That might not be a coincidence, right?"

"Maybe. But they were having a public meeting about a gala. How would she have gained access to these files? We have access to his devices, and we've never found anything like this on him," Eva counters.

She's right. I might be forcing pieces together, but Pippa wasn't managing gala details at The Vault last night—she was working McCarter. I know I'm right about that. I just don't know how to prove it or what it means.

"E, can we pull footage from the bar? I want to see where Pippa went after her meeting with McCarter."

Hudson clears his throat. "She went to Club14. We were together last night. All night."

Well, fuck me.

I try not to show my growing frustration, but I can't imagine I'm doing a great job at it. "Alright, well. I still want to follow my gut on this. Something is off here. E, let's set up surveillance on Pippa for a few days, see what we find. I know you've already been looking into TruthDrop, but look for ties between Pippa and this leak on McCarter. Let's look back into Bellamy and Trask, too. See if she's connected to either of them or any of the other politicians or celebrities who have been exposed by this group."

"I'm pissed we've missed this again," Eva says. "These men have been clients since Dad's time, but we always dig into the skeletons in their closets. I have access to their home security systems, for crying out loud. I added extra backend trackers after Bellamy and I'm *still* not finding this info. How is this group doing it?"

"I don't know," I admit. "I'm sure I'll hear from McCarter now that shit is hitting the fan. I'll make sure he knows he's off our roster."

"Bellamy and Trask died pretty quickly after their scandals, right?" Hudson chimes in, as if trying to work out his own clues.

"Yeah. Bellamy had an aneurysm; Trask a heart attack," I answer.

"E, who else had file drops linked to TruthDrop?" Hudson asks. "That tech CEO Silas Truve and the Hollywood producer Wes Thornwell—"

"Yeah, and Dex Hannigan," Eva finishes for him. "That bummed me out. I grew up watching his show—he was so funny," she adds.

"Right. So, is it just my imagination, or are all of those guys dead now?" I ask

Eva, he and I look at each other. I'm trying to track what I know of TruthDrop, of the media scandals of the last few years, and of the men who have been exposed. Are any still alive?

"Damn, yeah. Truve had a stroke, Thornwell had a blood clot, and Hannigan died of kidney failure. What the fuck?" Eva says, eyes on her screen.

"They *were* all older," Hudson says. "Those are all natural causes of death for men their age. They were under a lot of damned stress and pressure after these media leaks."

"They all died within a month of their media leaks. It could all be a coincidence—"

"I don't believe in coincidences," I say matter-of-factly.

"Agreed," Hudson says.

"So, what are we saying? That we think the vigilante group behind TruthDrop is not only exposing predators, but *killing* them? And we think your siren, Pippa Saint James aka 'Jane,' could be a part of it?" Eva asks.

We all sit in that statement for a moment.

"Feels like a leap," Hudson says.

"Yeah, we need to start digging into this," I say. "If McCarter dies unexpectedly, then we've got a bigger problem than a staffer who seems out of place or an anonymous group of hackers exposing pedophiles. We're talking widespread assassinations that no one seems to know about."

SIX

decided

Hudson

Monday Evening, Day 5

It's been a few nights, but the tension hasn't faded. Enzo's SUV idles like it's holding its breath—blacked-out windows, engine humming low. The kind of car that disappears sitting still. Luca's at the wheel, steady as ever. Niko rides shotgun, silent, alert. If something goes sideways, Niko will move first—he always does.

The air smells of gun oil and faint tobacco. The residue of Luca's last cigarette clings to the cab no matter how many damned air fresheners he hangs. Outside, the city pulses with horns, sirens, and footsteps on pavement.

Inside, the car is a pressure cooker. Silent. Focused.

All eyes locked on her—Pippa, Jane, or whoever the hell she's pretending to be today. She walks like a woman with a purpose. The sway of her hips in those high heels is all confidence and calculation, every step balanced between temptation and threat.

Eva had a set of Enzo's men set to trail her tonight, but Enzo wanted to handle this personally. He asked me to join, which I took as a good sign.

I snack on pretzels to keep my hands busy and sell the illusion that I'm fucking calm. It's easier than admitting to the nerves running through me as we tail the woman who's haunted my dirtiest thoughts for the past year. Knowing her real name feels... *dangerous*. Like I've crossed a line without intending to.

I'm not sure if my nerves are about seeing the "real" her or if I'm nervous about Enzo's new obsession with her. *Damn it.* I've never seen him like this about a woman, not even his ex-fiancée, Ciara. I'm not surprised Pippa captivated him—I understand the draw all too well—but I am concerned about a woman coming between our friendship. I know we wouldn't let it happen, but... *fuck*. This feels precarious.

Enzo breaks the silence. "So... Jane has a real name."

Here we go. I exhale, long and theatrical, in attempt to break the tension with humor. I want to let him know this doesn't have to be a problem. "Yeah, funny how that works. You fall for a mystery girl, and she turns out to have a LinkedIn profile. Complete with a sexy-as-hell corporate wardrobe she'd never be caught dead in playing poker."

Today, she's dressed in a high-end white designer suit that is tailored to her every curve. And don't even get me started on her heels. *Fuck me.*

Enzo forces a chuckle. "And that doesn't throw you?"

We both know he's opening a can of worms, but we've been friends too long to keep avoiding it. "Depends how this all plays out, doesn't it? She could be the woman of my damned dreams or the one whose secrets ruin me for all future women. Hard to know." I pause, then add, "Besides, Eva said that when you talked about the redhead from The Vault you sounded like the one who needed a cold shower. You doing okay over there?"

He shoots me that deadly look he uses to intimidate, but he knows it doesn't work on me. "This isn't about me."

I grin, knowing I've successfully baited him. He started it. "Says the guy who sounded downright poetic when he described her sitting at the bar wearing… What was it you told Eva? A dark green jumpsuit that matched her eyes?" I chuckle. "Don't worry, I get it. She's…" I take a breath.

"*Remarkable*," we both say at the same time.

Luca flicks his eyes to the rearview.

Niko doesn't move, but I clock the tension anyway.

This, whatever the fuck this is, is new territory for all of us. Enzo and I have never gone after the same woman before. Now, we're in his SUV basically stalking one. Luca has every right to wonder what the hell is going on.

Then, because deflection is my love language, I add, "Also, just to put it out there… As your token bisexual best friend, I'm not opposed to a little sharing. And spoiler alert, neither is she. We've…done that several times."

He looks at me for several long beats without saying anything. No immediate dismissal. No scoff.

Interesting.

When I learned Pippa's real name, I was ecstatic. I couldn't believe my luck. I immediately thought about showing up outside her office—perhaps even pretending it was a coincidence—and finally introducing myself. My *real* self. Having her name felt like an opportunity.

I haven't known how to feel since realizing *why* Enzo and Eva sent me her name.

I can't blame my best friend for being drawn to her—I can't blame anyone for being pulled in by her orbit. Shit, I understand it better than most.

Images have entered my thoughts without permission since last night. Fantasies I try not to think about too often. Enzo knows I'm bisexual, and he's too good-looking to fool himself into thinking I've never thought of him that way.

The idea of him *and* Pippa? *Fuck.* I remind myself not to get hard in the back of this SUV just thinking about the three of us together.

Unfortunately, our line in the sand has been well-established for a long time. Enzo is straight. He's never once indicated otherwise.

I'm lost in these thoughts and daydreams when I spot Pippa take a turn on her walk. "The hell? Is she going to the Old Wharf?" That area is about half a mile south of respectability, and way outside the Capital's comfort zone.

"Yeah, this isn't the side of town where a woman like her would usually spend time. Alone," Enzo grumbles as he watches her round a corner flanked by graffiti-tagged brick and a flickering streetlamp.

"This is giving serious back-alley rendezvous energy," I say with a wink at Enzo, just to get under his skin.

Niko exhales then coughs to clear his throat.

Luca doesn't laugh, but he fights a smile.

"You're an idiot," Enzo mutters.

"Correct."

We let the conversation fade as we follow her.

Jane—*Pippa* is walking deeper into the abandoned warehouse area of the Old Wharf. She seems locked into a destination, navigating this area like it's her second fucking home. She approaches one of the larger warehouses and disappears behind a side door with a keypad lock. And shit, just like that, I know Enzo's hunch about her is edging closer to correct. No one walks into a warehouse locked with a keypad in the Old Wharf unless they're hiding something, damn it.

"Well, brother, those instincts of yours may have hit the mark again," I say.

"What do you think's inside?" he asks.

I keep my eyes locked on the entrance. "Something she doesn't want on the Hill."

He grunts in response.

"What's the play here?"

Enzo calls Eva. She picks up on the first ring.

"You're on speaker," Enzo says. He gives her an update, then asks, "Think you can give us a peek inside?"

She makes a sound halfway between a cheer and a gasp—pure hacker glee. "You know just how to make a girl's night."

I tell her the address, and I hear keys clicking on a keyboard.

"I'm tapping traffic cams, alley feeds, anything in a five-block radius . . . " she says, then, "Hm. That's odd."

"What?" Enzo and I ask in unison.

"The cameras in that area seem to be on loops. Someone's overridden the code. Anything that could have eyes on that block has been hacked or disabled."

Enzo and I share a glance. Luca and Niko cast their gazes back our way.

Damn, Jane, what are you up to?

Eva rattles off some options we have for overriding the cameras in the area or setting up our own, when we see another woman approach the warehouse.

I gasp. "Holy shit! That's Luna!" *What the actual fuck?*

Eva and Enzo both ask me if I'm sure. "I'd recognize her hair and bright-pink glasses anywhere. It's even her backpack. I'm telling you, Luna Steele just entered that warehouse."

"I tried to find any connection between them. I couldn't," Eva says, "but neither of them has much information to even find. Luna certainly has the skills to keep their identities protected. And to keep this warehouse block out of sight of prying eyes."

The car is silent as we process what we're learning here.

Enzo asks if there is anything Bureau-related that might have

Luna here, and I'm not sure. It's a possibility she's on a case I know nothing about, but when our agents are on classified assignments, the ADs are usually informed. We can't know details, but I'd know if she wasn't available. The new case with Stone is on the West Coast and she hasn't been pulled from any other cases yet. I explain that I'd expect to see other agents here if she was on a case. She wouldn't be in the field alone; she's not an undercover agent of any kind.

A third woman approaches the warehouse. None of us recognize her. I snap a photo and send it to Eva to see if she can run facial recon to find out who she is. "Sorry, Eva. Not sure how good the quality is going to be. We aren't that close and lighting is bad."

"Let me see what I can find. Hey, Luca, does your console still have that lock kit with the pin scrambler?" she asks.

Luca confirms.

"Perfect. Enzo, does the keypad look standard?"

He confirms it does.

"Then the scrambler should gain you access. If you want to walk in and ask some questions—"

"You think we should ambush them? We have no idea who else is inside," I say.

Enzo looks deep in thought. He can't think this is a good fucking idea.

"Enz?"

"Yeah, no. That's a bad idea, for sure." I'm relieved, but then he adds, "But I think we should go in."

"Okay, what am I missing here? You think it's a good fucking idea to just go unlock their private warehouse they clearly don't want anyone knowing about and what? Storm in and demand answers?"

"I don't know. Let's play it by ear," Enzo says.

"Never once in the twenty-plus years I've known you have I

ever heard you say we should play something by fucking ear. Enz, let's get more info. Eva said she can put cameras here overnight. We can keep an eye out and learn more. We have no idea what we'd be walking into. I know that at least Luna is armed. They're in the Old Wharf, for fuck's sake, they better all be packing if they're smart."

I think I'm getting through when Eva breaks in. "I can't find anything on the third. The pic has too many hits, she has a common dark hair look that is really standard and her face is too grainy."

"Makes sense. Hudson, I hear what you're saying," Enzo starts, "but something is telling me this is our window. If we don't go in there tonight, we won't get another shot to learn what is going on."

Fuck. I know this look, I know my best friend. He wants to go in there, guns blazing. When he wants answers, he can be stubborn.

I slip into my FBI field persona. "Let me be devil's advocate here. Let's say we charge in there to simply ask questions. Best case scenario, they likely tell us to fuck off. Worst case, they shoot us. But let's say we get past all that and we learn what they are up to—and to be clear, I don't think they will tell us jack shit, but let's just pretend our good looks and charm can get us some answers—then what? What's the goal here?" In this situation, outside of wanting to know more about Pippa, and now Luna, I really don't see the benefit of rushing in there.

I spot the moment Enzo decides and resign myself to the inevitable.

"You each deserve an answer to that question. I don't have it, though. I'm just telling you I know I need to get into that warehouse. I can go alone or you can come with me, but I'm going in."

Niko and I nod to each other as we check our guns. If he's going in, so are we.

"Stay safe," Eva says over the phone. "I don't have eyes."

"Appreciate it. We've got it from here."

"Go get your girl, boys," she tosses out with a chuckle sweet as poison. She hangs up.

Maybe it is as simple as that. Maybe Enzo just needs to be near Pippa, make his presence known. He and I may not understand how to handle this fucked-up dynamic, but one thing is clear: She's pulling us deeper into her web and neither of us seems to be willing to stop it.

And Luna? We've worked together for years. She's like a little sister to me, similar to Eva. I have to admit I feel a responsibility to confirm she's okay. Whatever they've gotten into, maybe we can help.

SEVEN

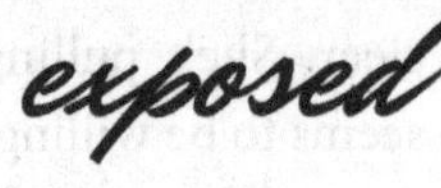

Pippa

Monday Evening, Day 5

The warehouse hums with energy, like a storm about to break. The whiteboards in front of us are covered in names, colored thread, intel dumps, and coded shorthand. Our own war room built from secrets, sacrifice, and the kind of pain most could not endure.

Jules hovers over Luna, her posture all control and command.

Luna sits at her workstation, scrolling through files to find our angle into Victor Malin's house. Our next operation is to take out the head of the secret service.

With the Speaker dying within the week, Malin's death the following week will give us the opening we need for Jules's security firm to be contracted as part of the gala's security team. I'll also get pulled further into gala planning. Each domino carefully planned and pushed at the *exact* right time to give me the access needed to take out Magnus Troy.

I pace the floor, restless energy pent up—a combination of

anxiety, being so close to my own personal vengeance, and an uneasy feeling about being on the FBI's radar. It feels like a bad omen, but I know we've worked on this plan too long to pivot now.

"I know we said we wouldn't, but I really think we should put someone from my team on surveillance. Getting access to his house may be too hard for the three of us to figure out in time." Jules has made this case in each of our last few meetings. Malin's house is a fortress. Luna was successful in hacking his security system, but we still don't have enough information to enter his place safely next week.

"It's too risky, Jules. Victor Malin isn't your client. We'd expose your team if something went sideways," I repeat my position. "Maybe we don't need to do this at his house. What other angles could we work?"

"By next week?" Jules asks with her brow raised skeptically. She's got a point.

"Maybe we have enough information already," Luna starts. "Sure, there are still some unknowns, but if you let me join you in the field—"

"No!" Jules and I both bark in unison.

Luna huffs and rolls her eyes. "I do work for the FBI, for crying out loud," she says under her breath as she returns her face to the screen. "I've had just as much combat and arms training as the two of you. I don't see the problem."

This has been an ongoing point of contention for the last couple of years. Luna thinks we are overprotective about her safety. She's right. Jules and I are aligned to protect Luna at all costs.

BAM!

The warehouse door slams open.

Luna curses and turns to the security feed.

Jules and I whip around.

Enzo Luciano storms into the warehouse, gun raised, eyes locked on us.

Trailing right behind him are two more men with guns. I recognize the dark-haired guy from the night at The Vault. And the third guy…

John?

Our eyes lock and my heart stumbles.

Holy shit.

Enzo radiates masculine energy that feels more reckless than deliberate.

John's tension reads like he's trying to slow a crash he can't prevent. They are twin storms colliding in the same space, and my sisters and I are standing in the crossfire.

I don't even realize I've raised my gun. Next to me, Luna and Jules have mirrored the motion. Our three guns raised to their three.

"John?" slips from my mouth.

"Hudson?" Luna asks at the same time.

"Enzo *fucking* Luciano," Jules hums, ready to go head-to-head with him.

Enzo doesn't flinch. "Easy, ladies. We just want answers."

"That's rich, given you just stormed into *our* space, guns aimed. We have the upper hand here," Jules fires back.

It's a standoff. Six people, six guns, zero exit strategy.

Everyone starts talking over each other, shooting questions and accusations in every direction.

"Everyone shut the fuck up," I yell, slicing through the chaos, and everyone obeys.

"Luna, did you say Hudson? Hudson-from-work Hudson?" I ask.

"Yes," she confirms.

"The blonde or the brunette?" I ask, staring into the eyes of a man whose body I know almost as well as my own.

Luna confirms the blonde.

John/Hudson's smile takes over his whole face.

I decide to ignore that particular clusterfuck for a moment and turn my attention to Enzo. "Hi, again. Couldn't stay away, huh?" I feign flirtatiousness as a means of distraction. My sisters and I need a beat to make sense of what the fuck is going on here.

Jules jumps in. "Enzo, you working with the FBI now?"

"More importantly," Luna follows, staring daggers at John—Hudson—whoever the fuck he is, "why are you walking in with Enzo Luciano?"

I can't help but laugh. "Please. Of course, the head of organized crime is in bed with the mafia. Fucking Washington."

"You know I'd much rather be in bed with you," Hudson says with a wink at me.

Well, fuck, here we go.

I maintain my death-glare at him.

"Pippa?" Luna and Jules ask in unison.

I sigh. "John Doe from the casino."

Jules closes her eyes for a moment, taking a calming breath, then opens them again.

Luna's face goes ghost white.

Nearly imperceptibly, Enzo seems to flinch at that admission.

Hudson looks too proud of himself for a man holding a gun. "So, it seems my reputation precedes me," he says as his smile widens. "*Jane,* I'm flattered."

I roll my eyes.

"You've been hooking up with the head of the FBI's organized crime unit?" Jules hisses sharply.

I shrug. "Technically, I met him as John, underground poker degenerate. You know I don't put much stock into my random hook ups."

"Ouch!" Hudson teases, though it's lined with a hint of hurt.

"Who's this guy?" I ask.

Luna answers, "Enzo's head of security, Niko Moretti."

Jules turns to Enzo. "Let me guess: After you met her at The Vault, you asked your buddy here at the FBI to run a file on her. You didn't have enough information, so you decided to tail her?"

The men don't reply, but we are all on the same page here. Enzo clocking me at The Vault was a bigger problem than any of us realized. Now we've been exposed.

Hudson's tone turns serious. "The real question is, why are you here, Luna? Who are these women to you? And why the hell are there so many boards covered in what looks like high-profile targets and classified intel?"

My stomach sinks. He's seen the target list. They all have. *Shit.* I take a deep breath. "Do we kill them?"

"Seriously?" Hudson snaps.

I tilt my head as my finger grazes the trigger, motioning I'm ready to pull it.

Instantly, everyone squares up, sights aligned. The air goes razor-thin, pressure about to snap.

"Everyone, calm down," Luna pleads, stepping forward and raising a hand. "We're not killing anyone."

Enzo's mouth curves, something dangerous flickering in his eyes. "That's a relief."

"You likely have more men outside, and I have no doubt your sister knows exactly where you are," Luna responds in a commanding tone, showing she's not to be underestimated.

Enzo stiffens at the mention of Eva.

"Luna is an expert in organized crime," Hudson interjects before Enzo can react. "It's her job to know about you, Eva, and your whole crew. I don't believe Luna intended that as a threat."

"Something tells me I've only seen half the picture with the Luciano family all these years, now," Luna quips. "Shit, Hudson, I really thought you were one of the good ones."

Hudson/John/whoever-the-fuck doesn't respond, but his eyes soften.

I try to rack my brain to remember what I know about Assistant Director Hudson Cross. Luna talks about him regularly, but I can't remember seeing any photos. How the fuck did I not know the men were one in the same?

"If Enzo disappears," Luna continues, "Eva and the entire Luciano organization will come for us. And if Hudson goes missing? We'll have the Bureau crawling all over town." No one disagrees. "I think we can all agree, it's in everyone's best interests to just take a breath. We should all put our guns down."

Silence follows as everyone mulls over their options.

Hudson lowers his weapon first, slow and deliberate. "I'm not going to hurt Luna or Pippa," he says softly.

Jules squares her shoulders, taking control. "Here's what's going to happen—Pippa and I will lower our guns at the same time as Enzo and Niko. I'm going to pat you all down and take your weapons while you sit at that table. You're going to give the three of us a minute to chat before we join you. Then we'll figure out what the fuck to do next."

Enzo tilts his chin up, and one by one, the guns lower.

The tension doesn't disappear, but it shifts. Like the first breath after a long dive.

Jules, ever the calm military-turned-security professional, shows the men exactly who is in charge as she takes their weapons and phones. Enzo negotiates a quick text to his driver, and the men are led to the lounge in the warehouse—where we have couches, tables, and chairs. She directs them to the long meeting table.

The three of us head to the opposite side of the massive space, behind the room dividers where I manage my chemistry lab.

When we are out of sight, Luna whispers, "This is my fault. I wasn't watching the camera alarms, and I should have had the audio on, and—"

"Luna," I cut her off, "this is clearly my fault. I had a tail I didn't clock. This situation is bad enough without beating ourselves up."

We hold eye contact, agreeing to let the blame pass between us.

Jules turns to me. "You never looked into John Doe from poker? You've been hooking up with him for a while. Luna gave us Hudson's file."

She's calling me out, and I don't like it. I throw up my hands. "We vetted Hudson Cross when Luna joined his unit, like five years ago! I only met him last year. You know what I'm like after a takedown. I'm half-manic, half-feral. The club's my off switch. I don't exactly have a filing system when I'm Jane Doe." I rake my hands through my hair. "Shit. I'm going to have to rethink how I unwind."

Luna and Jules exchange a concerned look, but they don't press. "And why the hell is Hudson here with Enzo?" Jules asks. "None of our research showed those two were connected."

"Yeah, but with a man on the inside, there wouldn't be a record, would there? They probably had Hudson in play before we even arrived in DC. Only way it could have worked," Luna says with her arms crossed, clearly unnerved. Her fingers tap against her arm.

"What do we do?" I ask.

Luna sighs. "We might get away with telling them the bare minimum."

"Excuse me? Bare minimum of *what*? The operation we've been working on for over a decade? What are you even talking about? You think we can trust them?" I huff.

Luna and Jules exchange a glance. "Maybe," they say together.

They've lost their damned minds. "Are you kidding me? They saw the boards, they're probably memorizing them right now. The names, the intel. You think those men just walk away from that? You know they won't."

Jules exhales, rubbing her temples. "Look, I'm not talking full disclosure, obviously. I'm saying strategic honesty. Enzo is not involved in trafficking. We've confirmed it a hundred times. He moved their business away from sex work when his parents died. And it's widely known that he doesn't take hits on women or children. He's not our enemy. If he knows *why* these men were targeted, he might let it go."

Luna agrees. "Hudson worked in anti-trafficking prior to his promotion to organized crime."

I laugh, short and bitter. "So, what? That makes them heroes or something? Jesus."

"Focus," Jules warns.

"I am focused. You two are talking about trusting three men who've seen us unmasked. Just the fact that they've seen us together is a huge fucking problem. And you want to hand them a partial confession and hope they…what? Walk away?"

"Control," Jules says evenly. "We decide what story they get. And we control their next steps. They don't want to be exposed any more than we do."

"Pippa, we seriously can't kill them," Luna adds. "I wasn't just saying that."

"We've killed much more dangerous men than them," I retort. I can't believe they are considering sharing *anything* about our plans with these men. *Am I in an alternate reality right now? Did I jump timelines?* I am beginning to feel fucking unhinged.

Luna steps closer. "Yes, we've killed predators, Pippa. Would you really be okay crossing the line into taking out innocent people from our real lives?"

"No man is truly innocent." I scoff.

Luna continues, "If we give them nothing, they'll dig on their own. They won't let this go."

"She's right," Jules agrees. "We tell them enough to stop them from asking questions. And then we keep them out of our way."

"What if I whip up some sort of memory-blocking toxin?" I ask, looking around my lab, grasping at straws.

Jules and Luna just look at me with blank stares.

I take a deep, cleansing breath. "Fine. But the second they start sniffing around, we disappear. No hesitation. If we can't take them out, we protect ourselves. We have protocol on this for a reason."

"We go with the Regina Phalange protocol," Luna affirms, voice steady.

"No personal links. No family ties. No mention of Maribel," I confirm.

"Or Dad," Jules adds.

"Never Dad. To anyone," I whisper.

Jules glances between us, grounding us again. "We share just enough. Nothing more."

"Then you'd better lead, Jules. You'll sell it best." I'm too amped up to figure out the right role to play in this scenario.

We all square our shoulders and start toward the men waiting at the table.

"We'll tell you what you need to know," Jules says as we approach. "And nothing else."

Hudson leans back in his chair. He wears a façade of easy charm, but his eyes are razor sharp. "That's a good start, because I've got a shit ton of questions."

"Don't we all," Luna shoots back.

Jules continues, "Those names on the wall aren't what you think."

Enzo tilts his head. "Oh? So, it's not a hit list? One that

includes a mark that looks a hell of a lot like President Magnus Troy."

"Then maybe you should stop assuming and listen," Luna cuts in. She's calm, but I know her pulse is pounding. She hates confrontation.

He meets her stare, seemingly both wary and impressed. "I'm listening."

"We're not about to explain our entire operation," Jules begins. "You stumbled into something that wasn't meant for you. And now we have to make sure everyone walks away intact."

Enzo leans forward. "Meaning?"

"*Meaning*," she says evenly, "we'll give you enough context to understand why you can't interfere. Nothing more."

Luna adds, "We don't owe you anything—least of all trust—but we're offering clarity. Take it or leave it."

Hudson glances between us, his grin absent now. "Guess we'll take it."

No one moves for a long beat. Finally, Jules gestures for us to sit. We take our places across from the men, the whiteboards of names and red thread looming behind us like a confession on their own.

For the first time in a decade, we're not the only ones who know what lives inside these walls. As the words start to come, slow and deliberate, I can feel the ground shifting beneath us.

Something tells me that once the cracks form, we won't be able to close them.

EIGHT
embedded

Hudson

Monday Evening, Day 5

The women take their seats at the long oak table where we were told to wait. Enzo and I sit on one side, Luna and Pippa across from us. The one I don't know anchors herself at the head of the table, with Niko rounding out the table at the other end. No one has offered formal introductions yet.

Kind of rude, if you ask me.

I scanned the room while we waited and found myself both impressed and a little giddy. It's a luxe version of an FBI war room—even fancier than anything my billionaire best friend has built at his estate. State-of-the-art tech owns a back corner with workstations, monitors, whiteboards, and meticulous files that line the wall. We are in the corner across from that area in a lounge. The long table is offset by leather sofas and chairs that scream luxury.

Luna's fingerprint is woven throughout both spaces—her

pops of bright color and '90s nostalgia cutting through the otherwise lethal aesthetic. Just like her desk at work.

A third corner is an arsenal big enough to arm a small country. Concerning to say the fucking least. The corner they hurried to for their huddle sits behind room dividers through which I can see stainless countertops and pristine lab stations peeking through. I guess that chemistry minor of Pippa's wasn't just for fun.

The one who is clearly in charge starts. "The three of us work together."

Obviously. I don't like how calm they are for people whose operation just got exposed.

"Professionally," she adds. "That's all you need to know for now."

Enzo asks, "Who do you work for?"

All three scoff. My Jane answers first. "What, because we're women, we must be working for someone else? Fuck you."

God, that fire of hers is such a fucking turn on.

Their leader cuts in again. *Seriously, anyone planning on any introductions?* "We don't work for anyone. We've been using our positions in Washington—mine in security, Luna's at the Bureau, Pippa's in political ops—to take down trafficking networks. Quietly. Off the grid."

"How?" Enzo asks, echoing my thoughts. He's using his deep mafia-boss tenor, which usually means he's trying to intimidate or he's worried. I'm not sure which this time, but I clock that no one at this table flinches. *Damn.*

"No one knows us," the brunette replies. She has this whole military-chic vibe going for her. "Not really. We do well in our fields, but we stay off the radar. Luna's hacking got her recruited by the FBI. I built Redline Solutions to serve the rich and powerful. And Pippa swims through DC secrets like it's her private pool."

Redline is a top name in private security. It's run by an ex-CIA agent named Sinclair. *Damn,* is this her? Admittedly, I should know this. But she's right, they do know how to stay off the radar. They aren't on the FBI's watchlist for nefarious purposes, like many other private security firms in the area.

Luna cuts through my thoughts, steady as ever. "We use what we find to pick targets, then we take them down. Digital, legal, financial—whatever we need to do to guarantee they can never hurt anyone again."

This aligns with Eva's theory about TruthDrop. If Luna has a hand in those file dumps, it's no wonder no agencies have been able to track them.

Pippa taps her long, perfectly manicured nails on the wood tabletop as she stares at Enzo. "We hit them where they're weakest—their ego. Nothing like a tall redhead with an Ivy League degree and a fake crush to dismantle a power-hungry sociopath."

Damn, that's hot. I want her to dismantle my—

"So that's why you were with McCarter," Enzo says.

She meets his gaze and holds it. Neither confirming nor denying.

He arches a brow. "So," he says, voice dripping with condescension, "you sleep with them. Then what?"

I shoot him a look that says 'maybe don't insult the vigilante assassins who somehow convinced us to voluntarily give up our weapons.' *Christ,* that Italian hotheadedness of his is going to get us killed one day.

"Aw. Are you jealous, Enzo?" Pippa taunts, eyes glinting.

He refuses to give her the satisfaction. Enzo directs his attention to Ms. Sinclair, voice calm but probing. "Who else are you working *with?*"

She doesn't flinch. "What makes you think there's anyone else?"

I shift, aiming for less heat than Enzo. "It just seems big. For three people."

Pippa tips her chin. "You mean *women.* What you're really wondering is how three *women* could dismantle empires without a man behind the curtain."

Enzo starts, "That's not what I—"

"Relax," Luna cuts in, smile sweet and sharp. "We're used to men underestimating us. It's our superpower." Having worked beside her for years, I know she's right.

Ms. Sinclair leans forward, eyes cold. "We don't need a team. We are the team."

Pippa glares at Enzo. "And considering the bodies piling up, I'd say we're doing just fine."

Enzo's jaw sets. "One last question. Some of your targets are obvious—everyone knows Troy and his cronies are mixed up in this shit—but some of those targets are on my client roster." A statement, not a question.

The women wait, silent. They're good.

"How did you get intel we didn't? If any of my clients touched trafficking, we would have handled it."

Luna answers quickly. "Our research says you don't touch that world. Neither did the Lucianos before you. Even with Hudson running cover all these years"—she throws me an annoyed look—"your family's stance on the exploitation of women and children is loud and clear."

Enzo nods once. Stoic. But I know he's fucking livid that his clients were doing this right under his nose.

"These men have been doing this longer than we've all been alive. And they have powerful friends to cover their tracks. Your business is money, weapons, intimidation. Without the kind of dedicated focus we've had for years, anyone could miss it."

Enzo says nothing.

I know they aren't telling us the whole story, but I know they don't plan to either.

"Jules and Luna aren't giving you enough credit, boys," Pippa says sweetly. "You told a bunch of politicians not to hurt women and children. You probably said it all *big and bad like,* too." She does a slow clap, and I can feel the heat rising off Enzo's skin. "That did it! That solved the whole problem. Let's give these boys an award."

"Pippa," Jules hisses.

Luna levels a glare her way.

"No, ladies, come on. These men are the *real* heroes. They laundered the money of criminals, provided them with weapons and protection, all while turning a blind eye. Probably assumed these dirty politicians were just using your protection to help the poor, right? Tell us, how many millions have you made this year alone? Surely with all that bravado about not harming women or children, you used some of that profit to help victims, yeah?"

Seeing my Jane all fiery has me ready to put her over my knee. *The few times she's let me do that—*

"You're right," Enzo surprises me when he quietly responds. "We haven't done enough."

"So where do we go from here?" I ask before Pippa can fire back.

The silence says we are all worried about the same thing.

"We told you what we can," Pippa says. "Are you going to stay out of our way or be a problem?" She says it like a dare, like she would enjoy the wrong answer.

Enzo answers too eagerly. "We'll help."

"What now?" I blink at him.

Around the table I hear a chorus of "no, thank you," "no way," and I am pretty sure an "oh, fuck no" from my girl.

Enzo shrugs, as if it's already been decided. "We have reach, resources, direct lines to several of these men. If we can help take them down, we should. As you said, we're not doing enough."

"And because your savior complex is acting up, we're supposed to let you in on the action?" Jules asks pointedly.

Damn, she clocked him. Impressive. Enzo calls it protection, honor, even duty. I call it his Achilles heel. The compulsion to take care of those around him burdens his every move. What I don't know is when he decided these three needed his protection.

If Enzo is ruffled by Jules calling him out, he does not show it. He doesn't respond, either.

"I am sorry your pristine criminal empire got a little dirty," Jules continues, cool as ice, "but we did not ask for backup. We do not need rescuing."

Enzo tries another angle. "If you do not want our help, fine. Don't confuse that with our continued ignorance. I can't unsee this. I will not sit back."

Pippa smiles without warmth. "On the record," Pippa says in a tone sweet enough to rot. "Was that a threat?"

Niko stiffens and so do I.

Enzo's tone is even but not calm. "No. It is a promise that if you do not let us in, someone else will come sniffing around."

Huh. He's worried someone else will find them. Savior complex in-fucking-deed.

The women look at each other, contemplating.

I aim for reason. "He isn't wrong. If we found you, others can, too."

Jules scoffs. "Just because Enzo got hot and bothered by Pippa does not mean we are on anyone's radar."

Enzo's jaw ticks at the comment, but he doesn't deny it.

"Pippa, Jules, maybe it's worth considering a controlled partnership, a trial alliance," Luna suggests. "It could—"

Pippa folds her arms. "Are you serious?"

Right as Jules says, "Absolutely not."

Pippa turns back to us. "Next step is simple—you leave. If we need anything, we'll say so. Any pressure? We go dark."

I meet her eyes. "Oh, is that all?"

"No surveillance. No back channels. No reaching out to any of the men on that wall," Jules answers. "Violate it and this conversation never happened."

Enzo opens his mouth.

I put a hand on the table to stop him from making things worse. "We hear you."

Luna stands. "Good. Then we are done."

Chairs scrape. With that, everyone disperses from the table. Niko, Enzo and I take our leave. Jules escorts us out to where Luca waits by the car. She returns our phones and our guns, emptied of ammo.

Not exactly a win. More like a temporary ceasefire no one believes in.

Tuesday Morning, Day 6

Even the morning light in the Luciano mansion feels expensive. It slides through those tall windows like it's auditioning for an art film. Golden, soft, a little smug. The kind of light that whispers *old money*.

The Luciano mansion has been in their family for generations and it's the only place that has ever been a real home to me. Enzo and Eva have been unwilling to make any changes to the design after losing their parents.

We sit in the kitchen debriefing last night over breakfast. Vaulted ceilings, a black marble island big enough to land a small aircraft, copper pots suspended like jewelry above the stove, every high-end appliance you can imagine. A space too grand for the only two Lucianos left.

"So, let me play this back," Eva says, staring between us. "You tailed Pippa to a secret warehouse on the wrong side of town and in a plot twist none of us saw coming, my *idol* Luna Steele was there, and you uncovered some sort of vigilante assassin lair?"

"That's the short version," I answer.

"That's the *awesome* version," she says, grinning. "You're telling me it's three badass *women* out there cleaning up the trafficking scum who've evaded every major organization? Ours included. I love everything about this."

Enzo shoots her a look as he deadpans, "They almost shot us."

She waves a hand. "You *did* break into their warehouse. You two totally give 'shoot first, ask questions later' vibes. You can't blame them."

That gets a chuckle out of me. Eva is always keeping us entertained. "You're way too excited."

"Because it's *brilliant*. They're like modern-day superheroes. But even better, because they're *women*!"

Enzo rolls his eyes. "I take this to mean you agree we should help them."

She gives him a mock glare. "You're not one to ask dumb questions, Enz."

I raise an eyebrow at my best friend. "Pretty sure they made it clear they don't want help from us."

"*Us* as in *you*," Eva corrects, setting down her coffee as she hops down from the counter. "They might be more open to someone who isn't playing a double agent at the FBI or running a criminal empire. Or—more importantly—someone who isn't a man."

"Eva," Enzo says, his tone serious, "they made it clear that we are not to approach them."

On the drive home last night, I tried to get Enzo to open up to me about what he is thinking—about Pippa, about his offer to help them. He said he needed more time and would talk in the morning. I know him well enough to know pushing wasn't going to get me anywhere. So, he dropped me at home, and I headed here first thing.

"Yeah, but that's because they don't know how delightful I am yet."

"You only want to work with them so you can finally meet Luna," I say.

She smirks. "And what if I do?"

I laugh. "You've been obsessed with her since that paper you wrote about her in school." Eva has had a not-so-secret crush on Luna for a while. I have had to warn her more than once they are not allowed to *accidentally* cross paths.

"I prefer the term *professionally fascinated*," she quips.

We both give her disbelieving glances.

"What can I say? She's so ahead of her time. She's everything the hacker world pretends it wants women coders to be but actually punishes them for. It makes so much sense that she's behind TruthDrop. No one has ever tracked the sources. The media thinks it's a large international group, but *it's just her*. I mean, I'm sure the other two help, but she's obviously the tech-savvy branch of the whole operation."

Enzo mutters, "You sound like you're writing her fan mail."

"She's one of the few people doing something real—not waiting for permission, not pretending the system works."

"No one is under the illusion that the system works, E," I say.

"E, let's run a file on Jules Sinclair. Then, compile what you can find on Luna and Pippa with it. I don't think they are going to take us up on our offer, but if they do, I want as much info as we can find."

Eva perks up. "Enzo, you already told them we have clients that are on their hit list, right?"

"Right."

"Good. Then we start there. Let's offer to set up a meeting with a high-value client—someone they couldn't easily access without us. You give the girls the name, the location, the setup, whatever they need, and then you get out of the way. Let them handle it however they choose."

Enzo rubs his jaw, thinking. "It's not the worst idea."

"I know." She grins. "What about Jonathan Vale? He's been causing problems for our other clients ever since his son landed on Troy's ticket. You said Troy was on their list, so this could be perfect."

The suggestion lands heavily. Even the sunlight seems to dim a little. Jonathan Vale, father of the Vice President, advisor to world leaders, political kingmaker, and the kind of man who could make a phone call and ruin a life before breakfast.

"So, we open negotiations with offering them the father of the Vice President?" Enzo asks, incredulous.

"Relax. All we have to do is make the offer. See if it's the olive branch they need."

"Let's pretend this isn't a stupid idea—that it's *not* the kind of plan that is likely to get us killed by Vale's cronies. How exactly should we make that offer when they've specifically told us not to approach?" I ask.

"Last I heard, you and Luna still work together."

Enzo and I scoff.

"It's not like she can avoid you forever."

I sigh, rubbing my temples where a dull headache is starting to form. "So, I ambush her at work. Which, let me remind you, is the FBI *headquarters*...and offer a chance for her and her friends to take out a golden goose? Someone too tempting to ignore."

"Exactly!" Eva claps in excitement. "Even if she's mad, she'll realize what we are offering."

"And what's that? Besides our possible deaths?" Enzo retorts.

"A way to prove that we are in this with them, that we have skin in the game, and maybe a reminder that not everyone in this city is an enemy," Eva says. She clearly knows she has us hooked.

I look at Enzo.

He gives a slight tip of his chin.

"Fine," I say. "I'll see what I can do."

"How hard was it to admit I was right?" Eva teases.

Enzo and I both chuckle as we leave the kitchen.

I guess I'm going to find out if Luna Steele and I are still friends. That is, if she's even willing to talk to me after last night.

NINE
concession

Pippa

Tuesday Evening, Day 6

The uncomfortable chair I'm sitting on—the wooden seat pinching and pressing like it has a personal grudge—is a welcome distraction from the discussion about Magnus Troy and his upcoming ostentatious gala. When that distraction ultimately fails, I might try to decide if the smell in Senator Cramden's chambers is mildew or mold.

Cramden rambles on about the importance of getting face time with certain gala attendees.

I made sure I was on this committee so that I could secure an invitation. In the more than two years since our Predator-in-Chief was elected, I've managed to avoid meetings and events where he'd be in attendance. It was easily done since all the other staffers are clamoring for those opportunities. I played into Cramden's sexist nature to convince him that women (myself included) are great with event planning. *Asshole.*

With the event one month away, my ability to indulge in

conversations about the faux importance of the new ballroom and what it stands for is truly waning. I care more about the delivery method for the poison when I shake President Troy's hand.

I've been testing both a skin contact patch for my palm and a micro-point option on a ring. The capsule method I initially considered has too many risk factors, so I ruled that out last month. Skin delivery has its issues because he'll be shaking other hands that night and risking transfer seems unnecessary. Even though the formula I created is specific to his medical history (his *real* medical history, not the bullshit he feeds the press), there are too many old people on similar medications he could accidentally poison. The ring seems increasingly the way to go. I remind myself to test out more needle widths. I have to ensure it goes undetected while also injecting enough poison into the skin.

Unlike other marks we've run, the aim is not a delayed reaction. No, we don't need time to air his dirty laundry—the world knows exactly who this man is.

The plan is for him to have a stroke within thirty minutes of my handshake, at the event. At least it'll be one last hit to his ego before he dies. The man thinks the world believes he's in perfect health even though we all have eyes.

I'm trying not to worry about him recognizing me. It's been seventeen years. I don't look the same and he has dementia, but the issue keeps Jules and me going back and forth on our plan. She thinks she should be the one to deliver the poison no matter how many times I've told her I have to do this.

She just doesn't want me to have to face this monster again but knows I need to before I can put the island behind me.

"Pippa, does that work?" Senator Cramden's voice cuts in.

"Yes, of course," I respond. I have no idea what he said, but I've learned that men usually just want you to agree with them.

And if that doesn't work, I just pivot to the role of a silly, dumb girl. Works every time.

"Great. That's all then, team." We are dismissed.

I stack my papers neatly and close my laptop, setting both on my desk as I walk into the main bullpen.

I'm meeting Luna and Jules at the warehouse, and I'm already late. Luna has an update to share regarding Hudson.

So much for them leaving us alone. They lasted less than twenty-four hours.

I feel awful. I'm the reason they found us. I obviously had no way of knowing Enzo and Hudson were working together, but that doesn't change the fact that I led them both to our front door. *Literally*.

Twenty minutes later, I'm keying in the code at the warehouse.

Click.

The familiar scent of ink, dust, and chemicals hits me as I step inside. Jules and Luna are at the large table Enzo, Hudson, and Niko sat at just last night.

Jules looks my way and smiles in greeting as she continues writing in a notebook. Luna doesn't look up when I walk in. She's on her laptop, fingers moving fast, takeout likely cold beside her.

"Hey, sorry I'm late." I set my bag down and slide into the seat next to Luna. "You said you had an update."

She exhales, closing her laptop halfway. "Two, actually. Let me get through both before we dive into either, okay?" She glances between us.

We agree.

"First one's about Jonathan Vale."

Haven't heard that name in a while. A good friend to Dad and Magnus Troy back in the day. A frequent visitor to Maribel Island. He has stayed behind the scenes this past decade, while his son, Jackson Vale, has taken center stage in the political arena. He certainly called in those skeletons in Troy's closet to get his son on the ticket when Troy ran.

"Hudson and Enzo made an offer. They want to hand Vale over. Some kind of gesture of good faith." She pauses for a beat to let the words settle.

We have every intention of going after the Vale empire after we take care of Troy, but Enzo and Hudson would have no way of knowing that. He wasn't on any materials they could have seen last night.

"So much for them not approaching us," Jules mutters.

"I didn't think Hudson would talk about this at work, but I was wrong." Luna sighs.

"Well, I'm not surprised," I start, "they aren't the type to wait for instructions. Vale is an interesting offer, but nothing we can't handle ourselves."

Jules dips her head in agreement.

Luna clears her throat, her eyes flicking to her notes. "The second thing... Stone just looped me in on a new case. Celebrity parties in Bel-Air, suspected trafficking network feeding into Mexico. The details...they're almost identical to Dad's parties on the island. Overlap on the guest lists. Funding tracks back to the same shell companies. Even looks like Russian security teams running cover."

For a long moment, no one says anything. The only sound is the hum of the overhead lights.

Jules is the first to find her voice. "You're saying it's the same operation? Or a copycat?"

"I don't know yet," Luna replies, "but the pattern is too similar to ignore. Stone already had his suspicions before he brought me in. I haven't shared my findings yet, but he specifically asked me to compare notes to all our files on Jared Whiteman and Sophie Delacroix."

I press a hand to my temple where an old ache returns—the one that lives somewhere between memory and warning. *"Fuck."*

Luna watches me, waiting for me to say more.

I don't, because what can I say? That I'm not surprised Sophie may be operating under the radar? That we should have found her by now? Or should I lead with the fact that it's my fault Hudson and Enzo are circling us? That even knowing we shouldn't make an alliance with them, I'm not sure I can stay away.

I give a small shake of my head. "Assuming Bel-Air could be connected to Sophie, we should follow the Russian funding and ties to Volkov's old network. When was the last time we had eyes on Junior?"

"Good idea," Luna says. "I'll run searches on Volkov's old contacts. There is still no chatter on Sophie. It's been…a couple of months since I ran surveillance near Junior's estate—still no sign of him having left the estate, no systems I can hack into, no known crew on the streets. A ghost."

We keep hoping we'll catch wind of Junior Volkov leaving his fortress or find something on the dark web about what he's been up to since his dad died, but we've had no luck in the last decade. He certainly has enough money to stay hidden for the rest of his life.

Sophie was supposed to go to the Volkov estate after Maribel. So were we. Junior's dad was meant to protect all of us, but that was before Sophie turned evidence against Jared Whiteman.

Jules, Luna, and I have been back and forth on whether we think Konstantin helped Sophie turn Dad in or if he was as surprised as our father. All we know for sure is that he and Junior left unexpectedly that day, narrowly missing the raid.

Screams guilty to me.

Our assumption was that Sophie has been in witness protection this whole time, but someone as well-known and infamous as her staying hidden for nearly twenty years? When every powerful person in the country (and world) wants her dead? Seems unlikely. Yet…where is she?

Luna takes notes on her laptop, Jules flips through her notebook, but we are each caught in our own thoughts. Frozen between two current threats and haunted by memories.

Jules is determined to be the one to take Sophie down and I know the fact that it's taken this long to find her bothers her to no end. Luna can't let go of the image of Junior as the childhood best friend who took care of her. I know she hopes she finds him before his enemies can—his biggest enemy being Enzo Luciano.

Jules interrupts my train of thought, saying, "We can't go after Vale yet, not until after the gala. When he falls, we have to be ready to take down several other marks in quick succession."

"Whatever we decide," I say, "we can't let Hudson or Enzo get leverage. Maybe we meet them, hear them out, and come to the table with a counteroffer of our own."

"Wait, what? You've been the most vocal *against* partnering with them. Or anyone, for that matter," Luna responds.

"Oh, but that was before our possible allies included a hot mobster who is obsessed with her and the only man she's allowed to have multiple repeat performances in her bed," Jules deadpans. Her eyes meet mine in challenge.

Luna shakes her head. "I still can't believe John from the casino is Hudson."

We all make noises of agreement at that.

"Don't worry, Hudson won't be making any more appearances in my bed. And Enzo can get over his crush. I'm not interested."

Both my sisters roll their eyes at me.

"I *don't* want to hear them out, but I know they won't stop pushing their way in. The timeline between now and the gala is shortening. So, let's see what they have to say."

"What if we bring them in on Malin, instead?" Luna offers, like her brain is already thinking a few steps ahead. "Jules, you said a few times we could use more bodies."

"Yeah. I know. I just wanted *my* people on it," she grumbles. "I don't trust these guys and I don't know if we have time to bring them in on the plan. We need Malin taken out within the week."

"Agreed. But it would be easier if we had help. Malin is a mark that makes sense based on the story we told them. They already saw Troy on the board, they know we are going after him because he's a well-known predator. Taking out the head of the secret service to get to the President won't reveal more than they already know," Luna explains.

Jules adds that we should still discuss Vale with them, in case they have ideas we don't. Luna suggests that instead of them helping us take him down, maybe they can get his office bugged, or intel that we can use down the road. We all like that idea.

Everything feels like it's spiraling, but with my sisters beside me, hashing out all the angles, the chaos fades. We've survived worse. We'll survive this, too. Anyone who comes after us will just have to learn that the hard way.

TEN

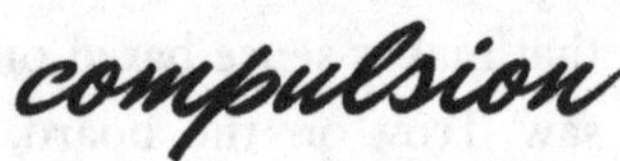

compulsion

Enzo

Tuesday Evening, Day 6

Everything in Pippa's condo is deliberate—clean lines, quiet luxury, nothing wasted. And I can't appreciate any of it because I'm fuming about how damned easy it was to break in.

Yes, I'm a professional criminal and breaking into a private residence is second nature, but the fact that it wasn't harder? That gets under my skin. She should know better. She shouldn't leave herself exposed, not with the kind of enemies she's collecting.

Hudson spoke to Luna today, but I decided I could sell the alliance better if I could talk to her privately. At least, I've convinced myself that's the reason I'm here.

Where the fuck is she? She left the Hill over two hours ago.

Is she with a mark?

Is she with Luna and Jules?

Is she on a fucking date?

Does she date?

Fuck. I need to get this boiling rage under control.

I look around her place again. It's exactly what I expected of her. Modern elegance. White marble countertops. Luxury cream walls and drapes softened by gold accents. A scent from the peonies on the table and something spiced lingers in the air. There's a decanter of bourbon on the sideboard, next to a glass sculpture that looks fragile enough to shatter if I breathe too deeply.

And beneath all that polish, there's heat. A crimson velvet blanket draped carelessly over a cream sofa. A painting that's all chaos and color—a burst of flame against an otherwise polished room. It's her in visual form: all refinement and clean edges, but underneath? Wildfire.

I give myself a healthy pour of bourbon as a reward for my patience before sinking into one of her leather armchairs. Tension coils in my neck and shoulders.

The seconds stretch, turning into long moments. And then I notice it.

An almost imperceptible red dot winking from the corner of the ceiling.

Cameras. Of course.

I take a deep breath, letting some of the tension out of my neck.

Eva didn't find any tech she could hack in this unit, but I'm glad to see Pippa is smarter than I gave her credit.

No sooner do I realize my break-in didn't go unnoticed than the lock clicks.

"Honey, I'm home," Pippa's voice rings out, light, amused, the sound of a match striking. She steps into view with a slow, knowing smile. "Your stalking tendencies are becoming worrisome, Enzo."

And just like that, the fury I'd been nursing finds something new to burn on.

Her.

How is she sexier every time I see her? How does the mere sight of her make my pulse race? And why does every outfit she wears fit her like it was custom made for her flawless fucking body?

Her white pants are tailored impeccably and starkly contrast a black blouse that drapes in all the right places. Red lips. Red heels. A wet dream.

I use every bit of my waning self-control to remain seated. "You should change your security system."

Her brows lift, teasing. "Should I? You worried about me, hot stuff?"

"Worried," I echo. I lean forward and place my elbows on my knees. "No. Frustrated, yes. You circle dangerous people and you're too reckless for your own damned good."

That gets a flicker of seriousness from her, maybe annoyance—brief but telling. Then, she smirks and slides out of her heels, but she doesn't leave the foyer. She's waiting for my next move. "You're here for a reason, Enzo. Spit it out before you start lecturing me about my safety."

I exhale, drag a hand through my hair. "I'm here to discuss Vale."

There is a long beat of silence. I wonder if she's going to acknowledge what I said.

We hold eye contact like a dare.

"Ah yes, the offer of 'good faith,' I believe it was. Didn't Luna tell your lap dog we'd be in touch?"

"Should I let Hudson know you called him a dog?"

"Whatever does it for the two of you. Look, I get that you're used to people falling at your feet, desperate for your protection and help. I'm sure waiting for us to come to you is *killing* you."

"I'm not known for my patience. I have to admit, though, I'm surprised you're not jumping at this offer."

"I bet you are," she says, voice cool, chin tilted like she's the one with the upper hand.

She is.

I force a slow exhale and rise from the chair, setting the bourbon aside. "Then enlighten me, Pippa. Because from where I'm standing, delivering Vale to your doorstep looks like the fastest way to get what you want."

"What I want?" She laughs—sharp, cold, dismissive—as she walks past me to the kitchen counter. As she walks, she flips open the clasp on her designer watch like the conversation bores her. "See, that's where you're already wrong. You think Vale is a chess piece. A token. Something you slide across the board to negotiate a truce."

"He's leverage," I counter.

"He's a landmine," she snaps.

There it is. That fire under her polished exterior.

She turns, leaning a hip against the counter with her arms crossed. "You don't understand what he is. What he *was* to us. What he's capable of. You think handing him over makes you heroes, but it doesn't. It makes you naïve."

A beat. My jaw ticks. *What he 'was' to them? Did she mean to let that slip?* "You think I don't know what Vale is capable of?" I ask quietly.

"I think you don't know what happens to the people around him," she replies. "I think you're walking into a storm you've never seen before and assuming your power will carry you through." She pushes off the counter and closes the distance between us. "But this isn't your world, Enzo. This isn't the mafia. This isn't dirty politics. This isn't money and compliance and bending people to your will." Her voice drops to a whisper when she says, "This is hell. And you don't walk into hell offering gifts."

My pulse jumps. Not at the warning—at her. At the heat radiating off her, at her closeness, at the fury vibrating through every elegant line of her body.

"Even if we agreed to Vale," she continues, "even if we accepted your alliance, you'd be stepping into something you can't control. And when it blows up—and trust me, those odds are high—you'll put your entire business at risk. Your family, your crew. These aren't the kind of kills that can be allowed to find their way back to you. You wouldn't survive it. It's why we work alone." She begins walking to the front door, as if she's seeing me out.

Something inside me snaps. I step toward her and grab her arm. I turn her around and crowd her, forcing her backward until her spine meets the wall with a soft *thud.*

She gasps. Not in fear, in challenge. Her eyes blaze up at me. "Don't."

"You think I'm afraid of your warnings?" I growl, hands planted on either side of her head, caging her in. "You think I don't know exactly how dangerous this is? How dangerous *you* are?"

Her breath hitches. I watch her tender neck move as she swallows. I can see her pulse quickening and it's taking everything in me not to lick that pulse point in her neck.

"You keep pretending you're warning me off," I say, lowering my voice, "but what you're really doing is trying to convince yourself you don't want this—that you don't feel anything."

Her jaw flexes. Her gaze drops to my mouth for half a second. Half a fucking second, but I see it. And I can't unsee it.

I lean closer, then lower my hand to hers. I hold our two hands between our chests. "Tell me you don't feel this, Pippa."

Her other hand goes to my chest, not to push me away, but to steady herself. The slightest tremble betrays her.

She swallows hard. "I d—" Then she closes her eyes, collects herself, and when she opens them again, the ice is back. "I don't have the luxury," she says, quiet but fierce, "of making decisions based on how I feel."

The words hit me harder than if she'd laid hands on me.

She presses her palm to my chest and pushes just enough to signal me to step back. Not enough to break the tension. Not enough to breathe. But the small space between us might as well be the Grand Canyon.

"I don't make decisions based on how I feel, either." I tilt her chin up, forcing her to look me in the eye. "But I don't seem to have the luxury of staying away from you."

Our breathing grows noticeably heavy.

"And what about Hudson?" she asks defiantly.

I shake my head and take a step back. I release her hand and it feels painful to not touch her. "Yeah, this is complicated, you're right about that, but it doesn't seem to be keeping me away, does it?"

"Does he know you're here?"

That question makes me pause. I didn't tell him. I had Eva help me locate her address, but didn't loop him in. I told myself it wasn't a big deal, but it seems like one now that Pippa is calling me out on my own bullshit.

Fuck.

After a few beats, she says, "I didn't think so. You should go." She points to the door. "We'll be in touch about Vale."

"Pippa—" I start, not sure how to finish that sentence. I step closer. I have to close my fists to stop myself from touching her. "This isn't over."

"I know," she breathes out. "But you know this is a bad idea."

"The worst."

"Then tell me why you're really here, Enzo. I know it's not about an alliance."

"I wish I fucking knew, Pippa."

We are staring at each other, both vibrating as we breathe in and out, using all our restraint to not touch each other again.

"Fuck it," she says and then her lips are on mine, her arms around my neck. My arms wrap around her waist to pull her deeper into the kiss.

We are ravenous—tongues colliding, breathing each other in, kissing like we might not survive the next moment without them.

I move one hand into her hair, pulling slightly at the nape of her neck.

Her breath hitches as she moans into my mouth. Her arms drop to my waist as we begin our exploration of touches, caresses, squeezes.

My erection presses into her stomach. "Pippa, I need—"

"Yes, I—"

More moans, more touches.

"Fuck. We should stop." I need to stop this. *Can I stop this?*

"Mm...probably," she says as she kisses my neck.

My already racing heartbeat speeds up. Hudson's face enters the forefront of my mind. I find my last ounce of self-control and pull back.

I can't do this.

Not yet. I need to know what he wants.

Her eyes clear from a haze of lust as she stops. She shakes her head. "That's for the best."

"For now," I say.

Pippa hums and runs her hands through her hair. She checks her outfit, tucking her shirt back in. "Luna, Jules, and I met tonight. We agreed to a meeting. Luna plans to tell Hudson tomorrow."

Disbelief curls at the corner of my mouth and I shake my head. "I can't tell if I'm winning or losing with you. Or what the rules are. Which should send me running, but instead I want all in. Drives me crazy."

I earn a smile from her. The first real smile I think she's ever sent my way. That smile could talk me into anything.

"Crazy suits you. Me too."

I return her smile and we just stare for a beat.

"One last thing: Luna, Jules? Who are they to you?"

"None of your business."

I smirk. "That figures. You're sure you can trust them?"

She laughs. "More than I can trust you."

"We are far from trust, I know that, but how do you know you can trust them?"

She looks at me for a while, assessing, then sighs. "Thank you for being worried. I want to be more annoyed by your protector alpha vibe, but I know it comes honestly."

I offer a small smile, appreciative of her genuine observation.

"You don't have to worry about Luna or Jules. They are the only two people I trust with my life."

"But how did you all meet? How did this all start? There is no real information to be found about any of you."

"Enzo—"

"I know. I know. I just—"

She puts her hand on my bicep. "I appreciate your concern." She means it.

I just haven't earned any answers yet.

As I open the door to leave, I clasp her hand in mine and raise it up to kiss the inside of her wrist.

She lets out a shaky breath as she closes her eyes.

Then, I release her hand and walk away, hoping it's not too long before I see those green eyes again.

ELEVEN

Pippa

Sunday Morning, Day 11

I still don't think we should go.

JULES:

You've made your position clear.

LUNA:

I don't know, I'm starting to feel good about it.

Love you, but you're too positive about most things.

LUNA:

Fair. But doesn't it just feel better to be positive?

JULES:

Chaos and conflict are her happy place.

As the oldest, I really don't get the respect I deserve.

My sisters and I arrive at the Luciano mansion on a Sunday morning like this is a normal thing we do. We are united, but unsmiling. The air feels heavy as we walk into enemy territory, even if the enemies say they want to help.

Niko greets us while he and a few of his men check us for weapons. Without coordinating, we all dressed in black tactical attire—most fitting when you're not sure if you're forming an alliance or starting a war.

Tactical black may be an everyday look for Jules, but definitely not Luna or me. Luna's colorful wardrobe is the perfect match for her personality, the same way my tailored suits create the armor I don to rub elbows with Washington's elites.

But the three of us have an alias for every occasion, and today I've stepped into my fighter persona. Sharp-eyed and ready—as if I'm entering a ring, not a meeting. Jules is not the only one with ninja assassin skills in our crew. We all have them. Luna and I are just as scary as her when it comes to a physical fight.

And make no mistake about it: This is a fight.

While we've decided to share a small part of our truth with these *possible* allies, we are still playing characters today. No one can ever know our true identities. We'd be as dead as Jared in that jail cell—no doubt about it.

The Luciano mansion is exactly what you'd expect from a mafia dynasty. Stone walls, high ceilings, a fireplace that could swallow a Fiat, and enough security cameras and men with guns walking the perimeter to make Langley nervous.

We didn't want them back at the warehouse, so meeting here made the most sense and offered the most privacy.

Don't love it, though. Which is why we made them agree to no weapons and no guards in the room. Security have been informed we are free to leave any time we want.

Niko reiterates this as he guides us into the sunroom, where

Hudson, Enzo, and Eva are waiting, and then he steps outside, presumably to take guard at the door.

It looks like they got the black tactical gear memo, too. Good. We are all ready for battle, then.

While technically sunlight is coming into this room, nothing about it feels particularly bright. It's grand and moody, with iron-framed windows, stone floors, and enough expensive furniture to host the Queen of England.

Enzo takes a moment to introduce everyone to Eva as we settle into a loose circle, sinking into couches and high-backed chairs arranged like a council no one asked for.

Jules and Enzo are positioned at either end, staged like a boardroom brawl.

Hudson and Eva are on the far couch.

Luna curls up next to me, cross-legged, scanning the room like she's deciding who she might kill first. She may present sunny and bubbly, but she's as lethal as anyone sitting in this rag-tag group of possible-allies in the making.

"Thank you for the invite to this cute little mob brunch," I break the silence. "Should we jump right in?"

"Sounds good." Enzo's demeanor is calm. Very different from the other night at my condo.

Hudson sits back, relaxed, presenting his normal playboy energy.

Eva has a smile on her face that offers way too much excitement and eagerness.

Didn't expect that. Reminds me of Luna.

"We've discussed the offer of Vale," I continue. "We've come today with a counteroffer."

Enzo sits straighter and opens his mouth to interject but I raise my hand.

"Hear us out. We are willing to test a partnership, but we don't think Vale is the right first target. We need more in play before we take him out. With your access to him, though, we were thinking we could set up some bugs to get ears on his operation."

The opposing trio all agree, thinking through logistics.

"In addition, we are willing to share our next target to see if working together makes sense. We aren't convinced extra people will actually help, but we are intrigued about what you might bring to the table."

There's a heartbeat of silence. Then, they all speak at once.

"I'm in," Eva says enthusiastically.

"I like it," Hudson adds with a big smile.

"That makes sense," Enzo states with a small incline of his head.

Luna and Eva both chuckle and they exchange a drawn-out look that seems dangerously close to flirtation.

As if my history with Hudson or the heat brewing with Enzo wasn't already complicated enough. Sure, let's add another flirtatious entanglement. Why not?

Jules and I share a look that says, *that was too easy*.

I don't like it, but I continue. "Look, we've each got strengths. Enzo, you and Eva have reach and muscle. Hudson, you have a high-level network at the Bureau and a clean reputation." I gesture toward Luna. "Luna's the best hacker in the country, maybe the world. Although I hear Eva may be hot on her heels. Jules is ex-CIA. I have White House clearance and access. We're not amateurs playing vigilante. All three of us are trained in combat, weapons, chemicals, poisons, you name it. We didn't stumble into this. We built it."

Hudson lets out a low whistle, eyes flicking from me to the others and back again. "Damn. Glad I never got on your bad side, Jane."

I raise a brow, lips curving just slightly. "That's still up for debate." I slide the folder across the coffee table. It slows to a stop in front of Enzo. "Let's start with one op, one mark—Victor Malin. Head of President Troy's security detail. Publicly, he's an American hero. Privately? He's a broker, a buyer, and a protector of the worst kinds of men. We've had eyes on him for years."

Enzo flips it open. I see the question forming before he says it. "Is he on the list as your gateway to the President? Is Troy the final mark?"

I glance at Jules.

She doesn't blink. "We're not there yet."

Hudson leans in, half-smirk. "Yet?"

I meet his eyes evenly. "Magnus Troy has enough skeletons in his closet to fill Arlington. The world knows who he is. We've played a very active role in spilling his dirty secrets. Somehow, it hasn't seemed to matter. Taking out Victor Malin does help us to get to Troy, yes, but that's not the only reason he's on the list."

"I've always wondered if Malin is in with the Russians," Eva chimes in, "but could never find any proof."

Jules offers a small smile. "Good instincts. Victor with a C now, used to spell it with a K. He's no American war hero. He's a KGB double agent, planted here in the nineties. The Malin family has deep ties to the Bratva. In Russia the KGB, organized crime, and politics have always worked hand-in-hand. He was introduced to Troy in the late eighties and he's been building influence ever since."

Hudson leans forward. "How do you know this? He's not on the FBI's radar of KGB operatives. I've looked into him before; I couldn't find anything."

No one replies. Everyone looks at each other. Our silence makes it clear we won't share how we know—it would reveal too much.

Enzo lets out a low whistle and leans back. "Malin and Troy go way back. It's no secret Troy is in with the Russians. You'll get no argument from me. The Volkov family runs the DC syndicate, and I killed Konstantin Senior after he killed my parents. His son, Junior, has been in hiding ever since. He knows the minute I get access to him, he's dead."

The room goes silent at the heaviness in that admission.

We understand the history between the two families and knew leading with a Russian target would be a good test of this fledgling alliance. Or whatever the fuck this is. My sisters and I give nothing away at the mention of the Volkovs or Junior.

We wouldn't want the Junior we were raised with to die. It's hard to know who our childhood friend turned out to be. For all we know, he could be at the center of it all, just like his dad was. We can't let our complex pasts influence how we pursue these predators.

"So, this is where the crusade leads?" Eva asks. "From high-end predators to the world's most notorious Predator-in-Chief?"

Hudson raises his brows and tries to cut the tension with a laugh. "Awesome. So, what? We take out the head of the secret service and then...you simply go after the President next? Sounds like a solid plan. Zero red flags." His laugh dies in the quiet that follows.

I look at him, my tone flat. "If you're here to talk us out of it, you're at the wrong table."

Across from me, Enzo closes the folder and taps it once against the table. "So, Victor Malin's first. Fair enough." He dips his chin slowly. "Let's talk about how we make him disappear."

And just like that, a precarious union is formed. It still feels too easy, but I'm under no false assumptions it will be.

We spend the next hour detailing plans, threading logistics, and outlining blind spots. Enzo offers backchannel access to key members of Malin's inner circle. Hudson volunteers Bureau intel he can get through unofficial back doors. Jules, ever the quiet operator, points out a surveillance vulnerability on Victor's estate, sharing some of the challenges we've had so far.

When it comes to the digital front, Eva and Luna are already speaking in shorthand, bouncing ideas off each other like they've worked together for years. Watching them click into sync is almost scary. Eva is all sass and sarcasm mixed with impressive genius. And I'm sure Eva's movie star looks aren't going unnoticed by my sister. I can tell Luna is impressed. Eva is a tiny, female version of Enzo. The genetics in that family are extremely generous.

I sit back, watching the room with curiosity. This isn't trust. Not yet. Maybe not ever. But I'd be lying if I said it didn't feel good having smart, talented people to bounce ideas off. There is this little bubble in my chest, something like…excitement? Hope? A light at the end of the tunnel?

I pride myself on trusting my instincts and right now, this feels good.

I'll try not to get my hopes up, though. If there is anything I've learned, it's that most people are wildly disappointing.

Including us. Because if anyone ever knew the DNA running through our veins, they'd run the other way.

An hour later, Enzo and Eva guide us to the dining room for lunch. A sunbeam slices through the antique windows of the Luciano mansion's very large dining room. It lands like a spotlight on a table full of criminals and vigilantes, pretending we're something closer to a brunch club. It's a surreal kind of sacred.

Luna and Eva sit together, chatting. Without encrypted language or shadowy threads, the conversation doesn't seem to flow as easily.

Luna is normally nonstop, a bubbly chatter box in most situations, but this time, she's composed. Watchful. Not uneasy but guarded.

Eva is a few years younger than Luna, in her mid-twenties, but she has the kind of confidence one *should* have when growing up mafia royalty. She has an ease and grace to her that I believe my sister would find captivating. I'll have to ask her about it later.

In the corner of the room, Jules is mid-conversation with Enzo and Niko, explaining something I don't need to hear to understand. Her gestures are precise, competent, grounded. The men listen more than they speak. They're asking intentional questions, taking her in.

Jules has always been like this—the quiet authority in the room. I'm glad they see it, too.

Hudson returns from the kitchen and sits beside me like it's always been his place.

"Different kind of meeting than you and I are used to," he says with a wink.

"Jane and John had more fun," I tease.

"Maybe, but at least now we are done pretending."

I glance at him. "Are we?"

"I am. You're harder to read now, but far more interesting."

"I was never easy to read."

"Definitely not at cards, but in the bedroom?"

My cheeks warm. "Sad those days are over?"

"Are they?" His puppy dog eyes contain a hint of pleading that somehow isn't pathetic, but rather endearing.

"Obviously."

"Agree to disagree."

I laugh before I can stop myself and Hudson cracks a wide smile.

Enzo approaches the table and takes the seat across from us.

"Gotta say," Hudson starts with a smirk, turning toward Enzo, "Pippa suits you much better than Jane."

I arch my brow. "Please. I much prefer John to Hudson."

Enzo snorts. "Straight to the jugular."

Hudson mock clutches his chest. "You wound me."

Enzo leans forward, arms crossed, shifting the mood. "Making sure this"—he points between Hudson and me—"isn't going to be a problem."

I sit back in my chair, squaring my shoulders. "What exactly would *this* be?"

"You two, your history," he says flatly. "We've got a delicate alliance on the line. We don't have the luxury of making decisions based on how we feel." He raises his eyebrows at me as he uses my exact words from the other night.

Poor guy, he really has no idea how to play this game.

Hudson is clearly amused. "That so? Isn't it *your* complicated feelings that led to this delicate alliance?"

I stare directly at Enzo as I say, "It's giving *jealous*, isn't it, Hudson? I think Enzo is jealous."

Hudson's grin stretches. "You may be right about that, Pippa, but what Enzo doesn't realize is he doesn't need to be jealous, does he?"

"No, he doesn't. Enzo, you're welcome to join us any time."

And just like that, Enzo's cheeks brighten to a shade just shy of the color of my hair. His eyes dart between Hudson and me.

"Johnny and I here have shared many times before… And we like it…*a lot*."

Enzo blinks and licks his lips. Then he clears his throat like he's searching for words.

The chef enters from the kitchen to serve the food and Enzo is saved.

Did I just tell Hudson our hook ups were over? Yes. Did Enzo's arrival bring my confrontational, teasing side out? Also yes. I won't dissect that.

Jules joins the table.

Niko leaves the room.

Chef Marco explains what he's prepared. Then, he pours us each a glass of wine before returning to the kitchen.

The conversation is easy as we eat—fun, even. Eva is the life of the party, cracking jokes, keeping us entertained with stories of their childhood or their work. Hudson and Enzo often jump in to "correct" her version of events. Hudson and Luna share a story or two about working together over the years.

Luna told me earlier she is still battling how she feels about the Hudson reveal. I know she always considered him a friend at work. Luna tends to turn inward in moments like this; she can be brutally hard on herself. Like it's a personal failure not to have seen it coming. Her scars from our past aren't as physical as mine, but I don't think she's ever forgiven herself for not comprehending the dark truth back at Maribel Island. Her obsessive attention to detail as a hacker ensures she never misses the obvious again.

Jules and I add an anecdote here or there to the conversation throughout lunch. We never reveal anything too personal but always find common ground—more than I would have expected, if I'm being honest.

But Enzo, Hudson, and Eva all spend their days playing various roles, too, so they just *get* it. It's…nice.

Hudson, Enzo, and I sneak glances at each other throughout the meal, though we all pretend we aren't.

I notice Enzo's attention keeps drifting, and not always back to me. I notice when it finds Hudson. I wonder if he's even aware how easily it settles there.

By the time dessert is served, I find myself wondering if Hudson and his best friend have ever crossed that line. If I didn't know better, I'd say Enzo's heated gazes after our joke weren't directed at me alone.

TWELVE

consider

Enzo

Sunday Evening, Day 11

Alone in my office, I stare out the window at the property grounds. Elijah Craig 18 is helping me drown the myriad of racing thoughts constantly battling in my brain these days.

Everyone except Eva left the mansion hours ago. After connecting with Niko and Luca on plans for the week, we retreated to our separate offices. I came here to get some work done, but mainly to make sense of everything I'm feeling.

Today's meeting went better than expected. A feeling of rightness lingers—the rare sense something aligned as it was supposed to.

I don't trust things that come too easily. I never have.

Especially not since Ciara.

The *easiest* of relationships. An arrangement between our fathers. *Another alliance.*

I grew up knowing I'd marry her—or someone like her—for

the mutual interest of our two families. I remember feeling relieved that I never had to worry about dating. Women seemed too complicated. Duty, loyalty, those were things I knew.

Romance, attraction, love all seemed too elusive, too hard to figure out. My father told me when I was seventeen that he had reached an agreement with Micky Donovan. Micky had a daughter one year younger than me, and we would wed when she was twenty. Our union would bring the Irish and Italian syndicates together. Seemed straightforward.

It was anything but.

It never felt right with Ciara. I knew it then, but I was young. Even if I had told my dad something was off, it wouldn't have mattered. It wasn't my decision.

She was beautiful. She was kind. I figured we had time to grow into it.

Neither Micky, my father, nor I could have imagined she and Junior Volkov would fall in love. Or that her choosing him would lead to a territory war that resulted in both their fathers' and my parents' deaths. It was madness.

The fact that I'm even considering another form of an alliance again ten years later should be a red flag—especially when the catalyst for this union is yet another woman.

I remind myself that today's meeting was the result of following my instincts several times over. There wasn't anything *easy* about this. These women would never allow it to be. Instead it has felt kindred, intended.

That realization settles slowly, like I don't quite believe it yet. I replay moments of the last week and a half again for the hundredth time. On paper, none of this makes sense.

My encounter with Pippa at that bar. Tailing her on the night she ends up in the warehouse. Barging in without a plan. Luna being with her and Hudson being with me. Their operation flying under the radar all these years. It all feels so unbelievable.

Doesn't that tell me what I need to know?

We crossed paths for a reason.

I don't even believe in that shit, but today's meeting has me reconsidering if fate is real. The pauses, the looks exchanged, the way no one reached for control just to prove they had it.

Instincts matter to me. They always have. They're the only reason I'm still here, the reason the Luciano family empire survived after our world imploded.

I was twenty-two when I took over the family business. An operation that spanned a dozen states and three countries. Many of my dad's rivals—and even more of his allies—saw me as weak, inexperienced. Saw my dad's death as their chance at power.

I had more attempts on my life in those first few years than my dad ever had in his almost-thirty years as the head of the family.

If I didn't trust my instincts then, I'd be dead. If I didn't figure out how to lead this empire, Eva could be dead. Or taken and used as leverage.

Eva and Hudson are the reason we survived—that we thrived. Eva brought us into this modern era. Hudson protected us from government forces. He helped me get out of the sex work operations and expand our arms business. Eva learned more effective ways of managing assets and money laundering and helped me grow my crew with new technology.

I owe them everything.

And they seemed just as eager and open today as I felt on the inside.

My mind inevitably drifts back to Pippa. The same way it has since the night I met her. It hasn't even been two weeks since that night and she occupies more of my thoughts than I'm willing to admit.

I was impressed by her today. I'm not easily impressed by people, not in DC. I had no doubt she would be smart. But seeing her in action, the way she commanded the room, it was a major turn on. That and her black tank that somehow managed to be both simple and criminally distracting. I swear the woman weaponizes her wardrobe.

I brush my fingers over my lips as I feel the memory of her lips on mine. Of my hands on her hips, her ass, tight in her hair.

Fuck! I want her.

Hudson left with everyone else this afternoon, but we'll talk soon. The way he and Pippa so easily joked about a threesome… I can't get it out of my head. They said it so casually, like it was no big deal. Like the mere idea of it didn't make me feel like the ground was shifting beneath me.

The moment was gone before I could process it, let alone respond. Throughout lunch I couldn't stop myself from stealing looks at them both. There is no doubt they are comfortable together. She's different with him. Of all the personas I've seen her sport, she seems at ease with him. Maybe it's the closest to her real self.

It was captivating to watch.

Seeing them together felt different than I expected. I thought I'd be jealous or feel left out. I never thought I'd be open to sharing a woman with another man, but as I sit with the idea tonight, I'm surprised by how unbothered I am at the idea of sharing her with *Hudson*.

In fact, the idea of sharing her with someone who already knows her body, knows her edges and her triggers…and who also happens to be the person I trust most in this world… It doesn't feel threatening. It feels…*irresistible*.

Inevitable, even.

And I won't deny that seeing Hudson with her, all easy smiles, fast jokes, in his element…adds another level of appeal. Images and thoughts I haven't let myself think about in a really long time have resurfaced. Curiosities I had to shove deep down at a young age.

Knock, knock.

Eva lets herself in, laptop tucked under one arm and coffee in the opposite hand. "So today went well, right?" she asks, perching on the edge of my desk like she owns the place.

"You tell me. What'd you think?"

She watches me for a long moment. "We have time to talk about the mission later. First, I need to know if you're good."

"Define 'good.'" I hope she's not going to pry too hard.

"Sure. 'Good,' as in are you spiraling because you want to jump the redhead, but also maybe your best friend?"

I groan. "Jesus fuck, E. Really?"

"You're not that subtle, Enz."

I lean back in my chair, take a deep breath, and stare at the ceiling. Eva is the perfect person to talk to about this. We've always been able to talk to each other about the hard stuff, and she is way wiser than her years. Hell, she's way wiser than me. Christ knows spinning this around in my head isn't getting me anywhere.

"I don't know what the hell is happening. I want her. More than I've ever wanted anyone. How could I not? Jesus. She's... she's—"

"A goddess. She's a goddess, Enz. They all are."

I chuckle. The three have beauty, grace, intelligence, and grit. I've never seen anything like it before. And while they are all uniquely impressive, I'm drawn to Pippa in a way I've never been drawn to another woman before. "You have a point, but I don't want to screw things up with Hudson. I could never do anything to hurt him—you know that. And he's had it bad for her for a long time. Long before I was in the picture."

"And?" Eva raises eyebrows.

"Are you really going to make me say it?"

She confirms with a slight motion.

"They both threw me a grenade today about…sharing. As if it were no big deal. So, yes, I'm spiraling. There. Are you happy?"

Eva takes a beat before answering. "Big brother, you and I both know Hudson would never do anything to make you uncomfortable. And if all you want to do is share Pippa with him, even to just get her out of your system, you know he'd grant that wish. He'd grant you anything you want."

I know.

"And yes," she continues, "there is something between the two of them—chemistry for sure—but you and Hudson are thicker than blood."

"Which is why I'm not sure what to do," I admit.

"Is it the idea of sharing her that has you feeling confused? I have to imagine you've had a menage-a-trois before." She chuckles.

I glare at her. "I will not be discussing such things with my little sister." *Or anyone, if I can help it.* Intimacy avoidance is my cross to bear.

"If I may," she says in a voice I know is preparing me for a hard truth. She learned it from our parents. "I don't think sharing Pippa is what has you in your head." She pauses.

I wait silently for her to finish.

"I think you're more curious about Hudson than you're willing to admit. Even to yourself."

The statement hangs in the air. I let it. A few moments pass as I ask myself if that is true. I love Hudson. He's family. I've always been curious about his bisexuality. How could I not be? He had freedom to explore. That was never on the table for me.

Is it the freedom? Is it attraction?

I don't deny or confirm.

She breaks the silence. "I think you're feeling real things for the first time in a long time. Can you see yourself feeling more now? With her? Him? *Them*?"

I close my eyes. On a whisper, I admit, "I don't know. It all feels too big. They seem so casual about it, but to me, it's…*huge*."

She smiles and pats my arm. "Life's short, Enz. Especially for people like us. Don't waste time pretending you don't want something you do. Go after it. You deserve happiness." With one last glance, she leaves my office.

And I'm alone again, realizing I'm not unsure. I know exactly what I want. The question is whether I'm ready to take it.

THIRTEEN

tangled

Hudson

Sunday Evening, Day 11

I should be asleep.

Instead, I'm sprawled across my bed, one arm flung over my eyes like that'll somehow shut my brain off.

Spoiler alert: It's not fucking working.

The mansion was quiet when I left. Too quiet, considering the bombshells that dropped throughout the day. The six of us made a plan, agreed to trust each other. At least enough to take down one very powerful, very dangerous target.

Victor Malin. Secret Service golden boy. Whose real secret is that he's a Bratva legacy. He's a KGB-bred snake hiding in plain sight in a damned designer suit.

I'm also thinking about Jonathan Vale, and Eva and Enzo's offer to bug his house at their next meeting. It all feels too fucking risky and my skin feels itchy thinking of all the shit that can go wrong. But we laid out skills, aligned on tactics, and paired teams, like this was some twisted murder version of *The*

Bachelor. Somehow, it was seamless. We left with a plan, with assignments, with *possibility*.

Then there's *her*. Pippa fucking Saint James.

Who, for the record, should come with a goddamn warning label. She's chaos wrapped in silk. She was definitely playing mind games with Enzo earlier, and while I jumped in on the fun, I now feel a little guilty. Not so guilty that I stop thinking about her sharp tongue, however.

Or fantasizing about sharing her with Enzo.

Fuck. If I keep picturing that, my dick is going to get harder than it already fucking is. And I already jacked off thinking about them tonight.

I need to sleep.

But she was fucking brilliant today. Her command, her sharp mind, her fearlessness—I was obsessed before I knew anything about her. And now I'm somehow supposed to pretend I'm not addicted to her while sharing air with a man who might want her just as much as I do?

Not any man—*Enzo*.

My best friend of over twenty years. Enzo, who didn't say a word when she made that crack about the two of us sharing.

Didn't flinch. Didn't scoff. Just…stared. At me.

Enzo Luciano doesn't look at people that way—not men, not publicly. But he looked at me as if he was hungry. And I'd be lying if I said it didn't *affect* me.

I've spent many nights lying in bed secretly wishing Enzo would give me *any* fucking indication that he might be open to exploring something with me. It's never been there. I know it hasn't, because I've searched high and low.

And in one comment, Pippa fractured everything I thought I knew about my best friend.

Bvvvt.

UNKNOWN NUMBER

Still up, Johnny?

As if my thoughts conjured her.

You miss my charming personality?

MY JANE

I miss your hands, mouth, tongue, and certainly those piercings of yours. But sure, it's your charm I can't stop thinking about.

I chuckle. Christ, she's the exact kind of trouble I want in my bed tonight. I debate pretending nothing's changed, but that's not me. Not with her. Despite never sharing our names or work details, over the past year, I've been comfortable being my real self with her. So, I call.

She picks up on the first ring. "Eager, are we?" Her voice is silk and smoke. It settles into my bloodstream.

"You know I am, Janey." I let the nickname roll off my tongue.

She hums. "You calling me that invokes some very fun memories."

"How interesting. You sound just like this captivating woman I used to sneak around with, back when things were simple."

"Simple's overrated," she murmurs.

"So, you want to get together tonight?"

"I do," she says plainly. No games. "I'm feeling a little reckless and you're an expert at—"

"Pip," I cut her off. I rub my hand over my face, surprised by my own resolve. "Things are…*complicated*."

"Yeah, I thought you might say that."

"Yeah."

She laughs, low and throaty. "And what if I want both of you?"

"I don't think the desire or chemistry between you and us is the issue." My mind short-circuits. Visions flash behind my eyes of her between us, *under* us. The heat, the chaos, the goddamn possibility of it all. "You know I'm game," I admit, "but it's different with Enzo. He's not a nameless third, like the others. He's been my best friend since we were kids. I owe him a conversation first."

"Then have it," she says, like it's that simple. She takes a deep breath. "I get that it's complicated. And frankly, I should be avoiding both of you. I know that—we all know that. But laying here in bed—"

I groan at the image.

She chuckles, then continues, "*Exactly*. I'm only human. I know we were teasing Enzo today; I know we were riling him up, but…the mental images it's created—"

"Yeah. Yup… Fucking same." I mindlessly cup my growing erection.

"And PS…" Pippa adds, "I don't think I'm the only one Enzo's craving."

I laugh after a beat, but it's not convincing. "Don't project your fantasy onto me, Saint James."

"You sure?" she purrs. "Because I'm starting to think your best friend might want to do a lot more than share me with you. I saw some looks today that made me think he might want to share both of us."

Click.

She hangs up before I can respond.

What the fuck?

For a boy from the wrong side of town whose mom's absence always made him feel unwanted, the idea of Enzo and Pippa *both* wanting me…

It has my heart racing in a way I'm not prepared to dissect.

Thursday Evening, Day 17

We've been parked a block outside Victor Malin's estate, staked out, for a couple of hours. Luca sits up front with Niko, while Enzo and I have been working in the back, waiting for Malin to get home. We've been clocking the rotation of his security team and discussing our roles of the upcoming op.

"In addition to us, Niko and Luca, I think we go with Max and Gabe," Enzo suggests as he looks over the plans laid out on the back seat. "Both ex-military, both loyal. They know how to handle silent entries and won't ask questions."

"Agreed," I nod and flip open my tablet. "I dug into Malin again last night—or should I say Viktor with a K—I ran back through some old FBI archives. There's barely anything on him, just a handful of vague references from the '80s. Nothing that ties him to Russia. Nothing about the KGB."

Enzo's jaw ticks. "Sealed records?"

"Maybe. Or he was never officially flagged. He's like a damn ghost, but someone buried him well and that usually means government involvement or someone with reach."

"Someone like a President?"

Enzo and I exchange a look.

Someone, somewhere, didn't simply cover up the fact Viktor Malin is Russian, they *reinvented* him. Scrubbed the KGB ties, polished the resume, rebranded him as Victor Malin, an all-American war hero. And that really irks me, because it fucking worked.

"His US military records seem legit," I say as I tap a knuckle against my tablet, "but even those are limited. Frankly, they're easy enough to fake. Eva or Luna could've done it in their sleep, so I have no doubt the Russians have their own top-tier hackers who could've laid the groundwork long before Troy ever announced his first run. The Russians have been funneling money into US politics and corporations for decades. They were laying the groundwork for the right patsy to step up."

Enzo grunts, arms crossed, jaw tight. "Makes you wonder how Jules, Luna, and Pippa figured out his background."

"Yeah." I say slowly. "They don't exactly leave a digital paper trail showing their work. The shit they know? It's not surface-level. They've got layers-deep context. Like they've had eyes in places no one's supposed to see."

"Insider sources?"

"Maybe. Or maybe Luna's cracked systems we don't even know exist."

There's a beat of silence.

"Doesn't mean I'm not wondering who the hell they really are and what else they know," I finish.

Enzo looks contemplative. "They've got trust issues; so do we. But their intel's been too good to dismiss."

We move on to the framework of the plan—logistics, recon, timing. We keep eyes on Malin's place, waiting for his arrival.

I can feel the tension between us, strung taut. I close the file.

"So," I start.

Enzo doesn't look up. "So."

"I talked to Pippa the other night."

That gets his attention. His eyes lift, sharp. He puts his hand up to pause me, then rolls up the window between the front and back of the car.

Okay, we're on the same page.

"She texted. We flirted. She still calls me Johnny." I try for a grin, but it falls flat under Enzo's stare. "We ended up on the phone and...she said she wants both of us."

Enzo stiffens. "She did, huh?"

"Yeah. And look, I know this is a damned mess. I told her nothing's happening until you and I talk first."

"I need to tell you something." He leans back, arms crossed, jaw working. "I went to her house last week."

The fuck? Why didn't he tell me? Why didn't she? "So, you two already—"

"No, no," he says hurriedly. "Nothing happened. It was after you approached Luna at work about the Vale offer. I told myself I was going to Pippa's to seal the deal, but I was lying to myself. I just had to be around her again." He seems pained by that admission.

Fucking same, brother, fucking same. "I get that."

He shakes his head. "We kissed, but we both stopped it before it went further."

I blink a few times, trying to discern how that makes me feel.

When I hesitate to respond he says, "She's different with you. Seeing you two together…there is history there, ease. She fights me with every step. I don't know, maybe it's too messy."

"Shit. No, man, she's on guard with everyone. She was like that with me, too, for a long time, but there is a part of her that rebels against having to play the right part all the time. I think our history allows her to let go and find release. Enz, she's fighting it because she wants you. And she doesn't want to."

I chuckle to myself because I am not only describing Pippa, but also myself. We both want Enzo. "Look, I've given this some thought. I think we should explore it."

He flinches a bit.

I'm not sure what that means, but I continue. "We both want her, she wants us. The tension will continue building until it explodes. Better to just try it—see what happens." I pause. "Of course, it's up to you. I won't pursue anything with her, with or without you, unless you're okay with it."

"Are you serious?" he asks hesitantly.

"I am." I lean forward, elbows on my knees, hands clasped like I'm holding myself together. "We've been through everything together, Enz. You're not just my best friend. You're my fucking family. And I'd never, *ever*, do anything to break that." I meet his eyes—no smirk, no deflection, just truth.

"But I need you to hear me when I say this," I continue, "she's different. Shit, she got under my skin the first night I met her. I tried to brush it off. I told myself it was just sex, but it's not. You know it. I know it."

His silence is more than I can take. So I continue, "I don't know what this means—for me, for you, for us—but I don't want to bury it. And I sure as hell don't want either of us to blow this up out of pride or fear. So if there's a chance we could figure this out without wrecking everything, I'm in."

Another long beat passes.

Enzo's fingers drum against his knee as he thinks, then he stops. "My first priority is us. You and me. We don't fuck with that."

I nod. "Then maybe we talk to her together."

The air shifts. It's subtle, but I feel it. His eyes lock on mine and for a second, something unspoken pulses between us. The kind of spark where your heart stutters and your chest tightens.

I swallow hard.

Neither of us move.

Enzo finally breaks eye contact, scrubbing a hand over his jaw. "Yeah. Let's talk to her…together. It's a good start."

I nod again. My pulse is racing. *Just breathe, Hudson. Jesus.*

Damn if I don't already feel like we're standing at the edge of something we can't take back.

The window inside the car rolls down.

Niko says, "We have eyes."

We turn toward Malin's property where one of the security guards scanning the perimeter is looking our way. He has binoculars and his attention is focused on us.

"Let's head out, Luca," Enzo commands.

Luca slowly pulls forward, taking the next right turn. I have my eyes locked on the security guard, who is taking pictures of our vehicle. Fortunately, the tags will lead him on a wild goose chase.

"Fuck, we didn't get enough info on the rotation of his security detail," Enzo says. "I'll have Eva send a crew out tomorrow to install some cameras."

"I'm sure she and Luna will get better intel tomorrow when they hack the security system and cameras in the area, too."

He agrees and we remain silent until they drop me home.

My head is still reeling, both from our conversation and with concern that the Malin op is fast approaching and I'm not sure whether Enzo, Eva, and I are providing any real value to the mission yet. Enzo's insistence on helping them has been confusing, and whether they need our help or not is still unclear.

One thing *is* clear, though. I have a growing need to keep Pippa and Luna safe. Whether they need us or not… I'm not going anywhere.

FOURTEEN

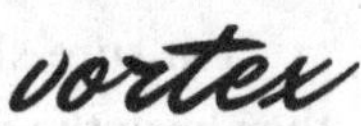

Pippa

Friday Evening, Day 16

I juggle a bakery box filled with extra cookies from my office as I key the code into the warehouse door. I'm hoping the extra sugar can help Jules, Luna, and me finalize this Malin op after an exhausting week. Working with a team has its benefits, but coordinating every moving piece has been more work than normal.

"Pippa, what's in the box?" Luna asks eagerly. Excitement floods her expression at the promise of sugar. I hand her the box and head to our kitchen for plates and napkins. I ask my sisters what they want to drink before joining them at the table.

"Ironically, Senator Cramden received all kinds of condolences in the form of baked goods and flowers today for the loss of his dear friend, Senator Max McCarter."

That makes us chuckle. It took longer than a week for McCarter's heart to fail. Yesterday I was freaking out that maybe my concoction wasn't going to work, but we finally got word he had a heart attack. What should have taken one to two weeks, took closer to three. But it is done.

His wife looked relieved as she made the rounds to the news outlets, clearly preferring to play the role of grieving widow rather than disgraced wife of a pedophile. I wonder how she's going to feel when she learns this weekend her husband's estate is worth a fraction of what she expects. Not only was her husband purchasing and abusing young girls, but it will also look like he was being blackmailed and had to squander his fortune to stay out of jail.

In reality, Luna funneled his assets to our estate—that's what we always do when we take these assholes down. We're female modern-day Robin Hoods—stealing predatory men's money and using it to destroy the legacy of them and their buddies. It's poetic, really.

"FBI got the autopsy report today," Luna reports between bites. "Coroner signed off on heart failure as the cause of death. No one is looking any deeper."

"We got word that they will hold the service Monday afternoon. I almost feel bad they will wake up that day to learn Victor Malin is also dead," I say sarcastically.

"On that note," Jules starts, "Enzo and Eva got the bug on Jonathan Vale's home office during their meeting with him earlier today. All went according to plan, and we should all have access to the data feeds by now."

Luna confirms. "I'll sort through the data tonight."

"Good." Jules flips open her notebook. "Enzo's crew conducted two days of surveillance on Victor Malin's property and set up cameras. Security runs a six-hour rotation. One guard at the gate, two roaming inside the property line. Eva's tapped into the city cams on the street, too, so we have full perimeter coverage."

"I took a look at the standard security protocol for secret

service directors and Malin definitely has more than the average number of guards at the house," I add, "which may support our theory that he'll have the intel we are looking for inside the house."

"Let's hope so," Jules says. "We haven't been able to find any paper trail on the women from Maribel. If anyone kept records, it would have been Victor."

We all nod. The weight of the mission—and hope for its success—settles in.

The three of us haven't spoken about our longer-term goal in a long time. We know we have to take these predators out, since no one in power seems inclined to hold them accountable, or to, *god forbid,* stop the trafficking of children. And we must find Sophie and end her miserable existence. But that doesn't mean vengeance is our only motivation.

We hope one day we can track down one or more of our mothers. Our understanding is that Jared got some of his victims pregnant in the '90s when he first moved to the island. For whatever reason, he didn't have the girls terminate their pregnancies, which was the standard by the time we grew up.

Knowing dear old Dad, his ego couldn't fathom the idea that anything carrying his blood could be unworthy. Sophie hated everything about his decisions to let the girls have their babies. She despised us and our existence, but Dad kept her around. I'm confident she made sure any future victims were on birth control or she made them get abortions behind his back.

We don't know what happened to our mothers. Young women and girls came and went through the island all the time. Did the girls who birthed us do the same? Are they somewhere in the world wondering what the hell happened to us after Jared was killed? Or did Sophie have them killed?

The latter is my hunch. I've always assumed Konstantin did

her bidding. Jules and I asked Jared once where our moms were and he got so angry it terrified us. Jared wasn't winning a Father of the Year award by any means, but he was very rarely cruel to us.

That was Sophie's job. She'd strike when Dad couldn't see or wasn't around.

Jared didn't hate us, but he did not love us. He loved no one but himself.

He must have thought we could be valuable one day, because he made sure we knew the importance of finding all the skeletons buried in someone's closet. He taught us the most powerful person in the room isn't the one with the most money, rather the one who could bury their opponents in blackmail and secrets. From a very young age, he taught us the art of taking down those in power.

We learned a great deal from him, and even more on our own these past ten years in DC. But we have never been able to find a way to track down the girls who gave us life. Deep down, I know we each need that closure before we can put Maribel Island behind us.

My focus shifts to Luna. "What's going on with your Bel-Air case?"

She closes her eyes for a beat, long enough that I know the answer isn't simple. "The bureau formed a special task force to investigate DeShawn Crown."

I blink. "The rapper? What is he called again? GoldT?"

"Yes—the rapper and mogul himself. The Bel-Air parties have been at his properties. The theory is that the private guest lists, the secure location, the weird invite-only 'charity events' he's running—they think his record label is a front for trafficking. The scope got big enough they moved Stone off as lead and brought in an outside expert. I caught wind that someone upstairs made a link to Maribel Island and Jared Whiteman."

I feel a cold twist in my stomach. "Sometimes I hate when our hunches are right."

"It gets worse." Luna's voice softens, but not in a comforting way. "The new head of the task force is Jax Novak."

Oh shit. Luna and I turn to Jules.

"He's in DC," she says slowly, testing the words, not believing them.

"Yes," Luna replies. "He's leading the investigation from here, but traveling to LA and New York, too. I'll be reporting all my findings to him directly."

"Why Jax?" I ask.

"After heading up anti-trafficking for Interpol, he went freelance for all the major agencies. He's considered a leading expert on—" Jules realizes we are both looking at her as we learn she has been keeping tabs on Jax. That's new information.

"Have you seen him since Russia?" I ask.

She shakes her head.

Luna leans forward slightly. "There is one more thing."

We both shoot her a look. "He asked me to pull info on all the private security firms with client lists that overlap with attendees of these parties. The assumption is they may have intel we'll need on the buyers and bidders. Redline was on the list."

Jules nods slowly. "Thanks. I appreciate the heads-up."

I take a deep breath, once again feeling like we are standing at the center of converging storms. Everything is crashing against the shore at the same time, from all directions.

Jules fell hard for Jax during her CIA missions in Russia and Ukraine. He was her Interpol liaison, and they ran anti-trafficking ops for over a year together. He was a man fighting the same demons and they had a whirlwind romance. She thought when her assignment ended, they'd find a way to make it work.

They didn't. As it turned out, he was married. He claims they had been separated for years, but it was a fucking mess. She returned from her missions completely destroyed.

I pat Jules's arm and Luna gives her a hand squeeze, but it's clear she doesn't want to talk about it.

"If you find out he's headed to Redline to see Jules, see if you can join, Luna," I suggest.

"I will," she agrees. "While we are on the topic of Maribel, I tried again to get eyes or ears on Junior, but no luck."

"It didn't seem imperative to know what he's been up to when we thought he was simply hiding from the Lucianos, but if these parties really do tap into Sophie's or Jared's networks, or the Volkov money trail, it opens a lot of questions about what Junior has been up to since his dad died," I say, vocalizing what we're all thinking.

I look to Luna to see if she'll share anything she's thinking or feeling. We were all friends with Junior back at Maribel. He was our *only* friend, the only other kid our age who was ever around.

He and Luna shared a special bond. They were inseparable.

I know she's tried to get a handle on his comings and goings for a long time. She doesn't take the opportunity to open up, though. She's played her feelings about Junior close to the vest for years.

She was upset when we decided not to wait for the Volkovs to retrieve us from Maribel. She was too young to understand why we needed to flee. She trusted us as her big sisters, but she'd also trusted Junior and his father her entire life. She'd trusted our dad, too, but she came to learn she was wrong about all of them. I think she's had a hard time letting go of the version of Junior she remembers.

"Okay, my turn." *Time to lighten the mood.* "Hudson asked me to go to his apartment for a meet up tomorrow night. Him and Enzo. They want to 'address the tension,' whatever that means."

"You should go." Luna wiggles her eyebrows.

Surprisingly, Jules agrees. "Honestly, yeah. You'll all keep spinning if you don't."

I point my finger at them. "First, I don't like being tag teamed."

"You sure about that?" Jules teases.

They both chuckle—*traitors.*

"Second, I really didn't think you two would be so quick to throw me to the wolves. Shouldn't we be keeping our distance from these men? Aren't we assuming this alliance isn't going to work out?" *Ugh.* I take a breath, ready to change the subject.

"It's nice having more people to work with," Jules says suddenly. "Enzo and his team are...solid. And Luna, I'm sure having another hacker to partner with is making it easier, right?"

I know Jules is right, but I hate hearing it out loud.

Luna doesn't respond right away, but then she lifts her chin. "I guess it's my turn to confess, then. Eva asked me out. Like, on a date."

"I'm sorry, what?" I ask.

Jules laughs under her breath. "Actually, that tracks."

Luna's smile seems calm and satisfied. "It does."

"I need so much more information," I say.

"I like her."

"She's great," I agree. "I like her, too. And I mean, I'm sure her runway-model looks don't hurt."

Luna blushes.

Jules smiles.

"Pippa, I understand what you're saying about Hudson and Enzo—it's messy, but I'm not sure I want to ignore how I'm feeling about Eva, and I don't think you should ignore your feelings, either."

"I get that." I really do. I take a deep breath.

Our little triangle goes quiet. Not tense, just full. Heavy with concern and secrets and anticipation of whatever comes next.

I raise my glass. "To…bad decisions." We laugh as we clink our cups together.

The three of us get back to work, locking in the plan for the Malin op. Jules will lead the ground operation with Hudson and Enzo's men. Luna and Eva will be back at the mansion running comms and tech. I will be in the van with Luca keeping an eye on the exterior.

Once Jules and Hudson administer the syringe I'm working on, they'll join Enzo in Malin's office to breach the systems and extract files with support from Luna and Eva.

We need Malin to die right away, which is different from the previous drugs I've concocted. It needs to look like he died in his sleep. Fortunately for me, you can take the guy out of Russia, but you can't take the Russia out of the guy. It seems he still drinks vodka like water. We decided on cardiac arrest, which will come as no surprise when they run his bloodwork and find that his liver is hanging by a thread.

The plan is solid.

For a moment, inside this warehouse full of screens and shadows, it feels like hope.

FIFTEEN

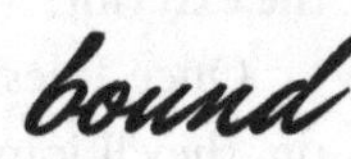

bound

Enzo

Saturday Evening, Day 17

Pippa agreed to meet with Hudson and me tonight to talk. Evidently, we all agree that is the right next step, but as I stand with my best friend in his apartment, my stomach, my chest, and my head have decided this is not a good idea at all.

What good could possibly come from talking about all these charged feelings? I don't know exactly where tonight is headed, but I know it's already on unstable ground. I should just step back. They are the two with history. I've only known the woman for two weeks. I'm considering telling Hudson as much when—

Knock, knock.

Hudson opens the door and the sight of Pippa causes my heart to stutter in my chest.

Her midnight-blue silk dress is cut low enough to make a man forget his better judgment. The silver stilettos look like they were designed specifically to tempt disaster. She wears confidence like armor, and tonight it's as sharp as glass. She wants the upper hand.

Bella, it's already yours.

Hudson clocks her outfit. "Well damn, Janey, you planning on giving me a heart attack before drinks?"

She brushes past him with a smirk. "Just trying to liven up what I assumed would otherwise be a very boring meeting."

I watch her take in the apartment, slow and assessing. Hudson's place is clean, polished, masculine. Expensive without trying. She's never been here before, I know that much. Everything between John and Jane happened on neutral ground—hotels, temporary spaces, places you don't leave fingerprints. Now the veil is half-raised, revealing real names, day jobs, hidden responsibilities, and apartments.

I stand by the window with a glass of bourbon, eyeing her appreciatively.

She smiles, but I can tell she's trying to read me.

"This feels incriminating. Mafia royalty spotted inside a federal agent's apartment? Bold," she smirks.

"I own the building. And the security system. Nothing gets in or out without me knowing."

She blinks. "Jesus. How much of DC do you own?"

"A lot."

Hudson drops into an armchair, feet up like he doesn't have a care in the world. "Yeah, it's super convenient. Mobster landlord, FBI tenant. We're like the shittiest sitcom premise ever."

I don't laugh. The operation is tomorrow night. Everything's set. Roles assigned. Contingencies planned. There's nothing left to talk about.

Except this.

"Well, gentleman," Pippa says, light but deliberate, "thank you for the invitation. I must say, I'm happy we've reached this inevitable conclusion. When I imagined the three of us together, this is exactly how it started. So, who's making the first move?"

I straighten. "Before anything happens, we need to talk."

"About the op?" she asks, innocent in a way that isn't innocent at all. "Or about logistics of a *different* sort? Who's putting what where?"

Hudson lifts his hand like he's toasting. "Cheers to that."

"We need to be smart. We can't let whatever *this* is mess with our plans."

"You think I'd risk our mission over a hookup? Cute, but no. Nothing to worry about on my end."

Hudson laughs quietly but stays out of it.

"I'm serious," I try again. "My friendship with Hudson isn't something I'm willing to sacrifice over a few nights of sex."

"Good to know where I rank," she says turning toward the door.

"Wait," Hudson says, standing. "Pip, come on. He didn't mean it like that."

She pauses, hand on the knob.

"He just thinks too damned much," Hudson throws a glare my way. "Me? I'm over here thinking maybe the three of us need to have a little less conversation, a little more action."

She glances back, mouth twitching. "Elvis would be proud."

I sigh and drag a hand through my hair, interrupting the wave of easy flirtation. "I just don't want to screw this up."

"Then don't," she fires back, closing the distance between us. There's heat in her eyes now, challenge sharp as a blade. "Don't screw it up. Stop overthinking and feel something for once."

"That's my girl." Hudson's grin falters when he notices I'm not smiling. "Shit. Pippa, Enzo is right." Hudson sighs, more serious now. "Like I told you on the phone, I'm not going to jeopardize our relationship. We all have to be on the same page if this goes any further."

The room stills. A standoff with an electric pulse. Complicated doesn't even begin to cover it.

"Look, I get it," Pippa says finally. "You two go way back. I'm not here to fuck that up." She shifts her weight, voice dropping, softer now but no less steady. "I respect your friendship and sincerely appreciate the fact that you're maintaining a focus on our mission. I'd never let anything come between Jules, Luna, or me either." She meets my eyes then Hudson's. "The way I see it, we've got two choices—we take this one step at a time and see if there's anything here or we shut it down now. Your friendship, our operation, none of it's worth screwing up over sex, like Enzo said. Even if the sex might be"—she smiles—"*spectacular.*"

Hudson chuckles, rubbing the back of his neck. "Damn, Janey. You really know how to kill the mood and turn me on at the same time."

The tension stretches, then settles into something precarious but livable.

"One step at a time," I say. "No drama. No games. If it gets messy, we walk."

Hudson confirms with a tilt of his head. "I can live with that."

She arches a brow. "Well, gentlemen...I'm glad we're all feeling adult about this. Now, who's pouring me a bourbon?"

Hudson beelines to the drink cart to do as the lady asked.

Pippa sits on the couch, crossing her sexy-as-sin legs in those damned stilettos like she owns the place, and I know I'm in trouble.

I need to take control of this situation before it takes control of me. "You've been with her before," I say to Hudson, "so maybe tonight, I sit back and watch and learn."

Hudson lifts a brow but doesn't argue. He sits next to Pippa on the couch. As they both look to me, I consider how drawn I am to both of them. Separately they are stunning. Together they are breathtaking.

Pippa tilts her head at me and smiles sweetly. "Learn *what*, exactly?"

I take a seat in the chair across from her. "What you like."

She swallows hard, her playful expression faltering just slightly.

I look to Hudson and I clear my throat, voice a little rougher than I want it to be. "Tell me what she likes," I say. "Show me how you touch her."

Hudson doesn't look caught off guard. He just angles slightly toward her, brushing his knuckles along her thigh. Casual. Familiar. Intimate in a way that draws me in.

"She doesn't want control," he says, voice low. "Not in bed. Not here."

My brows knit. That's not what I expected. Not from Pippa.

"She likes to lose herself," Hudson continues, glancing at me. "She likes to be told. To be pushed. Not because she wants to be dominated—she doesn't belong to anyone—it's the freedom of it. The edge."

I look at her.

Pippa's eyes are half-lidded, her chest rising and falling a little faster now, lips parted as if the sound of his voice alone is doing something to her. She's not denying it. Hell, she's basking in it.

"She craves abandon," Hudson adds. "Not safety. Not predictability. The rush. She wants to be wanted. Loudly. Unapologetically."

"And an audience?"

Hudson smiles. "That just makes it better."

Pippa lets out the softest sound, a breathy moan, and I swear to God, it tightens something in my chest.

I lean forward. My gaze flicks from Hudson's hands to the

look on Pippa's face. She's glowing—lit from within by anticipation.

"Stand, *bella*. Let Hudson show you how much he wants you."

And just like that, she obeys.

Fuck.

Hudson stands in front of her, his hands move to Pippa's hips like instinct, like he's done it a hundred times before.

My jaw ticks knowing that's probably true, but I don't move. I watch. I listen. I try to decipher what it is I'm feeling. Is it jealousy? Not quite. Possession?

Closer.

Pippa lets out a low moan as Hudson's mouth skims her neck, her fingers curling around his shirt. She's in her element, soaking in the attention like a flower with sunlight. And fuck if she doesn't deserve every ounce of it.

I shift in my seat, adjusting for the tension building in my pants. And in my chest. "Show me how you touch her," I say, my voice rougher than I intend.

Hudson turns to me slowly, his eyes narrowing just slightly, testing, not resisting. "She likes to be handled," he says, his voice just above a whisper, "with confident hands. Command but make her feel worshiped while you ruin her. That's the trick."

My gaze flicks back to Pippa, now watching us both like she's the flame, and we're circling moths. She bites her bottom lip.

My restraint damn near snaps. I've always needed control. Always. It's how I grew my family's empire after my parents were murdered. It's how I've managed to lead men who'd slit throats without blinking. But this? This isn't a battlefield. This is something else entirely.

"Then keep going," I instruct Hudson. "Let me see."

He obeys. Slowly, deliberately. His fingers slip beneath the hem of her dress, tracing her body as he removes her dress over her head.

She's not wearing anything under that damned dress. Pippa stands before us, totally naked in silver stilettos.

Okay, you beautiful minx...new kink unlocked.

Hudson and I are both stunned silent as we stare at her.

"Hudson," I say low and husky, to get him to focus, "touch her." As if coming out of a fog, he takes his hand and starts slowly rubbing her clit as he takes a nipple into his mouth.

Pippa arches, her head tipping back with a gasp.

My stomach knots. My fists clench.

I look at Hudson again. His focus. His touch. The way he reacts to her every breath like it matters. There's something magnetic about him, there always has been, but I buried that invisible force so deeply I almost convinced myself it wasn't there.

Until now.

Hudson glances up, eyes locking with mine. There's no mocking in them. No judgment. Just openness. Invitation. And something we've always had—*trust*.

"You coming, Enz?" Pippa teases, her voice breathy, lazy with lust. "Or are you planning to edge yourself in the corner all night?"

Fuck it.

I walk over and stand next to them. My gaze flicks between them as Hudson continues to rub her clit slowly, kissing her neck. I look deeply into her eyes as I take my hand and wrap it around the other side of her neck.

As formidable as she is, her neck is slender and delicate in my palm. My thumb reaches her mouth, and I use it to part her lips.

She darts out her tongue to suck my thumb.

I feel a rumble in my chest at the image. My other hand finds its way to her breast. It's heavy and full in my hand, supple. I pull her nipple between my finger and thumb, rubbing, pinching, and pulling. When she moans, lost in the pleasure of four hands roaming her body, I lean down to kiss her.

It's slow, unhurried, and deep. Our tongues fight for dominance. My whole body turns electric. I feel on fire for her.

For *them.*

I pull back and direct her to the couch. I have her lay across it with her head over the arm. I take her face in my hands and hold her gaze upside down. "Open for him, *bella*. Let me see how well you take his cock."

Hudson slowly undresses to his boxers. God, when was the last time I saw Hudson without a shirt on? I never noticed the way his abs flex when he moves, or the trail of ink down his side that disappears under his waistband. I must've been *trying* not to see.

Hudson grabs a condom and sets it on the couch, then he slips between her legs. While holding eye contact with me, he moves his mouth between her legs and licks from back to front. "Fuck, Enz. She's soaked for us."

My breath catches in my throat at the sight.

Pippa gasps, her eyes locked with mine until they flutter closed.

"No," I say. "Look at me."

Her eyes snap open as a moan tears from her lips, guttural and raw.

I kneel on the side of the couch so our heads can be closer.

Hudson continues to suck on her, adding his fingers inside her. When she's on the edge, breath hitching, I brush my mouth over hers, barely touching our lips together.

She trembles. Her hands grip me like I'm the only anchor she has. And then she shatters. Her orgasm hits like a storm, her cries muffled against my lips.

I hear Hudson shed the last of his clothes and roll on a condom.

Pippa and I slowly break our kiss to look at him. I watch him move like I'm seeing him for the first time. Every ridge of his abdomen taut, every inch of him impossible not to look at.

I see his large, hard, pierced cock covered in a condom and tell myself to catalog that image away. My own dick strains to be released.

When he settles between her thighs, I kiss her again, holding her face like it's mine to cradle, to protect, to possess. Pippa moans into my mouth as Hudson presses against her entrance. Slowly, he goes deeper.

"Jesus… *Fuck*," she breathes, the words tumbling out between kisses.

"Tell me how he feels," I whisper against her lips. My voice is darker now, more commanding. "I want to hear it."

She opens her eyes, glazed with desire, voice ragged. "He's… thick. Stretches me so good. His piercings—" She breaks off with a gasp as Hudson thrusts deeper, angling just right. "God, it's so good. Like a shock to the system every time he hits just right."

I press a kiss to her jaw, her cheek, her mouth again. "And here you are, taking him like you were made for it."

Pippa's breath hitches, and then she looks at me with fire in her eyes. "You have too many clothes on, Enzo. That's the only thing ruining this perfect fucking moment."

I smirk. She's right, and if I don't strip now, I might combust from watching them without entirely participating. I stand, maintaining eye contact with her as I undo the buttons of my shirt one by one.

Her gaze roams my body, drinking me in like she's already imagining what she's going to do with me next.

When I look up, I catch Hudson watching me, too.

I'm about to go all in.

I slide my shirt off, letting it fall to the floor. Their eyes trail my chest, hungry and unashamed, and something primal unfurls inside me. I toe off my shoes, undo my belt, and push my pants down, boxers following until I'm just as bare as Hudson, just as exposed.

And then...*fuck me,* my eyes lock on Hudson's. There's heat—not just lust, but something heavier. A challenge. An invitation. Something that makes my skin burn and I become harder than I've ever been.

I grab the couch's foot stool and position it near the arm.

Pippa's body is stretched open for him, glowing with sweat and need, but it's me she's looking at when she moans.

"Touch her," Hudson commands, voice low, ragged. "She wants you."

My hands slide down her sides, over her hips, then to cup her breasts, thumbs brushing her nipples. She arches, a whimper spilling from her lips.

"God, Enzo," she breathes. "I can't—"

"Yes, you can." I lower my mouth to her ear, lips brushing her skin. "You're doing so fucking good, *bella*. Let us take care of you."

Hudson thrusts harder, deeper.

She shudders in my arms, caught between us.

I kiss her again, slow and possessive, swallowing every sound she makes. Then I pull back, brushing her hair from her face. "I want your mouth. Can you do that for me?"

She nods quickly. Her whole body trembles.

Hudson shifts slightly, lifting her by the hips to hold her in place as I kneel on the ottoman and line my cock up with her mouth. Her eyes flick up, pupils blown wide, and then she takes me into her mouth, warm and wet and perfect.

"Holy fuck," I mutter, fingers threading through her hair as I place my hand around her neck. Supporting her head and feeling her throat work my cock.

Hudson groans, "She's so fucking tight. I feel her clench

harder the more she sucks you. And she's getting wetter. Fuck, she's so turned on, Enz."

Pippa moans deeper at his words, sending vibrations straight through my spine. She's pure chaos and pleasure, caught between us, owning us with every move she makes.

My head tips back as her mouth works me with a kind of desperation, like she needs both of us to breathe. Maybe we need her just as badly. It's not just the sex. It's trust. Surrender. The three of us locked in this impossible, burning gravity.

Hudson's rhythm speeds up.

Pippa's whimpers grow frantic, broken by the fullness in her throat.

My hips rock gently, letting her control the pace.

"Almost there," Hudson grits out.

I look down at her flushed cheeks, her tear-rimmed eyes, the sheen of sweat on her chest, and in an instant I know…

She's *ours*.

I lock eyes with Hudson and lean toward him. Our hands have been on her the whole time, but I reach over with one hand and clasp his neck. I lick my lips and watch him do the same.

Fuck, I want to kiss him.

I move my thumb across his neck and up his cheek, over his lip.

Connected, the three of us finish. Hudson first, gritting out Pippa's name like a prayer, then Pippa, crying out as she shatters between us. Finally, I come undone by the sound of her, the sight of them, the feel of everything we just gave each other.

The explosion is the best orgasm of my life.

Fuck. Is *that* what sex is supposed to be like?

I lift Pippa up and place her between us on the couch. She is boneless and flushed, her head tilted back against the cushion, hair wild, lips kiss-bruised. She looks wrecked. Sated. Beautiful.

Hudson leans back against the couch. He runs a hand through his hair, and his chest rises and falls like he's still catching up.

We don't speak. Because what do you say when everything has changed? Hudson and I didn't kiss, but from the way he held my gaze, we both seemed to know it was only a matter of time.

Pippa lets out a slow breath. "Well…that wasn't very professional."

We all huff a laugh.

And I know, at least for me, that nothing will ever be the same again.

SIXTEEN

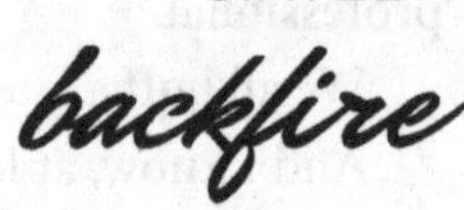

Hudson

Thursday Night, Day 22

The night tastes like rain is on its way—thick with tension, humidity, and the metallic bite of something unfinished. It's been hard to shake feelings of abandonment and isolation today. Enzo and Pippa both left quickly after our tryst on the couch. I tried not to take it personally. Neither of them handles feelings well and if they felt anything to the extent that I did, I'm sure as shit that they needed to process it all. I'm hoping after we complete tonight's mission, they'll at least be looking to blow off some steam. And maybe Enzo and I will—

"CCTV and adjacent security feeds are scrubbed," Eva's voice slices into the silence over comms. "No eyes on the property, no digital trail. As far as the grid's concerned, no one was ever here."

Jules, Enzo, and I are approaching the back door of Malin's house to disarm the alarm. Niko's team swept the perimeter of the sprawling estate. The heat signature indicates only one person on the property—Malin. And he has been lying still in bed for the last twenty minutes.

Pippa is in the van with Luca keeping watch. Eva and Luna work tech and comms from the mansion. If we do this right, we'll be in and out in ten minutes.

The plan is for Enzo to run a sweep in the office so Eva and Luna can tap in, while Jules delivers the fatal injection to Malin. I'll be with her to sweep his room and serve as backup. We are looking for any tech or safes we can hack into. Now that we know Malin works with the Russians, we are all hoping there might be intel that can serve everyone's various needs.

"You're good to enter," Pippa confirms. "Heat sig still reads one body, main bedroom, zero movement. He's either asleep or dead."

"Dead would save us some trouble," I joke.

We learned during our surveillance rounds that there's a nightly window when Malin is alone. His team takes off between one and six a.m., giving us the opportunity to keep casualties at a minimum.

As we enter the back door, Jules approaches the security panel. "Luna, Eva, we've got an NX2R touchpad. Mid-tier commercial grade, not hardwired. Secondary cellular backup."

"Copy that," Luna says, fast and calm. "NX2R has a six-digit override window, basic duress code, and…hold up, does it have the blue LED ring or red?"

"Red."

"Good. That's the older firmware. Eva, you got eyes?"

"Already tapped into the backend. Keypad's linked to a local node, not central dispatch. No video feed. You've got a ninety-second bypass before it pings secondary."

"Use the 3629 code sequence, hold the last digit down for three seconds," Luna instructs. "That'll stall the signal loop. Then swap to manual override and kill the ping. Easy peasy."

Jules nods once, fingers already moving. "On it."

No alarms. No lights. But the door doesn't unlock.

"No luck." Jules frowns and eases off the panel. She tests the handle anyway. It doesn't move.

Silence for a beat, then Eva says sharply, "Stand by. Signal went through. Panel reports unlocked."

Jules braces a shoulder against the door and leans in again, reporting that it's not budging. The three of us make eye contact, ready to consider our contingency options, if needed.

"Then it's not software," Luna says. "It's mechanical."

Jules shifts closer to the door. "What do you need from me?"

Luna answers without missing a beat. "We need to time the push with the input."

"Enzo and I can do that while you walk Jules through the keypad again," I say.

"When I say 'now,' you push. Not before. Not after," Eva says.

A pause.

Jules confirms that the three of us are ready and in place.

"Okay," Eva murmurs. "Rerouting LED power..."

The keypad's red ring flickers, dims.

"On my count," Luna starts, "One...two...now."

Enzo and I lean in, controlled, steady.

Clack.

It's muted, but unmistakable. The door gives.

"Nice work, team," Enzo says.

The three of us step into the hall. The mansion sprawls before us, drenched in shadows and silence. Malin's taste is gaudy and overcompensating. Gold fixtures, mirrored walls, furniture that screams wealth without taste.

We move silently, careful not to wake the sleeping dragon. We know our positions and responsibilities—all there's left to do is execute. *Literally and figuratively.*

Enzo peels off toward Malin's office. He'll work with Luna and Eva to scrape the hard drives clean.

Jules and I press toward the bedroom. I'm equipped with a syringe of poison intended for Malin in case anything goes sideways and Jules can't take him out. I agreed to it, but having this damned syringe in my vest isn't my favorite feeling.

"Bravo One, stop," Pippa instructs over the comms. "Target's on the move. Just got out of bed, heading to the bathroom."

Jules and I pause outside the bedroom door.

"Switch to shadow play," Jules whispers.

I nod once. *Shit*. This is getting a little more complex. Now that he's not in bed, we can't risk him having time to react and defend himself once he sees us. As long as it looks like he died of natural causes in his bed, we should be in the clear.

We enter the bedroom and approach the closed bathroom door. My job is to distract Malin as he exits while Jules injects him. He'll have immediate cardiac arrest, and we'll move him to the bed.

We aren't yet in position when the bathroom door explodes open. Malin charges out like a cornered animal, gun raised.

I try to pivot, but he's too fast.

Pop!

The crack of a gunshot splits the air.

Jules moves so fast, I don't register what is happening as I hit the floor.

"Hudson's been hit," Jules says into comms, calm and clear, so the team doesn't misinterpret the gunshot they just heard.

Then, I see Malin's body seize and twitch, folding to the ground next to me. I look up to see Jules placing the empty syringe into her vest.

Suddenly, pain blooms in my chest before I can register the blood pouring from my ribcage.

Jules kneels at my side, examining me. "Target down," Jules reports. "Hudson's bleeding. No exit wound. Chest hit."

"I'm fine." I have no idea if that is fucking true, but I gotta keep it light.

Enzo bursts in and drops to his knees beside me, hands moving, assessing.

My eyelids grow heavy.

"We need to move. Now!" Enzo shouts.

Jules and Enzo haul me up, draping an arm over each of their shoulders, walking me through the house.

"Niko, get to the house. Secure the scene. Cleanup starts now. Luca, we are headed your way, get ready. Eva, call Doc."

"Keep pressure on the wound," Pippa instructs in my earpiece.

I feel queasy and lightheaded as we make our way through the house. Pain spreads through me, keeping pace with the amount of blood I'm losing.

Fuck, that's not good.

My head lolls back, and Enzo adjusts his hold so my head rests on his shoulder. His hand is pressing into my chest, over the wound. Our eyes lock, and I see his concern. "Stay with me," he whispers.

Like I would ever leave this man.

"Van's ready," Pippa announces.

Niko and his crew are waiting at the door to help get me to the van.

Pippa runs up to us and places her hands on either side of my face. They're so soft. "You're not dying on me tonight, Johnny, okay? Stay awake."

"Wouldn't dream of it, Janey. I'm too pretty to die, we both know that."

She looks worried. It must be bad.

They pull me into the van. Jules reminds everyone that she, Pippa, and Luna have medical and EMT training. Pippa takes command in the van, while Jules takes command of the men outside.

"Listen, Hudson's DNA is on file at the Bureau," Jules says. "This must be the most detailed clean up job we have ever done, understood? It has to look like Malin died in his sleep. Let's get to work."

The van door closes.

Luca hops into the driver's seat and we speed off.

Eva's voice comes in tight and calm. "Doc's en route, ETA fifteen minutes. Luca, I'll have the south gate open." It's the fastest route to the clinic entrance.

"I'm not reading any police on your course," Luna adds. "Move fast."

"Jane, after you and Doc fix me up, will you give me a sponge bath?"

She snorts and shakes her head. "If you're still flirting, you should be fine."

I sure hope so.

I force my eyes open and tell myself to stay awake and keep fighting…because one night with Pippa and Enzo wasn't nearly enough.

SEVENTEEN

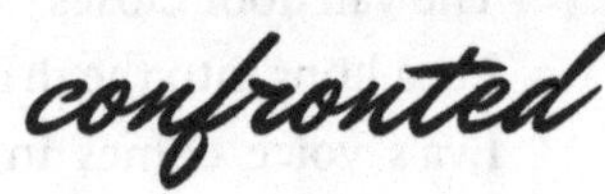

Enzo

Thursday Night, Day 22

Hudson's blood is hot against my hands. Too hot. Like his body knows it's losing too much and is working hard to inform me he's in danger. My brain and my heart are not willing to absorb that information.

In all our years as best friends, with Hudson running double ops between the FBI and the mob, he's never been shot, never had a serious injury. While I know what we do is dangerous, I've never faced the possibility of losing him in any real way.

And it can't happen.

I've got him propped up in the back of the van, his back to my front, head resting against my shoulder. Hudson's pulse thuds weakly beneath my fingertips and his breath rattles too loudly in my ear.

This is the first time I've ever held him like this—felt his body pressed against mine. Why did it take an emergency for me to have my arms wrapped around him? Isn't this where he's always belonged?

Pippa's pressed in on my other side, calm and focused as she works to steady all three of us. She has a small medical bag in hand. "It's all we've got until we hit the clinic. Pressure. Add more pressure," she orders as she snaps on gloves, tearing open gauze. "Enzo, hold that angle. Don't let his airway dip."

I'm so glad she's here.

I nod, jaw clenched, palms slick. I've seen men shot before. Hell, I've put bullets in more than a few. I've been around blood and death my whole life and I've always stayed calm and collected under pressure.

But this is Hudson.

My best friend.

My pain-in-the-ass second brain.

My sense of humor when one can't be found.

My— My—

My breath hitches. "Hudson, hey," I say, forcing lightness into my voice. "You still with me, pretty boy?"

His eyes flutter. "You think I'm pretty?" he mumbles weakly, too weakly. "I won't die on you if I'm finally getting you and Pippa to hold me at the same time."

Pippa lets out a small laugh, voice tight. "Stay awake and we'll make sure the touching is a lot more fun next time."

She and I make eye contact and share a million thoughts in the blink of an eye. We can't lose him and when he's through this, we'll stop wasting time.

Hudson coughs. "Don't threaten me with a good time."

That's Hudson. Always able to keep things light. Always able to keep *me* light. I feel anything but light right now, though. I press harder on the wound.

Stay with me Hudson. Please, please don't make me lose you, too. I won't survive it.

Pippa leans in, peels back his blood-soaked shirt. "Eva, let the doc know, pulse is 120, BP is dropping; tachy, shallow breathing. Let her know she'll need suction and blood units prepped. We'll need to decompress if we lose lung pressure enroute."

"Copy," Eva replies instantly. "Clinic is ready, and Doc is almost here."

Luca drives faster. We take a corner hard, and I have to shift to keep Hudson upright.

He groans.

"Sorry," I whisper, hand pressing harder on the gauze. "I've got you. You're gonna be fine, okay?"

He doesn't respond, his eyes are closed, and all my efforts to remain calm are about to fail.

I met Hudson on the playground on the first day of second grade. Much to my dad's concern, I was a quiet and soft child. Too much like my mom in those early years. And the kids on the playground didn't care much that I was the son of the head of the Italian mob. I'd later be crafted in Lorenzo's image, but at the ripe age of seven, I was picked on just the same as any other shy, quiet, awkward kid.

I was sitting by myself on a bench at the edge of the playground. Some kids came to make fun of me for reading instead of playing, but Hudson wasn't having it. He approached the group and acted friendly with them, charming them—like he charms everyone. Right when they thought they had another ally in bullying me, he dismantled them.

Not physically. Verbally. Even in second grade, he seemed to understand everyone's insecurities, their little-kid-secrets. He exposed all this embarrassing stuff, totally mortifying them. Then, he spoke of my dad, me, and my family in a way that made us sound formidable.

I'd later come to realize my family was exactly all the things he believed them to be, but he seemed to have reverence for my place in the world long before I did. I didn't understand until we were older that he knew about my family through his mother. She talked highly of the Lucianos and Hudson followed suit.

He became my best friend that day and we've been inseparable since. He's been by my side through every moment in life—all the good and all the bad. He kept Eva and me going when our parents died. Always treating her like his own sister, protecting her. The two of them are just as tight as she and I.

I can't remember a time he wasn't there when I needed him.

"Hudson, listen to me—keep fighting. You don't get to die on me," I whisper into his ear, urgent, desperate. "I finally figured it out. Please give me more time with you to do it right."

Pippa slips her fingers between mine. Her hand is blood-slicked and trembling, but strong. We're both applying pressure to Hudson's wound now. A triad of tension and fear and something sacred.

"Enzo's right, Hudson. You're not done here, okay? You've got to stay." She pulls her hand back to take his pulse again. "He's going to crash."

"Not today," I murmur, forehead pressing to the side of Hudson's. "You hear me? Not today. You're too charming to bleed out in a van."

The gates to the mansion are open by the time we round the final curve. Security floodlights cut across the driveway, guiding us to the large, open garage where the clinic is attached.

Dr. Alessia Romano, who we have affectionately called "Doc" since I was a teen, stands waiting. Her family and mine go way back. She's in her early fifties and has sharp eyes and steady hands. She's patched up half my crew at one point or another and right now she looks like a war general.

We screech to a halt.

Luca leaps out, runs around the vehicle and opens the door.

We all haul Hudson to Doc's clinic as Pippa calls out vitals and wound info in a sharp stream.

Doc and her two nurses surround him instantly, and I feel his weight disappear from my arms.

The absence is brutal.

Pippa stumbles slightly as they carry him away and I catch her.

Neither of us speak. We just stand there for a breath too long, covered in blood that doesn't belong to us, watching the team rush him inside.

He was staring into my eyes as he passed out—like he was trying to remember something in case he didn't make it.

I don't realize I'm shaking until Pippa wraps her arms around me and holds me like I'm the one bleeding out.

I let her. I let her comfort me, because for the first time in a long time, I don't have a plan.

Friday Morning, Day 23

The clinic smells like antiseptic and copper. It crawls into my lungs and stays there. Hudson's form stretches across the narrow bed, his chest rising and falling in time with the machines. The bullet's been removed. It missed all major organs or arteries. The doctor said that with rest he should be okay, but he hasn't woken up.

I need him to wake up. If I think hard enough, stare long enough, I can will him back into himself.

Pippa and I have been posted on either side of his bed for hours. At first, we held his hands, spoke to him, talked to each other. Filling the silence felt like something solid to cling to.

Then we rotated showers as Eva, Luna, and Doc drifted in and out.

Jules and the team returned about an hour ago and reported everything had been handled. They cleaned up, checked on Hudson, then peeled off to rest.

Dawn is fast approaching. By morning, Malin's death will make the rounds. Jules curated the details, ensuring the story ends with "died in his sleep." Clean. Final.

The raw desperation from the van is gone. The version of me that let Pippa hold me in the hallway while Hudson was carted away, that man has been sealed away. I've been quiet too long. I know it. I can feel something grinding inside me. A different Enzo sits here now—the onc people know. The one who took over after my parents were murdered. The one most men are smart enough not to cross.

"You should get some rest," Pippa says softly. "You've been holding your breath since we got here. Hudson needs rest and so do you. I can stay with him."

My jaw tightens. "I'm not leaving. I'll be fine."

She comes over to my chair.

I don't look at her. Her hand lands on my shoulder and my body goes rigid. Not with anger, but with distance. A wall slams into place before I can stop it.

"Don't," she whispers. "Don't you dare pull away from me right now."

My eyes cut to hers. Dark. Flat. Everything is locked down tight. "This isn't about you, Pippa."

"Then what is it? Because five hours ago, you and I were both fighting to keep him alive. Together." She squares her shoulders. "I care about him, too, Enzo. And now you're shutting me out. Don't pretend you're not. You think I don't notice you putting up walls?"

I turn back to Hudson. It's safer to look at him. "I should've seen it coming. Should've kept him safe. My head wasn't where it needed to be."

The truth sits heavily in my chest. I don't need her to say it—I already know. I've made this mistake before.

"You think this is your fault?" she asks.

"It is." The words scrape on the way out. "I let myself get distracted." I pause, drag in a breath. "By you."

She steps back. Stung. Her own walls fly back up; I can feel it.

"I just *had* to follow you into that warehouse. None of us would be here if it weren't for me." My hand drags down my face, what remains of my control slipping. "And now look at him. Hudson is fighting for his life. Because of me." The words land hard. Not because they're cruel, but because they're true. Just like when my broken engagement ended with the destruction of my family. I'm repeating history.

"This…us…" I shake my head. "It's too complicated. I can't risk him again."

"So that's it?" she challenges. "What if Hudson and I don't agree?"

The air between us snaps tight. For one heartbeat, I almost break, almost reach for her, almost say the apology clawing its way up my throat.

Instead, I straighten, armor up. "Get some rest."

Dismissal—clean and final.

Her hands curl into fists.

I don't look at her, but I feel the heat of her stare.

"You can run all you want, Enzo, but this thing between us? It doesn't vanish just because you say so. And if you think I'm the type of woman you can shut out, you really haven't been paying attention."

I don't reply.

Click.

The door closes behind her and the air shifts.

I remain where I am, eyes on Hudson, guilt heavy and familiar. I don't know how to untangle the three of us. I only know one thing for certain—I will not let anyone else get hurt because of me and my *feelings*.

Never again.

The steady beep of the monitor is the only thing keeping me anchored as I build my walls brick by brick. Each sound tells me Hudson's heart is still fighting. Each rise and fall of his chest under the blanket feels like a fragile promise I don't deserve.

"Vitals look good," Eva says softly from behind me.

I didn't hear her come in. I don't know how much time has passed.

"Steady. Improving. Doc says he's strong enough to pull through."

I don't look at her. "He hasn't opened his eyes."

"That's because Hudson likes the attention," she says with a forced lightness in her voice. "He knows the whole house is spinning around him and he's milking it."

I drag a hand over my jaw. "You don't get it, Eva."

"I don't?"

"No." My voice sharpens despite myself. "I pulled him into this. Into *them*. This is on me."

She blinks, then lets out a dry laugh. "So now you're rewriting the rules of cause and effect? A man gets shot in the middle of an operation and somehow your crush on Pippa pulled the trigger?"

I stiffen. "This isn't a joke."

"Then stop acting like one." She leans forward. "Hudson knew the risks, same as you, same as me. You didn't force him into this. You two have been ride-or-die since you were kids. He wouldn't want you sitting here turning yourself into the villain."

I don't answer. My silence is thick, furious.

"So let me guess," she continues. "It's your fault we all agreed to help them out. And in addition to blaming yourself, you're going to go into protector mode, right? You're planning to tell the team that Hudson, you, and I won't join any future missions. Am I missing anything?"

I straighten in my chair. "It's not our fight."

"*Wrong*. You can make decisions for yourself all you want, Enz. But so can Hudson and so can I. And their fight became my fight the second they trusted me with it. The second Luna let me in. You don't get to decide otherwise."

"The hell I don't!" I snap, the old Luciano authority filling the room—the very one our father drilled into me.

She stares me down, unflinching. "Last I checked, Hudson and I are adults. And you and I both know Hudson won't let this stop him from working with Pippa or Luna. He cares about them. He's all in on this, you know he is. And so am I." She looks just like our mother.

I curse and drag in a breath. "I know you're right, E. I know you and Hudson are in deep with this." I hesitate, then add quieter, "But what do we really know about them? We jumped in too fast."

"Maybe we did, but we jumped in all the same. Are you really telling me you can walk away?"

That hits harder than I want it to. I stare at Hudson, fighting something inside myself, unsure which side will win. "I can't argue about this right now, E." My voice gives way to exhaustion. "I just need to know he's okay."

"Can I ask you something?"

I want to say no. I agree anyway.

"Assuming Hudson recovers like Doc says—he wakes up with all his normal bravado and shenanigans—are you really willing to walk away from what you have with him and Pippa?"

"Why would I have to walk away from Hudson?"

The look on her face tells me that wasn't the answer she expected.

"Do you think Hudson will want to walk away from Pippa?"

I don't answer.

The silence stretches. Then, quietly, more vulnerable than I'd like, I ask, "Do you think he'd pick her over me?"

Eva's face softens. "Never, Enz. Hudson would never leave your side."

Some of the tension drains from my body.

"But after all this," she continues gently, "are you really willing to ask him to choose? You know he cares for her, too. And while you might be beating yourself up for getting us involved, you can't tell me you don't care about her. Could you really walk away?"

"I have to. I have to keep you and him safe, E. You're my family. The only family I have left." My voice cracks on the last word.

"I know, but no one ever said our family couldn't expand." She crosses the room and hugs me. I hold on longer than I expect to. I tell my sister I love her and she says it back.

When she turns to leave, she pauses. "Try to get some rest."

I nod, though we both know I won't.

I turn back to Hudson, grip his hand tighter, and wait for the next beep.

EIGHTEEN

Pippa

Friday Morning, Day 23

The patio outside the back den of Enzo's house carries the smell of pine trees and the coffee my sisters and I have in our hands. The air is damp, charged, like the world hasn't quite decided yet if it's going to forgive us for surviving the night.

None of us have slept. We refuse to leave the Luciano mansion until we know Hudson is awake and okay. He is still unconscious one floor down, but Doc expects he'll wake soon.

Every time I blink, I see him in the back of the van, bleeding. Watch the stain spreading under my hands.

Sitting around an outdoor table, Jules, Luna, and I plan for the day. Luna and I both know we'll be called in to work as soon as the news hits. Only a couple of hours likely remain until the chaos begins.

Luna sits cross-legged in a bright, oversized hoodie with her curly hair in a knot at the top of her head. She's vibrating with leftover adrenaline, one leg bouncing as she nurses her third cup of coffee. Her laptop glows between us, containing spreadsheets and code.

"In Malin's files I found receipts," Luna says finally. She taps the trackpad, a scanned ledger glowing in the dawn light. "A warehouse in Ivy City, paid for in cash through one of his shells. He's been making regular payments for over a decade."

That piques our interest.

"My gut tells me if Malin had anything about President Troy or Jared and Sophie, or records on the girls funneled through Maribel Island, that building is where he'd have kept it."

A chill ripples through me, sharper than the dawn air.

Magnus Troy—the man sitting in the Oval, powerful and seemingly untouchable.

Jared Whiteman—the beginning of it all, the predator whose sins we were born to bear.

Sophie Delacroix—the woman in hiding pulling the strings.

And the girls—the ones lost to men like Whiteman, Malin, and Troy, their futures stolen before they began. Their children ripped from their wombs and raised in the hands of monsters.

"If Malin is the key, like we believe he is," I say slowly, "then that warehouse could be the lockbox. And we need to break it open before anyone else knows we've found it."

Jules arches a brow. "Meaning we don't loop in the mafia siblings or Hudson when he wakes?"

"Exactly."

Silence stretches. Luna stares into her coffee like it might give her an easier answer. Jules weigh the pros and cons in her mind.

"Enzo's already pulling away," I whisper. "He blames himself for getting Hudson and Eva involved with us. He regrets getting close to me, I can tell."

"He'll come around—" Luna starts.

I shake my head. "Maybe, but we promised we'd never drag anyone else into this mess. We broke that promise and it's gotten someone I care about hurt. We sacrificed too much to get here to risk our goals and the lives of innocent people."

The truth is even heavier than that. Jared's ghost still haunts us. Sophie's absence mocks us. Now the celebrity parties seem to be in operation again. And the gala is fast approaching.

In just over two weeks I face my past—once and for all.

"How do we walk away now?" Luna asks, interrupting my thoughts. "And what if I don't want to?" she whispers.

"That's the problem, isn't it?" I ask. "We weren't supposed to want any of this. Not Enzo and Hudson. Not Eva. Not Jax, who is suddenly back in the picture." Jules starts but I raise my hand. "He'll be at your door any day, Jules, we all know it. And you probably want to see him again—no one would blame you—but *wanting* something means weakness. And weakness gets us killed. Or worse, it could get *them* killed. None of us are invincible against these men and their proximity to power. We learned that again tonight."

It's the real reason Jules walked away all those years ago. What she and Jax had was real, his ex was just an excuse. She got so close that she wanted to tell him the truth. She considered it then, but she knew it was too dangerous. So, she let him go. And she's never let anyone close again.

None of us have.

I fold my arms across my chest, keeping my tone clipped. "We walk away because that's what we've always done. Walls up. Circle tight. Survival."

The three of us fall quiet. The sun edges over the horizon, painting us in light that feels too fragile for the mess we're in.

Jules stands. "Here's the plan. We focus on the warehouse for now. Luna, you'll also need to find a way to cover Hudson at work. Keep him off the FBI's radar until he's walking again. I say Luna swings by the unit on the way back from HQ. Quickly. Quietly. No one sees you."

Luna beams.

I put my mug down. "It should be me. I can do it."

Luna interjects, "It's an easy warehouse in and out, Pip, no reason it can't be me. The warehouse is closer to my office, anyway."

Jules and I always keep Luna out of harm's way as best we can. She's the youngest of us, and we've always protected her more than ourselves, but this is important to her. I want to argue, but I choose not to. I'm fighting battles on too many fronts right now. "It's your find, Luna. I agree, you should do it."

She smiles with a small glint of appreciation.

"Pippa will be backup for you, and you'll keep us apprised of your steps. Call if you need anything, at all. And I'll keep us steady here and send updates on Hudson," Jules says.

We all nod in agreement and the plan is set.

The sun crests the horizon, streaking gold across the stone patio, catching in Jules's dark hair and Luna's tired eyes. For a moment, we look like normal sisters drinking coffee at dawn, waiting for the day to start.

Average.

Safe.

But we're not normal, and safety is an illusion I stopped believing in a long time ago.

Friday Morning, Day 26

The clinic is quiet except for the steady hum of monitors. Pale sunlight slips through the blinds, painting stripes across Hudson's chest. I've showered and dressed for the day, but I didn't want to leave until I'd seen him again.

He looks better than in the dark hours. His color has returned and his breathing is even, like the dawn has bargained him a little more life.

I'm holding his hand when the door opens.

Enzo steps in. His broad frame fills the doorway. He pauses when he sees me, then clears his throat.

I feel the air change.

His eyes land on my hand holding Hudson's.

I pull back reflexively, as if burned. I push up from the chair. "I should—" I start.

He lifts a hand. "Stay." The word sounds heavy. He doesn't move closer. We're awkward satellites, orbiting Hudson but avoiding each other's gravity.

Before I can find something safe to say, Eva breezes in, tablet in hand, expression tight. "News cycle's spinning. Malin's death is everywhere. Threads connect him to half of DC."

"I just got word," I add. "Cramden's office called me in. Damage control, I'm sure."

"I'll sit with him," Enzo says. An escape route offered to both of us.

Jules strides in and gives Hudson a once-over.

I keep my eyes on Hudson, on Eva's tablet, on anything but the man across the room.

Enzo hasn't glanced my way since he walked in. If ignoring me were an Olympic sport, he'd be taking gold before breakfast. I don't want it to bother me. I don't let men crawl under my skin, but somehow, I've ended up with two lodged there anyway—one I'm begging to wake so I can finally breathe, the other staging a world-class disappearing act from six feet away.

"Anyone seen Luna?" Jules asks, breaking me out of my pity spiral.

"Right here," Luna says as she pushes through the doorway with her phone in hand. "FBI wants me at HQ. I'm guessing Hudson will have received the same message. I can cover, keep them from sniffing too close, and see what chatter they're pushing about Malin."

Jules seems to be contemplating if anyone should leave . . . Surprisingly well-acted, given that we've already decided to get out of here. "Any word from Cramden's office yet?"

Someone give my sister the Oscar already.

I tilt my chin in confirmation.

The room fills with voices. Eva lists several cover stories, Luna questions how deep Troy's people may already be digging and what Redline can look into, and Enzo paces near the window.

No one questions why Luna or I decide to leave. The new plan is holding.

Good.

Suddenly, a low groan cuts through the noise. Hudson shifts, lashes fluttering. His lips part, voice rough but familiar. "Didn't realize I was this popular."

Relief cracks the room open.

Luna mutters something about grabbing the doctor before slipping out. The rest of us pile closer, like kids at a birthday party.

Hudson opens his eyes to find himself mobbed. At once, we all fire questions and relief in unison. He groans like we're torturing him, but I know he loves it.

I smile genuinely for the first time in the last sixteen hours.

Eva gets him some ice water. By the time Luna and Doc return, Hudson's holding court like a bullet to the chest is just another story to brag about.

Typical.

That's when I know it's safe to slip out. He's alive, surrounded, and safe for now. It's my cue to follow Enzo's lead and put my walls back up, too.

I can't afford distraction, either. I need distance. I need armor. I need to remember what happens when I let myself care too much.

Although, it's probably too late for me to stop, because somehow the people in this room got under my armor. I already feel like they are mine to protect. Even if it's me they need protection from.

NINETEEN
atlast

Hudson

Friday Morning, Day 23

"Good news," Doc finally declares, pulling off her gloves. "You're healing faster than expected. You'll live to annoy another day."

Eva laughs and bends to hug me with surprising strength for someone so petite.

Enzo claps my shoulder, firm but careful, though his eyes say the most right now.

One face is now missing. *Did I dream seeing her only moments ago?*

I scan the room, frown tugging at my lips. "Where's Pippa?"

Luna, who's been leaning against the doorframe with her arms crossed, shrugs. "She had to head to work. So do I. Don't worry, I'll cover for you at the office."

There's something in her tone. It's tight, deliberate, like she's smoothing over a wrinkle she doesn't want me to notice. She crosses the room and drops a quick kiss to my forehead and slips out before I can push.

I glance at Enzo. He's begun pacing, jaw locked, a storm building behind his eyes. Something has shifted while I was out, it's fucking heavy in the air now.

Eva lingers a beat longer, fussing with my blanket until Enzo shoots her a look. She sighs and presses a kiss to my temple, like Luna did. Jules mutters something about being tougher than I look. Then everyone disperses one by one, leaving me to decipher whatever Enzo hasn't said yet.

He moves to the foot of the bed, arms folded. He looks like he wants to punch something but doesn't trust himself not to break me instead.

I let out a dry laugh. "You can relax. You heard Doc, I'm not dying today."

Nothing. Not even a twitch.

"Seriously, man. Don't look so grim. You'll give yourself wrinkles and then where will your brooding reputation be?" I give him a slow smirk.

Still stone-faced.

I sigh, shift against the pillows. "What? You're gonna fucking stand there brooding until I guess what's eating you?" I know Enzo better than I know myself, and I know exactly what is going on here. "Let me guess: You're blaming yourself for getting us mixed up with our very own Charlie's Angels and pushing Pippa away?"

"You think I don't see it?" Enzo asks, voice low. "That you'll joke your way through the pain, keep us all smiling, so none of us notice how close we came to losing you?"

Well, fuck.

Enzo's hand grips the rail of my bed. "I was scared, Hudson. In that van, holding you as you bled out, listening to your voice fade, feeling your pulse drop... I realized I couldn't lose you—not you, Hudson."

My chest tightens. Surprise cracks through whatever shitty mask I had left. I can't tell if he means this the way friends care for each other. Or the way I've only recently allowed myself to hope for.

Enzo sits beside me, takes a deep breath, and finally looks me straight in the eye. "Hudson, I love you. I've always loved you. Most of that time loving you has been as a friend, as my family, but it's also always been a little bit more, too."

My heart stutters. Panic and hope collide in equal measure. "Enzo, don't— Shit, you don't have to—"

"Yes, I do," he cuts in gently but firmly. "Please let me say this. I've been sitting here for hours worried you'd never wake up and I'd never get the chance. So I'm going to say my piece."

I offer a small smile, encouraging him to continue.

"When we were growing up, I knew I'd be married off to some mafia Don's daughter. It was the path I was born into. I remember when you told me you were bisexual, I was jealous of you. I never told you that, but I was.

"I was jealous of your freedom. Jealous that you got to go explore who you were and what you wanted. I was jealous of all the men I thought would steal you from me. I remember that the most—feeling like I wish you didn't need anyone other than me."

My throat closes.

"I didn't understand my feelings at the time. I didn't even really let myself explore those thoughts. I was seventeen when I was first introduced to Ciara, and even though I never loved her, I believed she'd be my wife and that meant something to me.

"And after that blew up, after my parents... I was so young. I was so scared. And I was so grateful to have you and Eva in my life. For years now, I haven't thought about much more than survival. But I only knew I *could* survive because you were by my side."

I swallow hard. "I…I don't know what to say. I never knew you felt that way. I never thought that you might. I—I never dared to even dream about it." A breath slips out of me, half a laugh. "Okay, that's a damned lie. I've dreamt about it plenty. But it always seemed a fool's dream. Not my reality."

His hand drifts and his knuckles brush my forearm—testing, careful.

I don't pull away. I don't want to. When his fingers slide into mine, it feels like something clicking into place after years of the almost-perfect position.

We stare at our hands like they're proof this is real.

"Hudson, I don't know how to do any of this," he says quietly. "I'm sorry it took Pippa coming along for us to talk about the possibility of us. I've been an idiot, but I'm hoping you'll forgive me for being blind to what was right in front of me. I want to give this a try."

"Pippa," I say softly. Not accusatory, probing.

His jaw tightens. "I didn't think the alliance through enough before inserting myself into their mission. We don't know these people, not in the way real allies should, and I'm not sure we can really trust them—"

"Not all alliances result in deceit," I say, watching him closely.

His chest tightens visibly at the name. I can almost see the memories clawing their way up. "Ciara fucked me up, it's true," he admits. "But I wasn't heart-broken when she left me for Junior. If anything, I was relieved. But then my parents died because of Ciara's duplicity. Last night, you almost died because of an alliance with people who might not have our best interest—and safety—in mind. It's too similar. I can't risk you or Eva. I just can't, Hudson."

I press my hand over his, grounding him, rubbing my thumb over his fingers. "Look at me."

He lifts his eyes to mine, tears barely contained.

"You're not going to want to hear this, but I need you to listen. Your father *chose* to go after Donovan and Volkov when the alliance with the Irish was broken. He put himself and his family at risk—"

Enzo starts to interrupt, but I place my hand to his cheek. He closes his eyes.

"Volkov didn't kill your parents because of Ciara's choice. He killed them because he's a mobster. It was a goddamned territory war, one they all died for and no one even fucking won. It wasn't your fault." I rub my thumb across his cheek.

His eyelashes flutter.

"It wasn't even Ciara's fault. You were forced into an arrangement as kids. I loved your parents like they were my own. And you know I mean no disrespect, but, Enzo, their lives were always at fucking risk from a rival family or the feds. We are, too. We're *criminals*. And I wasn't at Malin's estate last night because of your choice, man. Did you force me there?"

"I forced you into that warehouse two weeks ago."

I chuckle at that, returning my hand to my side. "Yeah, you sure as shit did."

He returns a slight smile.

"The minute Luna sent me that file, the minute I had Jane's real name, you think I was going to stay away from her?"

"Probably not," he agrees.

"Definitely not," I assert. "I'm sorry I scared you last night."

For a long moment, it's just us. The machines. The quiet. The fact that I'm still breathing and he's still here.

He raises his other hand to my face. His thumb brushes my cheek, reverent. I lean into his touch without thinking. When he leans down, closing the space between us, I don't hesitate. Our lips meet, soft and careful, like we're both afraid this might disappear if we move too fast.

Then, I tilt my head and open for him. A quiet moan slips from my throat.

Whatever restraint he had burns away, and suddenly it's as if he's been starving—tongue, heat, lightning. Everything we've buried for decades detonates at once.

My hand slides into his hair. His grip tightens at my jaw. Touch after touch, greedy and desperate, mapping what we've denied ourselves, *fuck*. It feels like coming home.

Eventually, we pull back before we do something truly stupid in a clinic bed.

I smile crookedly. "At least you wouldn't have to worry this time about Pippa leaving you for another man."

He arches a brow, wary.

"She's already with the other man." I smirk.

He groans and drops his head against the side of the bed.

I chuckle, then wince in pain.

He laughs, just a little. "Maybe, but that doesn't change the fact that we don't really know her."

"You're right," I say. "I know protecting Eva and me is the most important thing to you. But, shit, maybe we should try to get to know her more instead of pushing her away."

"It may be too late for that," he admits.

I know him well enough to know whatever damage he's caused, this won't be resolved right away. "We'll talk to her when she gets back, then. Yeah?"

He nods.

"Did Doc say I was cleared for more than kissing?" I waggle my eyebrows.

"Absolutely not, pretty boy," he says as he gets up, smiling. "Let me get her again. You need some food and some pain meds."

"Enzo?"

"Yeah?"

"I love you, too."

We smile at each other a few beats.

He squeezes my hand one more time, kisses my forehead, and exits the room.

I close my eyes with the biggest grin on my face.

Enzo is mine.

Enzo Luciano. My best friend. My world. He's decided he can give me everything. Fucking everything.

Together, I know we can get Pippa back. I just wish it didn't take me getting shot to make us open our eyes. But now that they're open, I don't want to close them ever again.

TWENTY

Hudson

Tuesday Afternoon, Day 27

My first day back to FBI HQ is fucking chaos. It's been all hands on deck for federal and presidential security detail protocols. Malin's cause of death was ruled as natural causes, but President Troy has been frenzied in the four days since he died. It's clear Victor Malin was the only federal employee he trusted to keep him safe and now he's lashing out. He's been requesting different teams each day, fighting with our director, demanding private firms over federally vetted ones—a shitshow if I've ever seen one.

My unit has been tasked with assessing additional risks from organized crime groups that would want the president harmed during this time of perceived weakness. We've brought in agents from other offices and I'm just too tired for this shit.

I rested at Enzo's for three days before returning to work. He and Eva wanted me there longer, but I was getting restless. Luna could only cover for me for so long. She used my phone the morning after the shooting to text the director I had a stomach bug. I was able to keep the façade up once I woke and it bought me a few days off. Lucky for me, it aligns with the fact that I still feel like shit.

Enzo was angry I was returning to the office so soon, but Doc said I was fine. I needed to get back so I could talk to Luna. Jules left a few hours after I woke up, once it was clear I was going to be just fine. And we haven't seen any of our vigilantes since.

Three days of barely answered texts from me to Pippa. Three days of convincing Enzo to text or call her—with no damned luck. Luna seems to have been nominated as the go-between; she and Eva have been keeping all parties updated on the other. Jules, Luna, and Pippa knew I was healing well. And we knew they were "busy." They fed us excuse after excuse that everyone was caught up in the aftermath of the Malin and McCarter deaths hitting Washington.

All cover for avoidance. Our fledgling alliance seems to have evaporated into thin air before it really even started. My injury became the perfect excuse for everyone to return to business as usual.

I fucking hate it. I've let Enzo know as much.

Which means between my crankiness at the separation, his annoying stubbornness, and my healing…we've shared no more than a kiss here and there.

I'm hoping I can talk to Luna today. I know she, Eva, and I are aligned on working together on the next mark. I'm just unsure how Jules feels and I can't overcome the obstinate personalities of Enzo and Pippa on my fucking own.

Jesus Christ, those two.

I was pulled into the director's office as soon as I arrived and Luna's been behind closed doors with Novak and his team for a few hours now. I'm keeping an eye on the door to their conference room, hoping to catch her when they break for lunch.

"Hey, Boss," Alex Rios greets me as he approaches my desk. He's a junior analyst in my unit.

"What's up, Rios?"

"You feeling better?"

"Yeah, stomach bugs are the worst."

"Totally."

"Glad to be back."

"Awesome. Well, I had a hit on something I wanted to run by you."

"Shoot." I adjust my position in my chair with a grimace.

"Have you seen the headlines about TruthDrop?"

"Of course," I answer. Not a case that's landed on the desk of organized crime, but I was familiar with it before I learned who was behind it.

"Well, there is no proof that a group is out there doing vigilante expose work, but the media has been speculating about who could be behind the media drops on all these men, right?"

"Yeah. From what I understand, no one has been able to track where the files have come from, right?"

"Exactly. Which has led people to believe it has to be some highly skilled hackers."

"That's what I heard, too," I respond. "What does this have to do with organized crime, Rios?" *Hurry it along, man.*

"While you were out, I caught some chatter that maybe the group could be tied to the mafia. The assumption with this theory is the criminal organizations that have been protecting these men could be the same people now exposing them. Blackmail gone wrong—or something like that."

"Interesting theory. Could have some legs, I suppose."

"I thought the same thing. So, I kept an eye on the chatter to see if any other links came out of it. Pretty quickly, the forums dismissed it, saying they really think the group is composed of women. That only women would go after these powerful men like this."

I chuckle. *Christ, if only he knew.*

"And then people started talking about Eva Luciano."

Fuck. I try not to blink or breathe or give anything away. "Oh, yeah?"

"She's known for being good with computers, she's believed to be behind some past hacking scandals. No proof, but the rumors have circulated for years. I have no idea if she'd have the skill to pull this off, but it hasn't stopped people from talking."

"What are they saying?" *Calm Hudson, stay fucking calm.*

"Well, they think she has the connections to get dirt on these men—her family has been working here in DC for generations. She's believed to have the coding skills to send untraceable file drops, even if I'm not sure if that's true or not, but ever since her name was mentioned, the theory has really taken off, with hundreds of comments and posts pointing in her direction."

Well, fucking hell. "Is hers the first name anyone has linked to TruthDrop?"

"This is the first theory I have seen stick longer than a day. Even the hacker groups seem to think she could be behind it."

"Okay. Definitely interesting. Good job keeping an eye on this, Rios. I can take it to the Director from here. I'll get in touch with the team running point on TruthDrop and see what they have so far. Send me the files you have when you can."

"Will do, sir. One more thing… I mean, I know she's a Luciano, but, if she is behind this—or even if people just think she is—she could be in danger. Anyone else afraid of being exposed wouldn't hesitate to take her out if it saved their skin."

"I'll make sure we get eyes on her and see how Director Marsden wants to proceed."

Rios confirms and returns to his desk.

I won't be telling Marsden a *damned* thing.

When Luna gets out of that room, we have a hell of a lot more to discuss than how to keep our group from splintering. Maybe everyone will put their egos aside to make sure Eva is safe.

A guy can fucking hope.

Thursday Night, Day 29

Luna and I have managed to convince everyone to meet tonight at the mansion. We assured them it was an emergency, which has everyone around the table eager to hear what is going on. The tension is palpable as fuck and not in a good way.

The energy radiating off Pippa is borderline manic, although she's trying to hide it. She's fidgeting, clearly uncomfortable and ready to bolt. Enzo is a shield, Jules is unreadable. Eva, Luna, and I eye each other wondering what the fuck to do about these three.

"I'm so sorry," Luna begins, "this is my fault. I mean, it's our fault." She gestures at Jules and Pippa.

"No, Luna—" I interrupt.

"No, Hudson, just let me tell them. You all figured out pretty quickly we've been behind the TruthDrop files."

Enzo, Eva, and I confirm.

"I've been really careful—there is absolutely no way to trace the files back to *anyone*." She looks to Eva, then Enzo.

"What's going on Luna?" Jules asks with concern.

"The public's theory over the past several years is that it's been angry women or victims who have been sending files to the media. From time to time, people have made assumptions that it's someone on the inside. Someone in organized crime or trafficking who knows the ins and outs. Maybe family members of the predators even—"

She's rambling. I decide to step in. "What Luna is trying to say is that hackers and media alike have been grasping at straws because there is no real proof out there. Today, an analyst told me a group online is pointing fingers at Eva." I look directly at her.

"Me?"

"Are you fucking kidding me?" Enzo says.

"Some chatter started a few days ago that whoever is behind this would need inside criminal knowledge and hacker-level computer skills. You're a woman who fits the profile."

"Fuck!" Enzo slams his fist on the table.

"Eva, I'm so sorry."

"It's not your fault, Luna," Eva assures her.

"The fuck it isn't!" Enzo is fuming.

"Enzo, back off!" Pippa warns.

"Back off? Back off? Are you serious? Four nights ago, Hudson was shot, and now my sister is being targeted. And why? Why are the three of you going after these men?"

"We fucking told you why. We also told you to *stay out of it*. Don't you dare start blaming us for this shit." Pippa and Enzo are both standing now, facing off against each other across the table.

Luna, Eva, and I are trying to tell them to calm down. Everyone talks over the other. But it's Jules who silences the chaos. With one long whistle, the room quiets.

"Eva, we're sorry this is happening. Everyone sit down, let's figure out how to keep Eva safe."

"I can keep Eva safe, I don't need your help," Enzo snarls.

"Enzo, for fuck's sake. Stop!" I stare.

He stares back, nostrils flaring.

"Seriously, Enzo, this isn't their fault." Eva looks at him, but he's still staring daggers directly at me.

"We all agreed two weeks ago that these men needed to be taken down," Eva continues. "Even if our paths never crossed, this would have happened. And then we wouldn't have known anything about who was really behind it and wouldn't have had anyone to turn to. So just calm the fuck down," she commands.

After a few beats, Jules starts again. "Eva, I think between you, Luna, and me, we can find a way to quiet the chatter online. In the meantime, you're safest here in the mansion. Don't leave, but if you do, Enzo and Niko must be with you anywhere you go."

"She's not going anywhere," Enzo mutters.

Eva rolls her eyes.

Pippa huffs.

"Something funny?" Enzo directs his anger at Pippa again.

She doesn't take the bait. She remains silent as they engage in a stare off.

"Anyway," Eva starts, "I think that is a good plan, Jules. Enzo, I'll be safe and play by your overprotective rules. I'm sure this will pass."

"I think so, too, Eva, but you have our help until it does," Jules says tenderly.

"Thank you," Eva and I both say.

"Tell me why," Enzo says, directed at Pippa.

"Why what?" she responds.

"What is the real reason you are going after these men? Who are the three of you? Really? Who do you work for?"

She laughs. "Back to this? Jesus, if we were working for someone, don't you think you'd have figured that out by now? For fuck's sake, Enzo! Luna and Eva have been sharing code and files and cloud systems for a week. Eva has been to *our* warehouse twice. I'm sure she would know if there was anyone involved besides the three of us."

Enzo looks to Eva who simply shrugs. "Then why?" he asks again. "My best friend's and my sister's lives have been put at risk for your damned cause. I know why it matters, but I need to know why *you* and by extension, why *us*? I deserve to know who you are if I've put my family on the line for your vigilante justice."

"It's none of your fucking business." Pippa rises to leave.

"This isn't over," Enzo calls after her.

She whips around. "Over?" Pippa huffs a laugh. "It never even began. You made sure of that." And then she's gone.

Enzo excuses himself from the table and goes to his office.

The four of us look around the table at each other in silent agreement that those two are going to fucking kill each other.

Just my luck that the two people I want most would be this fucking stubborn. And hot-headed. And control-freaks.

Fuck.

Luna, Eva, Jules, and I head to Eva's office to begin damage control.

TWENTY-ONE

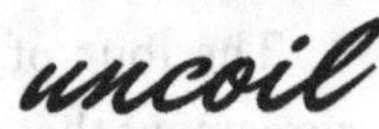

Enzo

Saturday Evening, Day 31

It's been two days since Hudson left my place after calling us all together to tell us about the suspicions raised against Eva. I haven't seen him and he hasn't answered or returned my calls. His text messages have been minimal at best.

Eva's icy interactions with me at the house haven't been much better. I've had some time to calm down and come to terms with the fact that I may have overreacted, but I don't think it was entirely unwarranted, damn it. My sister is in danger. How she and Hudson can't understand that, I'll never know.

What I do know is I need to lay eyes on Hudson today, so I'm outside his door. I've kicked up security at the house, this building, and Hudson's route to and from work. My anxiety is at an all-time high and I hope Hudson can understand that.

I raise my hand to knock when the door opens.

Hudson is standing at the door in shorts and T-shirt. It looks like he just stepped out of the shower.

My pulse settles as I take a deep breath and stare at him.

"My camera clocked your arrival like two minutes ago, wasn't sure if you were going to knock or not. Figured I'd put you out of your stupid misery." He gestures for me to come in.

"Thanks."

"Want a drink?" He heads to the kitchen.

"Water."

"Sure you don't want anything stronger?"

"I'm sure." I need to keep my wits about me.

He pours us both waters and we take a seat in the living room. I'm on the couch and he's in the chair across from me.

"I'm sorry," I start.

"For what?"

I let out a low chuckle. "You want me to list all the reasons?"

"I'm just curious if you actually know the shit you did wrong."

"Yeah, well, I've probably done a lot of things wrong this past week."

"Probably?"

"Can you take it easy on me? I'm not required to apologize in my line of work, okay? As a matter of fact, you and Eva are the only ones I ever apologize to. And frankly, I can't think of a time I've ever pissed the two of you off as much as I have this week."

"That's probably true," he agrees.

"I'm probably always going to be an asshole when it comes to yours and Eva's safety. I won't apologize for being overprotective."

"You know that isn't the issue."

"I know, I just don't know what to do about it," I admit, defeated.

"Me either." After a pause, he stands and joins me on the couch.

We face each other.

He grabs my hands. "Enzo, I want this with you. You know I do. I love you. I will never stop loving you."

I take a deep breath. I needed to hear those words.

"I don't want Pippa to come between us. I don't want the work that they're doing to come between us, but I do care about them. Luna has been my friend for years. I care deeply about Pippa. Even if nothing comes of the three of us, I don't want to lose them, either."

"I know Eva feels the same way. I just… I don't trust them."

Hudson starts to interrupt me.

"Let me finish. I believe what they've told us, but can't you agree they are hiding more than they are sharing?"

"Yeah, I can." He scoots closer.

Our legs graze. My body begins to warm all over. How many times over the years have our bodies brushed in this way? Did Hudson's body ever feel this way?

"I'm not upset with you. Thank you for your apology, though. You get a gold star for coming over here and trying to make things right," he says with a smile. "Now I need you to tell me you're not closing the door on Pippa. That you're willing to talk with her if she's willing to talk to us."

I shake my head yes. With that, his lips are on mine, and I feel like I can breathe for the first time in days.

Our hands roam. Our lips and tongues crash together. Our bodies shift closer.

"How are you feeling?" I ask him between kisses.

"Good. Really good."

"Your chest?"

"Enzo, I swear to Christ if you stop touching me, I'll fucking kill you."

I laugh and remove his shirt. His wound is bandaged, right below his nipple. I move my lips down his chest, across his collar bone. I kiss around his wound. I lick the nipple above it. I take my hand and caress the other.

"Enz— Fuck, that feels good." His hands are around my head, as I explore his chest, his shoulders, back up to his neck, and under his ear.

"Lay back. I've been fantasizing about exploring you, pretty boy."

"Oh fuck, really?" he stutters out on an exhale.

"Mhm." I continue kissing his neck.

He reclines into the couch. "I've had a lot of fucking fantasies about that mouth of yours, Luciano. That pretty goddamned mouth."

I stare into his hazel-blue eyes and run one hand in his hair. I wrap the other around his throat. I love the feel of his stubble under my hand—rough. "I hope I live up to your fantasies," I whisper.

"Hey, look at me"—he uses his hand to lift my chin and brings his nose to mine—"I'm going to love everything you do. Because it's *you*."

"But I haven't been—"

"I know," he says as he kisses me tenderly. "I'm so glad I'm your first. I'm honored, Enz. *Fuck*, so damned honored. I love you, okay?"

I nod. I'm nervous. Excited. My body is humming. I want to make him feel good. I want him to make me feel good.

I want everything with Hudson, but I'd be lying if I didn't say I wasn't also thinking of Pippa. Thinking of the last time Hudson and I were on this very couch, Pippa between us.

I take a deep breath and begin kissing him again. I run my hand over his cock to find he's just as hard as I am. I explore his piercings through his shorts, tugging lightly on each one, which he seems to enjoy.

"Fuck, yeah, babe, that feels good."

Hudson's ringtone plays, receiving a call.

"Ignore it," I instruct him as I reach my hand into his shorts, wrapping my hand around his cock. He curses at every flex of my hand.

Bvvvt. Bvvvt. Bvvvt.

It's my phone this time.

We look at each other.

"Shit. Fuck. Should we check it?" he asks.

I begin to say maybe, when Hudson's phone rings again. This time, it's Eva's ringtone. We both straighten and pick up our devices.

My missed call is from Jules.

Hudson answers Eva's call. "Hey, Eva. What? Fuck. Where? Okay, we're on our way."

"What's wrong?" I demand.

"Pippa's in trouble. Jules and Luna need our help."

My heart stops.

I'm grabbing my stuff and following Hudson out the door before I can think straight.

Hudson and I pull up outside what looks like an abandoned brick building off U Street. We're in the dodgy side of DC's clubbing scene. Jules and Luna are standing outside a van as we pull up. We have very little information. Hudson didn't ask questions after he heard they needed help with Pippa.

We exit the car.

Luca and Niko remain in the front seats while we approach Jules and Luna.

"What's going on?" Hudson asks.

"We tracked Pippa to this location. Luna hacked their cameras and we think she's been—" Jules starts to explain.

"Wait, back up. Tracked?" I ask.

"We haven't heard from her since—since we all left the mansion," Luna answers nervously.

"We had reason to be concerned," Jules interjects. "She wasn't returning calls, she didn't go to work, her phone was dead, she seemed—"

"If her phone is dead, how do you know she's inside?" I ask.

"We have other ways," Jules starts. "Listen, we don't have time to explain. Luna confirmed she's inside via the security feed. I think she's been drugged. It's a biker bar. She's in there—"

Hudson is already charging to the building and I'm right behind him.

Jules is hot on our tail. "Luna, stay with Niko and Luca," Jules shouts.

"Fuck you, I'm coming, too."

"Luna, she's right, it's not safe," Hudson grunts.

She doesn't listen, instead keeping stride with me.

I'm focused on getting into the building, gaining on Hudson as we approach when a thought dawns on me. "One second, everyone stop!"

Everyone turns to me.

"Hudson, we can't be seen going in there together. Luna, you either."

"I don't *fucking* care, Enzo. Come with me or don't—I'm going in." He storms forward.

With that, everyone continues after him.

Fuck. I can't think of a worse idea than us walking into a biker bar, armed, ready for a fight.

I spot Niko approaching from behind. "Niko, get back to the car."

"Boss, if you're going in, I'm going in. I have three men on their way."

Okay, so we're either saving Pippa tonight, or my whole crew is getting beat up. Or worse. Perfect.

"No one from Eva's detail, right?"

"No, Boss."

Hudson is first in. The rest of us follow close behind.

She's easy to spot. Her bright red hair stands out in the dark, dingy space. A rowdy group of men surround her, passing her around. She's clearly drunk or drugged. She can barely stand.

Hudson barges through the group like a wrecking ball to grab her.

Jules turns to Niko and me, whispering, "I count six in the circle, two behind the bar, and ten other sets of eyes on us. I assume they are all armed. You two ready?"

We nod.

"I have two weapons," she says. "You?"

Niko confirms he also has two.

I whisper that Hudson and I each have one Glock.

Two guys try to intercept Hudson, keeping him from grabbing Pippa. They tell him to back off.

"I'm getting her the fuck out of here. The only question is who wants to leave here tonight with broken bones and who doesn't," Hudson says to the biggest man in the group. Hudson is tall at six feet, but this guy towers over him and is twice his weight in muscle alone.

Smart move to go after the biggest guy, but that doesn't stop me from wishing he hadn't.

"Hey!" a guy from behind the bar yells.

I turn to see he has a gun raised.

Without blinking, all five of us raise our guns simultaneously.

Half a dozen bikers raise their guns and so does the other bartender.

Anyone without a gun backs away.

"Gentlemen, we aren't here for trouble!" Jules yells. "We're here for the girl. Hand her over, no one gets hurt tonight."

We hear a few chuckles from the crowd, some cat-calling, and some derogatory name-calling aimed at Jules and Luna.

"Enzo fucking Luciano. Fuck, it's really you. Guys, it's Enzo Luciano. Mr. Italian Mob himself," yells a voice from behind me.

I'm aimed at the bartender.

Niko quickly shifts one of his guns and his line of sight to the guy who spoke.

"Jules, cover the bar?" I ask. She shifts into position as I turn. "Do I know you?" I ask the drunk biker. He's over fifty with long, shaggy hair and a gut too big for his stick legs. Is he fucking serious? He doesn't even have a gun.

He laughs. "No, no. You don't know me. I just can't believe you're here. Did you really roll into a biker bar with two women? Has the mob changed that much since your daddy died, boy?"

"You knew my father?"

"Nah. Just of him. Saw 'im around town a few times. I did odd jobs for Donovan's crew back before they all took each other out. Damn though, you look just like him. Anyone tell you that?"

This drunk idiot. I learned long ago not to let anyone bait me by mentioning my dad, Donovan, or Volkov. Many have tried to rattle me with that shit—all have failed. "All the time. You and your friends going to cause us trouble? Or can we take the girl and go?"

"Johnny, is that you?" Pippa slurs her words.

Most of the initial group of guys have backed up. One druggy-looking scrawny guy is holding her, standing next to the big guy Hudson is squared off with.

"Yeah, Janey, baby, it's me. Ready to go?" Hudson says, never moving his eyes from the oaf.

"Janey? You said your name was Catherine?" The guy holding her asks.

She laughs and slurs a few words I can't make out.

"Who owns this place?" I ask the bartender.

"Who's asking?"

"Did you not hear your buddy over here? I'm Enzo *fucking* Luciano." That gets me a blink, like maybe he didn't believe his friend knew who I was. *Fair.*

"I—" He clears his throat. "It's my bar."

"What's your name?"

He hesitates before answering me. "Michael Dalton."

"Listen, Michael. You have two choices: The girl leaves with us and no one gets hurt. Or the girl leaves with us and your patrons get wounded, your bar gets trashed, and the place gets swarmed by police. The call is yours."

Druggy-guy holding Pippa speaks up. "Dal, don't let him talk to you like that! It's her choice. Tell them, baby. You want to be here."

I don't have eyes on what is going on, but I hear shuffling.

Then, Hudson says, "I got you, Janey. I got you."

I hear the same guy call her Catherine and ask her to come back to him.

Michael looks around before yelling, "We're letting them go, boys! Anyone causing trouble is on their own." After some grumbles and weak protests, guns start to lower.

I tip my chin to Michael, and we slowly walk backward toward the exit, guns still raised, Pippa positioned in the center of the group.

Pippa is saying "Jules" and "Luna" and mumbling something. I think I hear her say the word "sisters" a few times.

Niko's three backup men are outside the bar when we step through the doors.

"Make sure no one follows us."

They agree and take position.

I turn to Niko. "Hudson and I are going to ride with the girls back to the mansion. Go with Luca and keep us covered as we drive." He hesitates, but then tells the other three to follow us.

Luna takes the driver's seat. I'm not sure whether my presence will help or harm, so I take shotgun. Jules and Hudson crawl in the back with Pippa. Even though every cell in my body wants to be back there making sure she is okay.

No one from the bar follows behind us. We drive slowly with three other cars surrounding us for security.

Jules has given Pippa a sip of water, and she tells Pippa to swallow something.

"Stupid implants," Pippa mumbles. "I didn't want to be found." She's still slurring, but her regularly fiery demeanor is secure.

"You know better than to turn off your phone," Jules says.

I catalog the *implant* comment along with the *sisters* comments. I'm unsure if these are drunken ramblings or if they mean something more.

"I can't do it, Jules. He's gonna recognize me." She's nearly whining.

"Shh, let's get you home," Jules soothes, but Pippa repeats herself a few times.

"We're taking her to the clinic. I already texted Eva to get the Doc to the house."

Luna thanks me.

"No. I don't want to," Pippa murmurs.

"Oh well, Janey. We gotta get you checked out. Did you take anything?" Hudson asks.

"I don't take drugs!" she almost yells.

"Okay, I believe you," he says softly.

"Don't believe me, I'm a liar. I lie about everything," she mumbles.

I glance at Luna. She's looking in the rearview at Jules.

Okay. I don't want anything to be wrong with Pippa, but maybe loose tongues will open some doors here.

"Who is going to recognize you?" I probe.

That earns me a glare from Luna.

Jules clears her throat.

Hudson silently scolds me with a scathing look.

"Magnus. I mean, maybe he won't. It's been so long. My hair was different."

"How long?" I ask.

"Enzo, enough," Jules warns.

"No, we should tell them. Who cares anymore?"

"Pippa, sweetie, let's just get you home, okay?" Jules assures her.

"Maribel? I don't want to go home to that stupid island ever again!" Her voice rises with panic. She starts moving in the back seat. "Why would you take me back there?"

Luna curses and takes a deep breath.

"We aren't taking you there, Pippa, just to see Doc. We have to get you checked out," Jules tries to soothe her.

"No, no, not the doctor! Don't let them take me. They'll cut me open again. I'll die this time." Pippa starts fighting to get out of the car.

"Jules, what the fuck is going on?" Hudson asks quietly. He has her in his arms, trying to contain her, as she wails about not having another surgery.

"Hudson is here, Pippa. Let him hold you, okay. We are going to Enzo's, okay?"

Pippa begins to take deep breaths as Hudson whispers in her ear. She mumbles about being confused before she starts to pass out.

I distinctly hear her say "Maribel Island" a final time. *Jesus Christ.* Is she saying what I think she's saying? I make eye contact with Hudson—he's clocking the same thing.

"We're almost there," I say. "Let's get her to the clinic. Then, Jules, Luna, we're going to talk about Maribel Island and Magnus Troy."

TWENTY-TWO

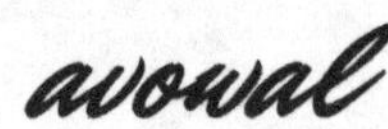

Pippa

Sunday Evening, Day 32

Water beats down over my shoulders, hot enough to sting, but I barely register the pain. I brace my hands against the tile and close my eyes, letting the steam fill my lungs. I can't seem to convince my body that I'm safe.

Last night I was anything but safe.

I didn't mean to put myself in such a dangerous situation—not again.

I hope Jules and Luna believe me. They seemed to. Doc finding Rohypnol in my system validated what I told them, at least.

I went to U Street to go clubbing, to get out of my head. I wanted loud music and flashing lights—anything to help me forget the strong arms and warm eyes of the two men I couldn't have.

Two men who found their way to each other and away from me.

I barely remember making it from the club to the biker bar. I must have been drugged at the club. *How could I have been so dumb? So careless?* That thought keeps looping through my brain, no matter how many times I remind myself I'm here now. Alive. Clean. Wrapped in borrowed comfort inside the Luciano mansion of all places.

The irony isn't lost on me.

I see flashes of last night when I close my eyes. Hands that weren't mine, the sour taste at the back of my throat, the way time fractured. I remember thinking, dimly, distantly, that maybe this was it—that I'd made one mistake too many.

And then there were voices. Familiar ones. Arms around me. Hudson. Jules. Luna.

Even Enzo.

They came for me.

The water runs as gratitude crashes over me all over again, sharp enough to hurt.

They found me. They pulled me back to safety, back to myself. I don't know how to reconcile that kind of loyalty with the danger that very loyalty keeps dragging them into.

Or the fact that Enzo made it very clear he doesn't want me around anymore only few days ago.

I shut off the water and step out of the shower, wrapping myself in a thick towel. My hands tremble as I dress. Not with fear, not exactly—anticipation, dread.

They're waiting for me downstairs.

All of them.

Jules and Luna told me what I had said in the van while I was drugged. Things I didn't mean to give voice to, didn't intend to expose. I put myself and my sisters at risk.

I guess Enzo and Hudson have tried to get Luna and Jules to

tell them more today, to explain why I was talking about Maribel Island, about Troy, and about doctors I didn't want to see again.

My sisters haven't shared anything further. They told them it was up to me what to reveal, but both made it clear to me they think it's time to tell the truth.

I can't imagine it. I can't see myself saying the words.

We agreed from the very beginning that no one could ever know.

Do I think we can trust them? Maybe.

Do I know they will never look at us the same again? Absolutely.

Knowing Jared Whiteman's blood runs in our veins…why would they want anything to do with us after they find out?

At this point, what does it matter? Enzo already wants nothing to do with me. Eva is at risk because of our actions. Hudson put his life on the line, *again*, last night.

I can confess, they will agree they want nothing to do with us, and my sisters and I can move on. It's for the best.

I finish dressing just as there's a soft knock on the door.

"Jane?" Hudson's voice. Gentle. Careful.

I open it and he's there. He looks tired and relieved and impossibly familiar. The sight of him hits me harder than I expect. My chest tightens.

"Hey," he says quietly.

"Hey."

He pulls me into a hug before I can overthink it. It's warm. Solid. Real. I let myself lean into it a moment longer than necessary.

"I'm glad you're okay," he murmurs, pressing a kiss to my forehead.

"Thank you for coming," I say, my voice rough. "For everything you did last night."

He pulls back just enough to offer me a kind smile. "It was the least I could do after you saved my life last week."

I offer a small smile, and we just look at each other for a few moments.

"Honestly, Pippa, it wasn't a question. You know that, right?"

I offer a small smile and say thank you.

"So, Marco is serving dinner and everyone is waiting for us." He doesn't push. Doesn't ask questions. Just offers me his arm to escort me downstairs. Hudson's presence grounds me as we walk.

Dinner is set when we enter the dining room. Enzo sits at one end of the table, Eva at the other. Jules and Luna are side by side, across from the seats Hudson and I take. The symmetry feels intentional. Unavoidable.

Plates are served. Polite conversation fills the air for a few minutes—compliments about the food, small observations—normalcy stretched thin over something much heavier. Eventually, Chef Marco retreats to the kitchen.

Hudson squeezes my hand under the table. "If you're ready," he says quietly. He doesn't let go.

My heart pounds so loudly in my ears, I'm sure they can all hear it, too. I clear my throat. "First, thank you—all of you—for coming to get me." My throat tightens. "I'm sorry I put myself in that situation."

"No one here blames you," Eva says firmly.

Enzo leans forward slightly. "But we do have questions." His tone is careful, measured. "You said some things about Maribel Island. I can make some guesses, but I'd rather hear the truth." He pauses, then adds, "I know the six of us haven't exactly had the smoothest start, but there's a lot not being said. And I think it's time we put all the cards on the table. That way, we can decide how we move forward."

Luna exhales slowly. "We didn't want to drag you all further in—not after Hudson was hurt, not with Eva being targeted as the leading suspect behind TruthDrop."

"If I tell you," I say quietly, "there is no going back. I don't say that to be dramatic. I promise, it has been safer for you not to know. No one in the world knows the truth but the three of us."

Hudson's hand tightens around mine. "We need to know."

Eva nods. "It seems to me we are already in danger. I'd like to understand why."

Silence stretches.

I take a breath, then another.

"Jules, Luna, and I don't only work together... We are sisters," I say.

A moment passes. No one speaks.

"Jared Whiteman was our father," I continue.

The room stills.

Enzo's face drains of color.

Hudson's hand twitches in mine.

Eva's jaw drops. She is the first to respond with knit brows. "I didn't know Jared Whiteman had children."

"Nobody does," Luna says.

"We were born on Maribel Island," Jules explains. "There's no record of us. No birth certificates. Nothing. We never left the island until after he died in jail. Pippa was seventeen, I was fifteen, Luna thirteen."

Hudson pulls his hand from mine to run both hands through his hair, before lowering his arms to the table, leaning on his elbows. "This doesn't make sense," he whispers. "Shit—I believe you, sorry—I just have so many questions. I've read those files so many times. How did no one find you on the island? You three don't look like sisters; you don't even look like him."

"We assume we each have different mothers," Jules responds. "We also assume they were victims, but we don't know. By the time we were old enough to start asking questions, no one was offering any answers. And getting off the island, well, it's a long story. We'll get to that part."

I continue. "Our dad wasn't *cruel,* not like Sophie." The name leaves a bitter taste. "But he wasn't good or caring, either. I mean, obviously he was a horrible human being. You'll get no argument from us on that. He cared about us because we shared his DNA. Like we were something he owned; we only held importance via our connection to him. Classic narcissist. We believe his ultimate plan was to pass his operation to us. We were still young when he got arrested, so we'll never truly know."

The silence deepens as everyone absorbs this information.

My hands curl in my lap.

Hudson's comforting hand doesn't return.

Time to rip the Band-Aid all the way. "The Volkovs ran security on the island. They didn't live there like us, but they were there most of the time. Konstantin, Sophie, and Jared were business partners for the parties and the trafficking ring."

Eva curses under her breath.

Enzo takes a deep breath and nods.

It's Hudson who speaks. "So, Volkov got you off the island and to DC?"

Jules, Luna, and I all say "no" at the same time, shaking our heads.

"We realized Jared's death was our way out. We were *supposed* to wait there for Konstantin, but we knew how evil he and Sophie were. Without Jared to protect us"—Jules shakes her head—"we needed to escape."

Enzo pushes his chair back to stand. He paces the room, tall and imposing as he walks. His face is dark and stormy, his hands clenching at his side. I can tell he's working out what to say or ask next.

The room waits in anticipation.

"I'm with Hudson. I have a lot of questions," he starts, "but only two matter right now."

The three of us nod our heads in agreement.

"Are you in contact with Junior?"

I answer emphatically. "No. We haven't seen him in fifteen years. He has no idea we are here in DC."

"How is that possible?" He's not asking the question like he doesn't believe our story. Our story is unbelievable and he needs to hear an answer.

Fair.

Jules takes it. "We weren't born with these names. There is no record of our births. When we left, we landed in Texas. We had plenty of money, but no identification. There were several years between then and our arrival in DC, but Luna found a way for us to repurpose the government paperwork of a few deceased girls around our ages. The Volkovs, Sophie, they don't know us by these names. Even if they think we are alive still, they wouldn't know how to find us."

Enzo nods. Admittedly, he is accepting this much more easily than I expected.

"That leads to my second question. Why come to DC? You escaped; you were free. Why put yourself right back in the path of all the people responsible for the atrocities at Maribel Island?" Enzo asks.

"You're right. We could have stayed hidden," I reply. "We had plenty of money. And we thought about it—trust me. At the time, we were still living in fear that Sophie or Konstantin would find us."

"This was before the fallout with your family and the Donovans," Jules interjects.

"Yeah, with Konstantin dead and Sophie on the most-wanted list, we could have remained in hiding, but we knew powerful men were still abusing children. We knew no one was doing anything about it."

"It started with exposing them," Luna says. "Jules went into the military and then the CIA. She was on the anti-trafficking taskforce. I went into hacking, sending proof to the FBI. That's how I got caught, by the way."

Hudson smiles. "I remember."

"Pippa wanted to go to school to be a doctor or a chemist—she's so smart," Luna continues and I blush. "But she thought studying politics at Yale would get her more access to the predators."

"We arrived in DC about eight years ago," I add. "We didn't come here to kill these men. It wasn't the original plan."

"What was?" Eva asks.

"To expose them, like Luna said," I answer. "Everything that happened during the pandemic, all the celebrity and politician scandals—that was the start of our work. When we first got here, we really believed that if we showed the world the truth about these men, it would be enough."

"But it wasn't," Enzo finishes. He's stopped pacing but remains standing. "Nothing happened to them—slaps on the wrist, maybe some fines or limited jail time—but nothing really changed."

We all nod.

"Then Magnus Troy became President," Luna says grimly.

"Everyone knew his past, knew his ties to Whiteman, and he still fucking won," Hudson adds.

Then Eva asks, "So, you started taking them out yourself?"

"Someone had to," I reply.

"All your intel, all your inside knowledge on Victor Malin, McCarter—it wasn't Luna's hacking skills, it was from your time on Maribel. You were witnesses. Victims," Hudson says.

"Yes," Jules confirms. "Jared kept meticulous records. We were smart enough to bring them with us when we left."

"Fuck. I don't even know what to say," Hudson admits.

Eva and Enzo murmur in agreement.

A few silent moments pass.

Hudson asks, "What's the plan for Troy?"

"The upcoming gala," is all I say.

"Do you need help?" Eva asks.

I look around the room, waiting for Enzo or Hudson to say they can't or won't help. Jules and Luna do the same. We expect a dismissal from Enzo, at the very least.

"My security firm has been pulled in for the event," Jules says. "That was why we needed Malin gone."

"Our plan is strong," Luna says, "but extra help wouldn't hurt."

"Let's hear it," Enzo says as he sits back at the table.

And just like that, we tell them.

We tell them Jules and I will be in attendance for work with Luna on comms. That I plan to ask for an introduction to Troy from my boss. That my handshake will be the method for poisoning him. And how twenty minutes later, he'll have a seizure right in front of all his friends and donors, as the event livestreams. No matter the medical attention he might receive, he'll be dead within a few hours.

They listen intently. Hudson volunteers to be on duty with the FBI for the event, sharing that they've been asking for agents to work it. Luna suggests she might volunteer as well, then. We all agree Enzo and Eva can't be seen in public at the event, but both could help on comms.

We tell them what Luna found on her other case regarding the Hollywood parties and that it looks like Sophie and the Russians are working with DeShawn Crown. His parties are the newest cover for trafficking, just like Jared's. We even tell them that there is history with Jules and Jax Novak, who is now leading the federal investigation to find Sophie.

We lay it all out, answering every question they have.

They never question whether we are telling the truth.

They don't run in the other direction.

They don't wash their hands of us.

They care.

To want to help.

And it feels… I don't even know. I don't know how it feels.

But I do know that for the first time in our lives, it isn't just the three of us against the world.

TWENTY-THREE

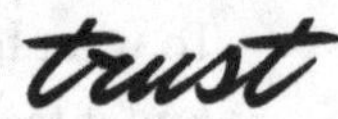

Enzo

Sunday Evening, Day 32

We sat at the dining table for hours, talking and plotting. Everyone went into operation mode. It seemed easier than dealing with the reality of what was shared.

Jared Whiteman had kids.

Not just kids—*daughters.*

The most notorious child predator and sex trafficker in US history, known for abusing young girls, providing children to his rich and powerful friends, had daughters.

Three daughters no one knew existed. I can't wrap my head around it, let alone everything these three women have been through—what every victim who went to Maribel Island endured.

When we wrapped our conversation, I asked Pippa if she'd stay to talk with Hudson and me. We said our goodnight to Jules and Luna while Eva retreated to her room.

The hug exchanged between my sister and Luna lingered in a way that reminded me I need to ask her what is going on with the two of them. In the chaos of the past couple of weeks, we haven't discussed her long-harbored crush or what it's been like working alongside Luna. Let alone my hunch that maybe something has developed between the two of them.

Now Hudson, Pippa, and I stand in the den. I've noticed none of us have been drinking tonight, but I offer to pour them a glass of bourbon. Both decline.

Can I have this conversation without liquid courage? I guess I'm about to find out.

We've taken seats in three different chairs, all facing each other. Pippa is dressed in sweats with no makeup, her hair in a ponytail. When I saw her descend the stairs for dinner, it caught me off guard. I've never seen her so exposed, so vulnerable.

Before tonight, I'm not sure I ever saw the real her.

"Pippa, how are you? Really?" I ask.

She doesn't look at us when she answers softly, "I'm not sure, to be honest."

Hudson and I tell her it's understandable to feel that way.

"I want to apologize," I say.

Her deep-green eyes look at me in surprise. I'm not sure we've made any sort of deep, meaningful eye contact tonight until this moment.

I catch my breath, then say, "I overreacted to everything with Hudson and Eva."

She shakes her head. "No, you didn't. You had every right to be upset."

"Maybe, but none of it was your fault."

She scoffs. "I think it was all my fault."

Hudson asks, "How?"

"What do you mean? The three of you wouldn't be involved in any of this if it wasn't for me."

"I'm pretty sure we forced our way in," I say gently. Pippa pauses, then gives me a small smile before she agrees. That smile lights me from the inside.

"Yeah, I mean, you did warn us," Hudson says, now smiling, too.

She laughs cautiously. "I really did."

After a beat, I say, "I have another question about last night."

This causes her to tense a little, but she waits for me to continue.

"You don't have to share anything you don't want to, but before we learned the truth tonight, when you were talking in the van about Maribel and Troy, Hudson and I jumped to a different conclusion. We thought maybe you were a victim of Troy's."

"You were really upset last night," Hudson adds, "and we don't want to force you to share anything, but…did anything happen to you or your sisters on that island?"

She swallows. "Yes." Her voice is low, quiet, raspy. My heart fractures apart. I see Hudson's eyes close. "To me. Not to Jules or Luna. Sophie made Jules help with…*recruiting* girls. And that traumatized her in other ways, but I was the only one who…" she trails off.

I tilt my head in understanding.

Hudson joins her on her chair. He picks her up and sets her on his lap.

Pippa lets him. This impossibly strong, formidable woman lets herself be held.

He wraps his arms around her middle, and she leans her head on his shoulder. They look gorgeous together. Truly stunning. "I'm so sorry, baby," Hudson says into her hair.

I sit, taking them in for a few minutes. Then I say, "It was Troy, then." Not a question, a statement.

She looks at me and, in that look, I know.

Magnus Troy needs to fucking die.

I already knew he was a predator. A fucking horrible president. An evil billionaire. But Pippa was right to call us out the very first night at the warehouse. We haven't done nearly enough. Fuck, we haven't done anything at all. All these predators walk the streets of my city, and I've sat back and let it happen.

No more.

"I know he and Jared were best friends, but how could Jared pawn off his own daughter?" I ask.

"It wasn't him; it was Sophie."

"The fuck?" Hudson curses.

She sits straighter in Hudson's lap. "I'm going to tell you everything. I don't want to, but I need to. I'm tired of secrets. I'm exhausted by all of it. I'll tell you everything and then it's up to you what you want to do."

I rise to join them. I lower myself to the floor in front of Pippa and take her hands in mine. The three of us connected. I know whatever she's about to say is going to be hard to hear, but I need her to know she's not alone.

A small tear leaves her eye and I wipe it away. She inhales a sharp breath, closing her eyes, and whispers a quiet thank you.

"Sophie hated that we existed. What Jules said is true—we don't know anything about our mothers except that Sophie hated them and us. She made sure we knew it every single day. I never understood Jared's relationship with her. He always referred to her as his girlfriend and they said they loved each other, but Jared…he was still always with girls. It wasn't a secret. Sophie would bring him girls. It was…*so* fucked up. Everything that happened was so, truly fucked up."

She takes a deep breath. "Sophie was cruel to us, and she and Jared were a package deal. When I was about fifteen, I started asking questions. I was angry all the time. I'd try to push their buttons because I wanted off the island. I wanted to attend their dumb parties, but we were never allowed to attend. I wanted to talk to literally *anyone* other than them, my sisters, and the Volkovs. I was going stir-crazy."

Hudson rubs her arms slowly. I caress her hands. We are hanging on every word.

"Jared would come and go from the island. I mean everyone did, except the three of us. One night, he was away and Sophie said she wanted to talk to me. She was so nice that night." Pippa laughs. "That should have been my first clue, but she played the friend, you know? Like she understood why I had been rebelling and she pretended to agree with me; I was 'becoming a woman,' she said. I needed 'to meet more people.' She told me one of dad's friends was coming over later in the week. She asked if I'd like to join them for dinner. I was so excited, I accepted right away. I was so stupid.

"The next night, she asked if I wanted to dye my hair. She acted like we were two teenage friends pulling one over on my dad. I *loved* the idea. I'd hated my red hair—it made me feel so different and she knew it. So, we bleached it blonde." She chuckles. "Dad was so mad when he got back, but by then, it was too late."

I feel my blood pressure rising. I'm working hard not to react, not to say anything. I can tell Hudson is restraining himself, too. I feel irrationally angry that someone else killed Jared before I had the chance. I want to tear the world down—hurt everyone who ever hurt her.

"I remember getting all dressed up, feeling beautiful. Jules begged me not to go. I told her she was just jealous. She's always been the leader of our group, even though I'm older. I should have listened to her, but I didn't want to hear it. I was expecting someone fun at dinner, someone close to my age, or maybe another girl, one in college. I remember thinking it was definitely going to be a girl, since so many were always coming and going from Maribel."

Her eyes flick between ours. "It didn't even occur to me… You have to understand, this was about two years before Jared was arrested. At this point, we didn't know what the parties were. We just knew there were these fun-looking parties every few weeks and that we weren't allowed to go. There were so many people we weren't allowed to talk to, and my sisters and I wanted desperately to talk to more people. When I got to the dining room, I was shocked.

"I knew who Magnus Troy was. I'd seen him on the island many times before. Jared and Sophie talked about him often. There were pictures of them together in the house, but I wasn't expecting to see him there that night. I knew right away Sophie had done this on purpose. I almost ran away. I wish I would have."

I squeeze her hands tighter. "I'm so sorry, Pippa."

"It happened a few times after that. She wouldn't let me dye my hair back because he preferred blondes. She told me I had to keep seeing him or she'd make Jules go instead."

"Fucking bitch," Hudson curses under his breath.

"I got pregnant," she blurts suddenly.

Hudson and I try not to overreact, but it's hard. I swallow, eyes wide, unsure what to say to such abuse and trauma.

"I just need to tell all of it, okay?" A tear slowly slides down her cheek.

Hudson wipes it away this time. We wait silently for her to continue.

"My sisters and I had never even been to a doctor. I barely understood periods, only that women got them. We had *some* homeschooling from Mrs. Volkov—" Pippa looks at me, eyes wide, realizing what she said.

I stiffen a bit.

"She was really lovely, Enzo. We were children and she was the *only* kind adult in our lives, like a mom to us three. She died when Junior was, like, ten. I think I was eleven or twelve. It was devastating."

I close my eyes. "Jesus. Didn't Konstantin have her killed?"

"We didn't know that at the time, but yes, that's the assumption. I'm not surprised—he was the worst. I'm glad he's dead," she admits.

I offer a small smile.

"And Enzo, I am not sure if I should say this, but the Junior we knew as kids… When she was alive, we were close. He was like family to us—like a cousin or a brother—he was a normal, sweet little boy. I have no idea who he became, but I can only imagine the control his dad had over him."

"I didn't know much about him before everything happened, either, but yeah, his dad was a piece of work."

She squeezes my hand.

What a complicated web this is. Christ.

"So, I got pregnant, but I didn't know that. I didn't know anything about pregnancy or missed periods. I was experiencing sharp pains and heavier-than-normal bleeding. I came down with a fever, and I guess it got really bad. My memories of that time are foggy, but I got so sick they had to get a doctor to the island on a helicopter. It turned out I had a miscarriage."

"Jesus, Pippa," Hudson pulls her in closer.

I move one of my hands up her arm. *Comfort. How can I give her comfort?* I want to wrap her in a cocoon and never let her out. She's been through too much. How did she survive it all?

"By the time they got a doctor to the island, he said I was dying. I had an infection that had spread and I needed surgery. I guess they found a surgeon they could fly in and pay off. When I woke, I was told they had performed a hysterectomy. I had never even heard that word before then."

I'm shell-shocked. Judging by Hudson's expression, he is, too. There are no words. I stand. I need to hold her. I pull her from Hudson's embrace and into my own arms. I tell her I'm so sorry.

Hudson joins me and puts his arms around her. We hold her for a few seconds when Pippa wiggles out of our arms.

I release her, confused.

"I don't want your pity," she says, stepping away, creating distance. Building her walls, protecting herself. "I know it's ugly and it's hard, but it was a long time ago. Now you know. And I understand if you don't want anything to do with me. I know I'm a mess and I know I'm broken, but I can't handle your pity, I just can't—"

"It's not pity." I lift her chin to look me in the eyes. "And you're not broken. In the few weeks I've known you, you've proven you're stronger than anyone I know."

She swallows, but I can tell she doesn't believe me.

"Look at me, Pippa. Really look at me."

She takes a deep breath and relaxes.

"Even if I never learned about this, I would still think you're the strongest person I know. But now that I do know? Fuck, *bella*... Not only did you survive literal hell, but you also escaped, you put yourself back together, and you came back and fought. You didn't have to do *any* of that, but you did. And why, why did you do all of it?"

She tries to look away, uncomfortable with so much vulnerability.

I don't let her, keeping her chin in my palm.

"To stop them from hurting more girls," she says quietly.

"Exactly. Not for yourself, not even for your sisters, not even for revenge. To stop them—something no one else was willing to do, even when the truth was made public, right?"

A tear slips as she slightly shakes her head, confirming I am right.

"So, I promise you, we don't pity you," I insist, "but do we hate that you went through that? Yes. Do we want to wrap you up and protect you from ever being hurt again?"

"*Fuck* yes," Hudson answers.

"We care, okay? We care about you. Is that okay?"

She stands still for a moment before offering a small shake of her head in confirmation.

I direct the three of us to the couch. We sit with Pippa in the middle. She pulls her feet onto the couch, legs to her chest. Hudson and I face her, and we take one hand each.

"Can we start over?" I ask.

"What do you mean?"

"We went about this all wrong. You are a force that came into our lives, and we acted on desire and lust—which I don't regret." I smirk. "But I want more."

"Me too," Hudson whispers.

"You do?" she asks.

We both nod.

She looks between us, probably searching for any lies or doubts. She won't find any. "I've never done...*more*," she says slowly.

"Me either," I say.

"Me either," Hudson laughs.

"But the two of you. Aren't you—"

"Yes," I admit. "After everything you shared, is it okay if I open up, too?"

She nods her head in agreement.

"Some of what I'm about to share, not even Hudson knows," I begin. "I was about sixteen or seventeen when I was told I'd be marrying Ciara Donovan at twenty-one. Our fathers wanted an alliance and the marriage was set. I knew it was my future before

I knew it was Ciara. Because of that, I never really...*explored*," I admit shyly. "Sexually."

"Wait, what?" Pippa asks.

"I'm not a virgin," I say with a deep chuckle, "but I promise you're both way more experienced than me."

"How is that possible? Have you seen yourself?" Pippa asks.

"Seriously," Hudson adds.

"Hudson and Eva can attest I was a shy kid. I didn't see the point in dating. If I'm being honest, I didn't have a crazy sex drive. I know that's odd for young men, and it always made me feel...different."

Hudson grabs my hand.

"Guys in high school were always talking about how horny they were. And I had this best friend who was *very* sexually free." I laugh looking at him. "I felt the complete opposite. I assumed when I got married, I'd figure it out, but then that blew up. Then my parents died. Then I had to keep my sister safe and take over the business, and I'll be honest: sex and relationships have never been a priority."

"That makes a lot of sense," Pippa says.

"It's not that I never thought about Hudson physically when we were growing up—I did—but you weren't an option for me," I say, looking at him. "No one was, so what was the point?"

"Yeah, I felt that way, too," he admits.

"Pippa, the night I saw you, you awakened something in me. I knew I shouldn't have approached you at that bar, but I couldn't help myself."

"She has that effect," Hudson says wistfully.

"I know it feels like Hudson and I have all this history," I continue, "and we do, but none of it had ever been romantic or sexual before you. And if you hadn't stormed into my life, I don't know if it ever would have been."

"Now that you realize your feelings for each other, why would you want me to complicate that?" she asks earnestly.

"What you call complicated, I call feeling alive for the first time in my life. I don't simply want you—I need you." I caress her face. I move my other hand to Hudson's face. "And I need him."

They both sigh.

"I hated pushing you away, Pippa. I really did. It was stupid. I was scared. I can't explain this feeling. But I know I want to give this a shot. Tell me we can give this a shot."

"Fuck yeah," Hudson says.

Pippa and I laugh. Then, she looks at me and says, "I'd really like to try. As long as none of us know what we're doing, it should work out, right?" She smiles.

I laugh. "Let's mess it all up together."

"I like that," she says.

"Me, too," Hudson adds.

"We don't have to do anything, but would you both like to stay the night? I need to know you're both okay."

They agree. By the time we finally drift toward the bedroom, the edge has worn off. The confessions are done, hard truths laid bare. What's left feels lighter—fragile, maybe, but real.

Getting ready for bed is strangely easy.

Hudson cracks jokes about my bathroom and closet being too pristine for a single man. Pippa laughs at his antics. The sound loosens something in my chest I didn't realize was clenched.

We're exhausted. The bone-deep kind that settles after adrenaline burns out and the emotional hangover takes its toll. We climb into my California King bed together like it's the most natural thing we've ever done. It feels right they're here, that I don't have to choose, don't have to draw lines or push anyone away. Tonight, at least, there's no fear of that.

Hudson sprawls like he owns the place, familiar as breathing.

Pippa hesitates for half a second before curling in between us like she's always belonged there. I wrap an arm around her without thinking. Hudson shifts closer, solid and warm on her other side.

Pippa's breathing evens out first. Hudson follows not long after. I lie listening to the rhythm. The steady calm of shared space settles deep in my chest.

Nothing has felt this right in a long time.

Maybe ever.

For once, the weight I carry doesn't feel so heavy.

TWENTY-FOUR

traction

Hudson

Monday Afternoon, Day 33

Completing normal tasks at the office feels like a sigh of relief after the chaos of the past couple of weeks. The mundane distraction is more than welcome. I clear emails, sit through a briefing that could've been an email, and skim a report I already know by heart. Muscle memory takes over, giving my mind something to hold onto.

Last night was heavy.

Sisters.

Maribel Island.

Jared fucking Whiteman and that cunt Sophie Delacroix, who is even more evil than I realized.

Young girls raised in the shadows of society's worst sins, inheriting baggage no one should have to carry. Choosing to make those predators pay when no one else would.

As heavy as it all is, I can't shake the sense that something fundamental shifted last night. Like a fault line finally cracked wide open, too big to ignore any longer, and the earth has reluctantly settled in its new place.

Written in the fucking stars, if I were to be poetic about it.

Waking up with them—*both of them*—easy, content…felt fan-fucking-tastic. Life-altering. It's taking concentrated efforts to avoid wearing the biggest smile of my life on my face all day today. I managed to fall for two very complicated, stubborn, guarded people. But last night, walls came tumbling down. And now we have a chance. That's more than I want to think about. It's too good and in my life good things have been few and fleeting. It's hard to believe any of this shit is real.

So yeah, work. Even if I've come to hate working at the FBI. Same corrupt fuckers the mafia services, just dressed up as public servants—at least the mob doesn't lie about what it is.

I wait until just before lunch before approaching Luna. "SCIF?" I keep my voice casual as I step into her line of sight.

She studies my face for half a second, then nods.

We don't speak as we walk.

Our friendship was cemented over many long hours in these halls. I know it can bounce back from its recent fractures, and I intend to make that clear.

We stop at a reinforced door marked SCIF, *Authorized Personnel Only*. I scan my badge and the lock gives a soft, electronic chirp. The door seals shut behind us with a heavy *click*.

We remain silent as I move with practiced efficiency, opening an app on my phone to scan for bugs. I do a slow sweep of the space, methodical, scanning the vents, ceiling corners, even the baseboards. The faint pulse of blue light from my phone screen bounces across the walls as I move around the room.

Just because a room says it's secure, doesn't mean it's not bugged.

Luna stays out of my way, drifting toward the far corner I've already inspected.

"We're clear," I say once I'm done, pocketing my phone.

Her shoulders relax, if only a little.

I lean against the table. "I wanted to check in. On you." I make deliberate eye contact, looking into her big blue eyes behind even bigger glasses. I wait.

She considers me for a beat, then relaxes her shoulders and says, "I'm better. Now that it's out. Lighter, I think, even if everything else feels heavier."

That fucking resonates. "I'm glad you don't have to carry it alone anymore."

She meets my gaze. "Me too. And—" She hesitates. "I'm glad you know. You, Eva, Enzo. The whole truth."

"Me too."

She gives me a faint smile.

"I'll be honest…I thought my childhood was rough. You make having a single mom who worked as an escort seem fucking beige."

Luna laughs. A genuine smile crosses her face. "You? Beige? Not possible."

"Phew. I was worried."

"How was Pippa after we left?"

Now it's my turn to smile. "I'm afraid to say this out loud, but…" A pause.

"The two people you want most in the world might be figuring their shit out?" Luna finishes.

That makes me laugh. "That's what I've always loved about you, Steele. You see the truth."

She stiffens and her smile falters a bit.

"Shit, sorry, what did I say?" I ask.

"No, Hudson—" She takes a deep breath then takes a seat at the table in the center of the room.

I join her but remain silent.

"I never knew. I had no idea who our dad really was. What the parties were. What Sophie and Konstantin did to find girls. I just… I didn't see it. I know once Pippa and Jules started to realize certain things, they protected me. I try to tell myself it wasn't my fault; I was so young. But I hate that I didn't see it."

"How could you have?"

She simply shakes her head. "I don't know, but the day he was arrested… I was such a mess. I didn't understand anything."

"Jules said you were like, thirteen."

She confirms and then continues, "I didn't just lose my dad that day—a dad I didn't know was a monster—but Junior was my best friend. I cared about him. I didn't want to leave him alone with his dad. We left him with a monster." A tear slides down her face. "It worries me that no one's seen him in ten years."

I nod slowly. "I didn't know him as a child, but Luna, he wasn't—"

"I know he's changed," she says. "I'm not naïve, but… I knew the little boy he once was, and I feel guilty that we escaped and he didn't."

Another tear falls and she wipes it away quickly. "Anyway," she continues, "I can't bring this up to my sisters. They have enough to deal with. Now that we're basically living at the Lucianos', I feel like it's disrespectful to them to even have these thoughts."

"What thoughts?"

"I shouldn't be worried about a Volkov. Not when Eva and Enzo—"

"*Yeah,* I wouldn't bring it up to either of them." I aim for a bit of humor. "But you can't help how you feel. Your caring heart is one of the things that everyone loves most about you."

She scoffs. "I thought it was my great taste in music."

"No one thinks nineties boy band music is great. Fucking no one."

She lets out a breath that sounds like relief. "Thank you."

I raise a brow.

"For listening. I know things have been strained—"

"It's been a weird few weeks, that's for damned sure, but you and I have been friends a long time."

Luna agrees.

"I'll always be here for you."

She offers me a smile and stands from her chair.

"And Eva?" I ask as I join her to leave.

She takes a deep breath. "It's new. And complicated."

"Just be honest with her. She can handle it."

"Since you're checking in on your family"—she turns to me—"my sister is also my top priority. So don't make me mad again, okay?"

"Oh shit. You were mad at me?"

"Duh!" she says with a smile.

"Fine, fine. Let's be nice to each other's families then? Sound good?"

"I like that."

Before I open the door, I say, "Oh, and we're on the security detail for the gala. Confirmed this morning."

"We have three days. I—I'm glad this part will be behind us soon."

Their scars may never heal, but Troy's death will be the start of a new phase. We unlock the SCIF and step back into the controlled chaos of the HQ hallway.

Jax Novak spots us and walks our way. He's at least five or six inches taller than my six feet, and his combination of dark hair and blue eyes is striking. He probably has a decade on me. And knowing he and Jules have history makes me very motivated to know this guy more.

"Cross, Steele," he says, calling to us both. "Good timing." He has a slight Eastern European accent that is very alluring.

Yeah, Jules, I see it. Yum.

I clock the look in his eyes—focused, purposeful.

"I need to scope a local security firm. Redline Solutions," he says. "I want to stop by today and thought you two could join me."

Luna glances at me, expression blank, then back to him.

"Jules Sinclair, the CEO," Jax continues, "I know her from my Interpol days. We partnered on some cases."

"Really?" I feign ignorance.

"Yeah. She's solid, but I need to see if she'll open her files."

"For client overlap?" I fake-guess.

He nods. "Especially anything tied to the gala crowd, the celebrity parties, or security cross-contracts. I think she could be an asset."

Yeah, hot stuff, I'm sure you do. I'm sure it has nothing to do with wanting to see your stunning ex. I see you, Novak.

"Agreed. When do we leave?" I ask.

"Now," Jax says. "Only a few days until the gala."

"Yeah. If Sinclair cooperates, we'll want Steele with us."

Luna squares her shoulders. "I'm in."

And just like that, we head for the elevators.

This is going to be fun!

TWENTY-FIVE

fusion

Pippa

Monday Evening, Day 33

The warehouse is quiet in the way I like it—humming softly with power, alive only with machines that do exactly what they're told. Unlike the idiots in Washington I'm surrounded by all day. I'm alone in my lab, hair twisted up, sleeves pushed to my elbows as I measure compounds into a vial. The smell is sharp, chemical. Familiar. Comforting, even, in its own way. Control lives here.

I think about last night more than I mean to—how sleeping between Enzo and Hudson didn't feel strange or dangerous or complicated. We didn't do anything; we didn't need to. We just slept.

I remember waking slowly, disoriented for half a minute, then realizing exactly where I was. Tangled and warm, Hudson solid at my back, Enzo's arm heavy across my waist like it had always belonged there. Safe. Content.

A new feeling for me.

They took care of me. Last night, this morning. Food, coffee, warm caresses. It was easy. No questions. No pressure. Just presence. Then, they drove me home like it was the most natural thing in the world.

I've had a smile on my face all day. And that's just unnatural. I think my colleagues were concerned. It was easier at the senator's office today. The gala was the main focus, as it's only three days away. I wasn't sure whether my anxiety would spiral again, and it wasn't completely gone, but some of the weight has lifted.

I know that whatever happens in the next few days, I'm not alone. I've always had my sisters, but expanding the circle feels much better than I imagined.

A heavy knock at the warehouse door interrupts the low hum of the space and my thoughts. I glance up, already smiling. I check the cameras and buzz them in.

Enzo and Hudson step inside like they've always belonged here, too—jackets off, sleeves rolled, eyes on me. Something loosens in my chest at the sight of them.

"You're early," I say, grinning.

"We missed you," Hudson says easily, eyes sparkling.

Enzo smirks. "I wanted to see you at work."

I laugh and cross the lab. They don't crowd me, don't rush.

Hudson leans in to kiss my temple.

Enzo's hand settles at my lower back, warm and grounding, before kissing my cheek.

I step back and gesture to the bench. "Come on, I'll show you where I'm at."

"I didn't know I had a sexy scientist fantasy, but, *fuck*, baby, I do now," Hudson teases.

I wink at him and then walk them through the setup. The vials labeled in my shorthand, testing strips, a small array of devices all laid out with deliberate spacing.

"I'll be wearing this," I explain, lifting a slim ring from its case. "Custom housing. Hollow band. Pressure-release mechanism."

I twist the solitaire gem slightly. A fine needle slides out of the band, barely visible.

"He won't feel the needle prick him?" Enzo asks, seeming impressed.

"It won't entirely penetrate his skin. It only has to make contact. The absorption rate is fast. It doesn't take much."

"Really? That's… Wow, shit, okay," Hudson laughs. "That's impressive, babe."

"We didn't really get into this last night, but can someone else deliver this deadly handshake?" Enzo asks. "Does it have to be you? I mean Hudson, Jules, and—"

I raise my hand. "It has to be me. Logistically, I've already worked out the introduction. I need to do this—I need to put this behind me and move on."

They both accept my answer. I can tell they don't like it, but they aren't pushing back.

I place the ring back in its case.

"So," I say lightly, "what's the plan tonight?" I eye the bag in Hudson's hand.

He sets the paper bag onto the counter. "Dinner. Hope you like sushi."

"Who doesn't like sushi?" I respond in mock horror.

"Good, because Enzo ordered the whole damned menu," he jokes.

Enzo's cheeks flush as he sets the food out. "I didn't know what you liked."

"Thank you. This looks great."

We move over to the lounge area to eat. Sitting on the couches, sharing bites, stealing smiles. Easy, flirty, and familiar in a way that feels new and exciting.

"You'll never believe where Luna and I went on FBI business today," Hudson says after a few bites. "Redline Solutions."

"Uh oh," I say, "now Jules is on the FBI's radar?"

"She's certainly on *Jax Novak's* radar," he says with a sly smile.

I let out a small laugh, more relief than anything. "I've never met Jax. What's he like?"

"Pretty dreamy," Hudson answers.

Enzo clears his throat. "Excuse me?"

"Don't worry, hot stuff, he only has eyes for Jules."

Enzo rolls his eyes.

"Really?" I ask. "So, you think he's still interested in her?"

"Oh yeah." Hudson takes a bite and wiggles his eyebrows.

"Huh. Interesting." I file that away. "I should check in with Jules later."

"You should," Hudson agrees. "She seemed less than pleased the FBI and her ex-lover showed up unannounced to her office."

"Also…either of you know what's going on with Eva and Luna?" I ask.

They exchange a look.

"No," Enzo admits. "I haven't asked. Eva doesn't share a lot with us about her dating life. I think she thinks we're overprotective or something."

I choke out a laugh. "Does she now? I can't imagine why she thinks that."

"No fucking clue," Hudson says innocently.

They both shrug.

I smile faintly. "Last I heard, they were planning a date."

They both seem surprised by that revelation.

Enzo's eyebrows rise and his grin turns sharp. "Interesting."

The conversation drifts into everyone's activities for the day and our thoughts on the budding relationships around us.

While we tidy after our meal, Enzo asks quietly, "What happens after Troy?"

The question lands heavier than expected, but I know what I want to do. "I want to quit Cramden's office," I say without hesitation. "I need a break from all of it."

"Good," Hudson says immediately.

Enzo agrees.

"You do?" Their encouragement surprises me.

"With Troy and McCarter gone, DC is going to be a mess. We should all take a break," Enzo says, which only surprises me more.

"The remaining marks from Maribel aren't in DC, necessarily —there are celebrities, corporate types, foreign dignitaries—but I don't think working for a senator will be necessary after Troy is gone."

"I think you're right," Enzo says. "And if there are more politicians to take down, any one of us can gain access. You don't have to keep burning the candle at both ends."

Hudson exhales. "I want out of the Bureau."

I blink. "Hudson—"

Enzo shifts toward him. "Really?"

"I hate the double life. I hate the people, the corruption. I know it helps you and Eva," he says, looking at Enzo, "and I'll stay—"

Enzo's jaw tightens. "No. Neither of you should have to play these roles anymore. *Fuck,* I don't even think I want to keep running the family business, either. Not like this. I don't want to launder money for these sick fucking men. They are all even worse than I knew. I won't be complacent in the trafficking and abuse of anyone."

A heavy silence settles between us. But maybe it's hopeful, too?

"What would we do if we weren't doing this?" I ask, trying to lighten the mood.

Enzo rubs his jaw. "Hm. Not sure I've ever given it enough thought, to be honest."

"What if we weren't surrounded by all this darkness? What if our lives weren't mapped out for us before we were born? What do you think you would have done with it?" I ask.

He takes a moment to answer, but eventually says, "Art."

I quirk a brow.

Enzo chuckles. "I don't have a single artistic skill. I've never painted or anything like that, but as a kid, I loved to doodle the world around me. I would have liked to learn more about art."

"Tall, dark, broody artist. I like it," I say rubbing his arm, smiling at him.

"Yeah, that's fucking hot," Hudson adds.

"And what about you, pretty boy?" I ask.

"Oh, I wanted to be Lorenzo Luciano, Senior when I was a kid. I idolized him," Hudson says with a big smile.

Enzo laughs. "You really did."

"The power, the respect. I envied it while we were growing up."

"Me too," Enzo admits, almost regretfully.

"What was he like?" I ask.

They look at each other, smiles crossing their faces as memories flash behind their eyes.

Enzo answers. "He had a tall, imposing presence—always serious or stressed—but he wasn't scary or mean. Not to us. He was kind to his men, to his family. Always fair, but also not caught up in stupid stuff. He never made us feel like we couldn't be kids. He thought our rebellions as teens were funny and necessary for growing up and growing wiser."

"Remember when Gabriella found us drunk the first time we skipped school?" Hudson asks.

Enzo laughs loudly. I don't know if I've ever heard him laugh like that before.

"Gabriella?" I ask.

"Enzo and Eva's mom. His parents always insisted I call them by their first names, instead of the formal Mr. and Mrs. Luciano. So, we're in high school and we decide to skip one day. It's important to know, Enzo was kind of a dork—"

"A dork?" he protests.

"I mean, you were hot, don't get me wrong, but yeah, you followed all the rules and made good grades and shit."

"You had better grades than me."

"I was smarter than you. Still am. But I wasn't a dork." They both laugh. "Anyway, I talked him into skipping school and stealing some liquor from his dad's stash. After a day of wandering around, literally doing nothing, we found our way back to the mansion drunk. Gabriella found us and she was so worried Lorenzo would be angry. It was like the first time Enzo was really going to be in trouble, you see. He was such an obedient little boy."

Enzo rolls his eyes.

"Anyway, when Lorenzo got home, he thought it was the funniest thing that we were drunk. He kind of interrogated us, to see if we had done anything to be concerned about, tried to freak us out a little, but overall, was entertained by our antics."

"I guess when you see the real evils in this world, some teenage boys drinking on a school day isn't a big deal." Enzo has a look of admiration on his face as he speaks.

"They sound like lovely parents."

Both guys agree.

"So, Hudson, do you still want to be like Lorenzo? Or, if you could do anything now, what would it be?" I ask.

Leaning back in the cushions, he ponders before saying, "Travel. I'd like to travel more. I've only left the country on quick work trips. It'd be nice to explore."

"I can see that about you," I say.

"Me too," Enzo says. Smiles cross their faces.

"And you, Pippa?" Enzo asks.

"I love the science and medical fields. There were times in college I considered becoming a doctor. I don't think I'd want a practice, though. I tend to need a little drama or adrenaline," I say with a smirk. "But maybe an ER doc or an EMT—I could see that being a good fit."

We talk a little more about our daydreams. My guys share more funny stories from their childhood.

Then an idea crosses my mind. "Don't we have enough money to never work again?" I ask slowly.

Hudson smiles. "Retirement?"

Enzo laughs. "In our thirties?"

"Why not?" I counter. "We could disappear after all this. Start somewhere new."

They look at me.

"Maybe," Hudson says softly, "we should."

Something shifts. It's quiet, curious, and hopeful.

Enzo joins me on my couch, sitting close to me.

Hudson mirrors him.

Their hands find mine, anchoring me between them again. No urgency. No rush. Just warmth. Choice. The sense that whatever comes next, we'll decide together. I rest my forehead against Hudson's chest, Enzo's hand warm at my back, and I let myself believe—for the first time—that the future might actually belong to us.

And nothing about that feels dangerous at all.

After a few moments, my skin starts to warm. Need thrums through me, heightening my senses. With them on either side of me, I slowly kiss Enzo. When I feel Hudson's lips on my neck, I let out a small moan.

"Mm, Janey baby, what do you want?" Hudson asks.

I look him in the eyes, licking my lips.

His eyes flare.

"I want to see you and Enzo. Together."

Enzo's hands tighten at my waist. "You'd like that, *bella*?"

I smile in confirmation and the guys lean over me for a searing kiss that has my desire spiking. I rub their legs. Each of our hands explore from one body to the next. I encourage them to switch spots, putting Enzo in the center.

"One second." I run over to our security desk and turn off the interior cameras. "Don't need the girls seeing this."

They both laugh.

"Hudson, have you tasted him yet?"

They both groan at my question.

"Fuck. No, I haven't. What does he taste like?" Hudson licks his lips.

I grab his head and kiss him, moving us to the floor in front of Enzo. I watch Enzo through my lashes as he rubs his crotch through his pants, watching us.

"You two are so hot together," Enzo says.

"I want to see you and Hudson. It turns me on." It really does. They are two of the most beautiful men. So tough on the outside, but so soft, caring, and protective on the inside. It just does something for me. Plus, their bodies are ripped. So many muscles, dips, and curves, and huge cocks. Yeah—they *really* do it for me.

I undo Enzo's pants and pull them to the floor. His cock springs free and Hudson and I are immediately mesmerized. He's thick and wide and so hard.

"You two keep looking at me like that, and I might not last long."

I begin kissing up one thigh, and Hudson follows my lead. We slowly tease him as we make our way up.

Enzo's breathing grows shallow. One of his hands softly lands on my head, his thumb rubbing across my cheek. He's doing the same to Hudson.

I take the first lick—his balls first.

He lets out a hiss.

I lick all the way up to the head, nice and slow, then take the head into my mouth.

Hudson's hand reaches up and wraps around the base of his cock.

"Damn it, you two, *fuck*. Shit."

"Your turn, Johnny," I kiss him, tasting both of them on my tongue.

Then Hudson pulls Enzo into his mouth, deep, rough, and fast.

"Holy shit. Fuck... Yes..." Enzo's head falls against the back of the couch.

As Hudson takes Enzo, I play with his balls and squeeze him at the base.

When Enzo says he's close, I encourage Hudson to pause. Both look at me expectantly. "I need him inside me."

Hudson and I have had many sexual encounters, but I've been dreaming about riding Enzo's cock, and I need him. Now.

Hudson pulls out a condom from his pocket, putting it on Enzo for us. I kiss Hudson again and rise from my knees to straddle Enzo.

"I've been dreaming of this, hot stuff." I kiss him with wild abandon.

As we pull back, he says, "I've wanted you since the first time I saw you, *bella*."

"We're all fucking aware," Hudson says, sexy and sassy. He's on Enzo's side now. They kiss next and I feel it in every part of my body.

Hudson lines Enzo up to my core and I start to lower. At the first inch, we both take a deep breath.

I lean in to kiss him as Hudson fondles my nipples. My body feels so alive, pleasure soaring through me.

I take him one inch at a time, adjusting as we go.

We all take turns kissing. One of Enzo's hands is tight on my ass, guiding me up and down. Hudson's hands have found their way south. One hand on my clit, rubbing slow circles, one hand on my back hole, doing the same.

"I want to take you back here one day while he's inside you, baby," he whispers in my ear. He knows how much I love ass play.

I hum in agreement.

"I want to take you while you take her," Enzo grits out. And we are all aroused by that idea.

I want it all with them. I want the wildly hot moments. I want the tender moments like last night. I want the stories and the laughs. I want to tell them all the shit I've been through. I want their protection when I am too tired to carry this by myself.

I want it all.

I deserve it all.

I deserve these men.

And I'm tired of running.

I guide mine and Enzo's hands to Hudson's cock.

He lays back against the couch while we please him together. The speed increases everywhere. Our hands, me riding Enzo. It's frenzied, hot, intense.

We all come loudly a few short moments later.

Breathing heavily, I lift off Enzo and we fall into a pile on the couch.

Hudson looks at us. "Let's do this in a bed someday, huh?"

TWENTY-SIX

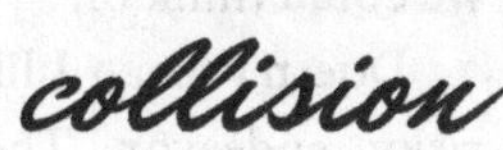

Enzo

Thursday Evening, Day 36

Three nights flew by too fast. I was pulled into more meetings at The Vault than I wanted. I had an itch to punch every dirty politician who insisted we needed to increase production of their laundering. I wanted to probe about why they needed more cash and faster. I couldn't help but think about these Hollywood parties and Jax Novak's hunt for Sophie.

I wanted to ask my clients, "What do you know about Sophie Delacroix?" "Have you seen her?" "Are you going to these parties?" and my favorite, "Should I fucking kill you now?"

I managed to keep a level head and resisted a killing spree, but it took considerable restraint. I knew supporting Pippa tonight was more important.

I sent Niko and a small crew to south Virginia tonight to deal with an issue we are having with our arms supplier. He's pissed that Eva and I are both in the field without him. Now he's checking in with me every fucking five minutes and I'm going to lose it if he doesn't calm down.

The comms van hums softly around Eva and me. The screens glow in the dark like watchful eyes. Feeds from inside the ballroom scroll past—wide angles, close-ups, security cams piped clean into our system—every angle accounted for. Every variable we could think of.

Doesn't mean I like it. I understand Niko's concern; this is a risky endeavor. There are more armed guards inside that building than there has any right to be. We are parked two blocks down on the south side entrance of the White House. Opposite of where all the celebrities and politicians arrive on the red carpet at the north entrance. Our van looks like any other media van stationed nearby tonight. We blend in, but that's still not enough to make me feel at ease.

Everyone I care about is involved in this op; I won't feel at ease until we are all back home. Safe.

Eva's headset hangs loosely around her neck. Her fingers fly over a tablet as she toggles between channels. Inside, Pippa, Luna, Hudson, and Jules move through the ballroom with practiced ease, calm voices, and clean check-ins.

I fidget and glance camera to camera, trying to keep an eye on all the moving pieces.

Pippa is easy to spot. She's wearing a stunning formal red dress in a sea of black gowns. When I first saw her tonight, she took my breath away. Her elegance and grace are unmatched. She told us she chose red symbolically, to reclaim her power from when Sophie made her dye her red hair blonde.

I am so proud of her. Every time she opens up, trusts me, shares with us, my heart expands for her. She's sunk her claws into my heart and I think I want them there for life.

Hudson, Luna, and Jules are harder to keep eyes on—they are meant to blend in. Each member of the secret service, FBI, and the contracted teams look exactly the same, but we are mic'd for anything urgent.

Eva and I can't go inside. We are too high profile, too recognizable. We are extra eyes, comms, and the getaway team, if needed. But I don't like being on the outside looking in.

Eva glances at me. "You good?"

"Yeah," I say.

She gives me a knowing look.

"No," I confess. "But I will be."

She waits for more.

"I don't think I want to do this anymore," I admit quietly. "The family business, any of it."

She studies my face, searching for doubt. She finds none. "Okay. I won't be upset if it all goes away."

That isn't what I expected. I thought she might feel sentimental over my father's legacy. "Really?"

"I want you alive. *Free*. Everything else is negotiable."

"Thank you. I'm sure that seems out of left field," I admit.

"Not really. It all seems, I don't know…dirty? Messier than before the veil was lifted?"

"Knowing what they went through, what thousands have survived at the hands of these fucking men," I hiss.

"And knowing our business helps them…"

"I can't unknow what we know now."

"Yeah," she sighs. "Enzo, we have enough money to never work again."

"It's not about the money… I guess I just worry that walking away puts us all at risk."

She tilts her head, pondering this.

We keep our eyes on the video feeds. Pippa should be introduced to the president after dinner. Her boss arranged the introduction for her and her stupid date, some idiot DC staffer with ambition.

"What if Niko takes over?" Eva suggests, snapping me from my murderous thoughts of Pippa's date.

"I've wondered that, too. It's an option. I think he and Luca could run things together."

She tilts her head, then exhales. "I've been thinking, too. Maybe I could focus on anti-trafficking work. Do something that actually matters."

"I really like that idea." I smile. "I wonder if Jules and Luna would have some ideas."

"Yeah, maybe," she agrees.

I swallow. "Things with Hudson and Pippa are good. Really good. We're taking it slow, but it's…well, it's really good." I break out with a smile I can't contain.

A smile curves her mouth, too. "I love that for you, brother. You deserve some happiness."

The last few nights have been…magical? Am I allowed to think that as a mobster?

Hudson and Pippa have spent every night in my bed. We've explored each other's bodies. We've shared meals together, showered together, and gotten ready together. Pippa has had moments of anxiety we've navigated well. She and Hudson went to Club14 to gamble two nights ago—she needed the adrenaline, the risk, and Hudson could ensure it was safely achieved.

When they returned to the mansion, Hudson and I helped her come down from her high.

The sex has been…amazing doesn't seem to quite express how it feels.

I worried I didn't have enough experience for them, but they've been so happy and excited just to be together. It's been… easy. Electric, fiery…and easy.

For so long, I truly believed I didn't have a sex drive. That I was just different than other people. I was sure as hell wrong about that.

Hudson and I haven't gone past blowjobs, but I'm eager to explore more with him. My first time going down on him was powerful. It rocked my world.

And the two of them are working me up to all the other possibilities for Hudson and me. I've learned a lot about ass play and toys in a few short days, but I want to take my time.

I've also wanted to focus on Pippa's mission until she is done with Troy once and for all.

"I want to date Luna," Eva blurts out.

That gets my full attention.

"She's taking it slow," Eva continues. "She's careful, a little walled off. I thought telling us everything—Maribel, all of it—would move things along, but she's been busy. I don't know. I don't want to push."

I think about Luna. About all three of the sisters. All they've been through. "Don't give up on her," I say. "Each of them will need a different kind of care. They've been alone their whole lives."

Eva nods slowly in understanding.

"At least we had our parents," I add, "even if we lost them too early."

A shift on one of the screens catches my eye.

I catch sight of Jax Novak deep in conversation with Jules near the bar. Their body language tight, guarded.

Eva frowns. "Something wrong?"

"Hudson mentioned he and Luna went to Jules's office with Jax Novak this week."

"She told me the same. I wonder how she's doing with this blast from her past. Just knowing he was in town seemed to stress her out. Looks like he's edging his way back into her life." Eva points to the screen.

No doubt that guy wants her attention. She reads like a blank rock, though, giving nothing away.

"Poor guy. Looks like if he wants back in, he has some work to—"

"Jesus Christ," Hudson's voice breaks through the comms. "Junior fucking Volkov is *here*."

Eva gasps.

"Are you sure?" I ask, trying to keep my voice steady. No one has seen him in ten years, he could be mistaken.

"He's wearing glasses like some Clark Kent motherfucker, but yes, I'd recognize him anywhere. Shaved head, but he hasn't changed much. It's him."

Eva and I look at each other.

My blood pressure rises. I haven't had access to this asshole since the night his dad died. No one in our network has laid eyes on him. And tonight, he strolls into a high-profile event at the White House? *What the actual fuck?*

"He's here with Lily Blackwell," Jules says. Lily is a seriously stupid-as-fuck congress woman who hitched her wagon to Magnus Troy. She'll propagate all his racist and classist policies if it keeps her in her seat.

That means it really is him. Jules would recognize him, too. So, would—

"Pippa. Is he going to recognize Pippa?" I ask, concern etched in my voice.

"What's his position?" Pippa asks. "I'll keep my back to him."

"Southeast corner," Luna says on a whisper.

"Luna, you okay?" Eva asks.

No answer.

"She's fine," Jules replies quickly. "Hudson, I need you to stay between Luna and Junior, so he doesn't see her."

"Hudson, did he clock you?" I ask.

He confirms he wasn't spotted and that he's making his way to Luna.

I locate Luna on the cameras and Eva zooms in. Luna looks shaken. Eva has her eyes locked on the screen.

"I'm sure she'll be okay," I reassure her.

Eva asks me off channel if I can spot Junior, but so far, I can't.

"What do we think he's doing here?" I ask to the group.

Hudson is the first to answer. "It's no secret Troy is a puppet for the Russians, but for him to show up here? That's...ballsy. I don't know, man."

"Luna, is Junior in the case file for Jax? Will he be recognized?" Eva asks.

No answer from Luna. On the camera, we see Hudson talking to her. They are in a back corner where staff comes in and out with drinks and hors d'oeuvres. I still can't identify Junior on the screens, but if he's in the southeast corner, he wouldn't be able to see Luna or Pippa from his angle.

Jules and Jax are in the northeast corner. My eyes scan every screen searching for signs of danger.

Hudson says, "Luna said yes. It's known that Sophie and the Volkovs were connected to Jared, but while Jax may know that, no one has seen Junior in a decade. We may be the only people who would recognize him."

Fuck. I don't like this. I don't feel good about it. *Why is he here?*

"They are seating us for dinner," Pippa whispers.

"Lily Blackwell's table will be close to the front, near Troy's. Pippa, your table is middle back. Make sure you sit with your back to the front of the room," Jules says. "Luna and Hudson, stay where you are."

I take a deep breath. Jules is in there. Hudson is in there. They are in control. Nothing will happen. Pippa and Luna are capable. They can take care of themselves. Everything is okay. I repeat this in my mind a few times.

I fucking hate that I'm stuck in this van.

I begin to vibrate with unspent energy and frustration.

"You can't go in there." Eva is eyeing me.

I look at her, neither confirming nor denying my intent.

"He may be hiding in plain sight, Enz, but you don't have that same luxury. You will ruin Pippa's mission tonight. Right now, everything is fine."

I know she's right, but my blood is boiling. I want him fucking dead, and I'm spiraling. Has he been coming and going from his fortress-of-an-estate this whole time? Have we missed that? The fucker has no tech or cameras we can tap into. He may be living in the medieval fucking ages, but we have eyes all over that neighborhood. Have for years. How did we miss this?

I take a deep breath.

I can't go in there.

I take a few more deep breaths. I focus on Pippa, finding her table, and keeping an eye on her.

Tonight is about her—she deserves to close this chapter.

I close my eyes.

"Can we get a clone on Junior's phone or put a tracker on him?" I ask. "What do we have inside the building?" We've got to take advantage of this sighting. If I can't be in there tonight, maybe I can use this as a chance to finally get tabs on this fucker.

Jules replies a few minutes later. "Great idea, Enz. I have the tech. I just don't know who can plant it. Maybe someone on my team."

"Jax," Luna suggests.

"No." Jules shuts it down.

"Tell him who it is—he'll want to do it," Luna pushes.

Eva and I look at each other. Is that a good idea? I don't know this guy, but he's hunting Sophie, and Junior is probably an important lead in his investigation.

Ultimately, Jules agrees with Luna and says she'll get it handled.

Shit… After tonight we might be able to track Junior Volkov. Finally.

The waitstaff is serving steaming dinner plates and politicians and celebrities have been announced to give toasts. All celebrate our idiot president on his stupid ballroom, that no one asked for.

As the minutes tick by, I feel myself slightly relax. I focus on Pippa.

Eva and I spotted Lily Blackwell at her table. We see a man next to her who fits the description Hudson gave us and confirm Junior's location. He has no line of sight to anyone on our team.

I zoom in on the image of Pippa's table and I see that fucking date of hers with his arm around her chairback. "Tell your date to keep his hands to himself," I mutter, not even realizing I've gone live on comms.

Hudson's voice comes back instantly. "If he doesn't, I may find myself escorting him out of the building."

Eva snorts.

I crack a smile.

The tension eases a bit more.

Jules whispers, "Guys, Pippa can handle herself. We need Jake to make the introduction. Behave."

Jake. Ugh.

As the speeches and toasts finish, the president takes the podium. He rambles on, making absolutely no sense. No doubt the guy has dementia—I don't know who his medical staff thinks they are fooling.

When he finally steps down, dinner has been cleared, and people begin to mill about again.

It's time.

TWENTY-SEVEN

reclamation

Pippa

Thursday Evening, Day 36

The decor of the new ballroom is gaudy. Gold light spills from chandeliers the size of small planets, refracting through crystal and champagne flutes, catching on sequins and polished shoes. Everyone here is dressed to be admired or feared—some manage both.

My skin has been crawling all night as I've had to smile and nod and rub elbows with criminal after predator after egotistical asshole.

My date, Jake, is a younger version of all these gross old men in power, and it's set me on edge all this evening. I've managed to keep things cordial and flirty, feigning interest in his boring, one-sided, and self-absorbed conversations all night. It's all been worth it, because we are approaching Magnus Troy.

My pulse ticks against the inside of my throat.

"Breathe," Jules says softly in my ear. "You're doing great, Pip."

I don't respond as Jake steers me forward with a proprietary hand at the small of my back.

"You're clear," Hudson says through the comms. "Junior is across the room—no line of sight."

Troy stands near the center of the room, surrounded by men who laugh too hard and women who tilt their heads just enough to look interested. He's thinner than the last time I saw him. Smaller. Age has hollowed him out, but the self-importance is still there, puffed up and polished.

Jake squeezes my waist. "There he is," he says, breath warm against my ear. "Try not to swoon."

I don't reply. My heart races. I picture myself outside of my body. Time for the role of my lifetime. I twist the solitaire stone just slightly. The motion likely looks like I'm fidgeting—nervous to meet the Pedophile of the United States.

You can do this, Pippa.

Do it for Catherine.

When we stop in front of him, Jake clears his throat, already smiling too wide. "Mr. President, may I introduce Pippa Saint James."

Jake gestures to me.

I step forward.

There's a beat—a fraction of a second where the room seems to dim, where the music dulls into a low hum—before Troy looks up.

When his eyes land on me, I freeze.

The air shifts. Not enough for anyone else to notice. Just enough that I do.

His smile falters. Comes back wrong.

He blinks once. Twice.

"Sorry," he says slowly. "Have we...have we met?"

My stomach drops.

Everyone in my earpiece says comforting, encouraging words. They remind me to stay calm, to not read into it.

I open my mouth. Nothing comes out.

I'm fifteen again.

He smells stale, like heavy cologne and something sour. I didn't know I'd be alone with him. I thought Sophie would be here. I thought...

His hand is too close; his voice is too low. He's saying things I don't understand yet—not fully—but they make my skin crawl.

"You're mature for your age," he says with a smile, like his compliment is the greatest gift.

I don't respond. I can't speak.

"I like your name, Catherine. It suits you. Timeless and royal."

Dad's best friend doesn't even know he picked my name for that very reason. Gross.

None of Dad's friends know about us—not our names and not that we hideout in the bunker during their parties.

It's for our safety, our dad says.

Safety from who?

His best fucking friend?

I wonder if Sophie could hear me if I call her name. Where did she go?

It's my fault for being so eager and coming in here. I should have known better than to trust her.

"Your hair is so pretty. Blondes have more fun, right?" He wiggles his eyebrows as he pulls at a lock of my hair. I know he wants me to interact with him, be charming, but I am frozen.

Tears prick my eyes.

Maybe Sophie will be back any moment. Lunch had been normal—boring, but nothing sinister.

Now this old man is sitting next to me...flirting. He's way older than dad. Too old to think I could want—

"Sophie told me you wanted to give me a tour of the estate," he says.

I blink my eyes a few times. In a small voice, I ask, "Haven't you been here before? Sophie said you and D—" I stumble. "Jared are, like, best friends, right?"

Sophie told me to refer to Dad as Jared. I almost forgot. But maybe if he knows I know Jared, he will stop. Or maybe I should tell him Jared is my dad, even if that bitch Sophie told me not to. Maybe that will protect me.

"Oh, I've been to some parties here, of course, but this estate is so big, I'm sure there are rooms I haven't seen." He's leaned in closer, but there is no room for me to lean back any more than I already am.

"Let's go, pretty girl, I want to see what you have to show me." He grips my arm to rise with him from the table. His hold is tight enough to keep me next to him as we walk out of the dining room and—

"Pippa?" Enzo's voice over the comms snaps me back.

Troy's eyes have gone wider, but not with confusion or alarm, with curiosity. "It's your eyes," he says. "I swear I know you."

The room tilts.

"Stay with us," Hudson says. "You're safe. You're in control."

I pull in a breath and lower my chin just slightly. When I speak, my voice is softer. Raspy. Practiced. "No, sir. We haven't met." I let a hint of awe creep in. "I'm sorry I'm so flustered. It's just an honor to finally meet you, sir."

Troy watches me like I've said something fascinating.

"I would remember meeting you," I add, equal parts demure and genuine.

This brings a smile to his face. Ego—always start with their ego.

"I guess that is true," he says, leaning closer. His smirk makes my skin itch. "You're stunning, sweetheart. Are you having a good time tonight?"

Disgust curls hot and sharp in my chest.

"I'm flattered, sir," I say. "Yes, the gala has been lovely."

He hums, pleased with himself. "Isn't it?"

He finally extends his hand to shake mine—to touch me.

I swallow.

He'll never touch me again after this.

After tonight, he'll never touch anyone else.

I take Troy's small, clammy hand firmly in mine. I ensure the ring makes contact with his swollen, bruised skin.

The poison transfers cleanly. Invisible. Perfect.

"Make sure you say good night before you leave, dear," Troy says with a smile as he releases his grip. "I'd love to set up some more time with you—and your friend here," he jerks his chin toward Jake.

I simply smile and nod.

As Jake and I walk away, I meet Jules's gaze across the room.

I lift my chin slightly, nearly imperceptibly.

Confirmation.

Jake laughs too loud. "What's it feel like to have the President of the United States *flirting* with you?" He squeezes my hip. "My date caught President Troy's eye. That man has great taste."

I say nothing. He continues to grope my backside. I still say nothing. No laugh, no encouragement. He thinks he's on a streak.

"God, it must be nice to be beautiful, huh? I mean I know I'm nice to look at, but beautiful women like you, you could have any man in here, couldn't you?"

His hand lowers.

Hudson and Enzo curse over the comms.

My smile dies. I turn to him slowly. "Take your hand off me." My voice is measured, but lethal.

His grin slips. "Excuse me?"

"You heard me."

His fingers tighten instead, digging into my ass.

Something in me snaps. Not loud, not messy. Clean.

I grab the arm on my ass and squeeze his wrist as I remove it. I squeeze—hard—placing his arm at his side and making sure he can't pull away.

"Listen to me. Being in this room has confused you. You think it means you matter. It doesn't. Men like you mistake tolerance for interest. You mistake entitlement for attraction and money for worth. No matter how high you climb, you will still be nothing. You don't intimidate me. You bore me. Touch me or any woman like that again, and I will make sure everyone here knows exactly what you are. Understand?"

His face reddens. "You think you can talk to me like that? I can end your career."

I step closer and flash him a lethal smile. "Go for it."

I cross the ballroom toward the corridor of single-stall restrooms. The bathroom is marble and mirrors and blessedly empty.

I brace my hands on the sink and breathe.

I did it.

It's over.

I look myself in the eye in the mirror and smile. *I'm proud of you, Catherine.*

Knock, knock.

My head whips toward the sound.

Through the comms, Hudson whispers it's him.

When I open the door, he slips in, locking it behind him. He pulls me into a hug. "You good?" he asks quietly.

I look up at him. Really look. And I start laughing. It bubbles out of me, shaky and bright and real. Tears well in my eyes. "I did it," I say. "I *actually* did it."

Hudson beams with pride. "Fuck yeah you did. I'm so proud of you."

"I'm proud of me, too."

He gives me a soft, tender kiss. Nothing steamy. Just care and something that feels a lot like adoration. Or maybe...*love*?

I wouldn't really know what a kiss or hug shared with love feels like, but as I stand in Hudson's arms, I feel cherished and safe.

He caresses my face and tells me I should head to the van soon. I agree. We embrace one more time and exit the bathroom one at a time.

Back in the ballroom, the energy has shifted. It's louder now —sharper.

I make my way to the bar and ask the bartender for club soda with lime, needing something cold and bubbly. The bartender delivers my drink, and Eva speaks over the comms.

"Pippa, I think Junior is heading to the bar—"

My skin prickles. I freeze as if my body knows I'm next to him again for the first time in fifteen years. My mind catches up when our eyes meet.

His widen.

My pulse spikes, but I don't flinch. Don't show signs of recognition. Years of practice, training, and self-preservation instinct activate. I won't give myself or my sisters away. I lift my glass to my lips to partially obscure my face.

I give him a small, polite smile, but nothing more than I'd give any stranger.

His shock is apparent as he stands less than six feet from me. The bartender asks him for his order, but his attention is locked in on me. He takes a slow, small step toward me. "Catherine?"

"Excuse me?"

His jaw tightens. "It's you."

As if on cue, Jax appears at Junior's side—a tall wall of a man now blocking Junior's view of me.

"Good evening," Jax says.

It takes a moment for Junior to realize Jax is speaking to him. He shakes his head to turn his attention to the imposing and lethal law enforcement officer next to him.

"You Junior Volkov?"

Junior calmly shakes his head, feigning confusion. "No."

"You sure about that?" Jax asks in a menacing, low tone.

I can't see Junior, but I see the shift as he lifts his hand to shake cordially. "Michael Grant. And you are?"

"I'm on security detail for the President tonight."

"Ah, well, if you'll excuse me, my date is waiting for me." With that, Junior turns and walks directly to the building exit.

Jax and I make eye contact. He's assessing me. I'm trying to decipher what Jules could have said to get him over here. I heard commotion over the channel when Junior was approaching, but I'd tuned it out. Now I wish I hadn't.

He gives me a polite, tight-lipped smile and simply walks away.

That works for me.

With my drink in hand, I scan the ballroom again. Jake is talking to Cramden—undoubtedly tattling on me—or sucking up to the senator. *Or both.*

I'm so ready to be out of here.

Thud.

Several shrill screams rise above the din.

Chaos erupts in the ballroom. All attention focused on the center of the room. On the collapsed President.

Secret Service rushes forward, moving people out of the way.

Medics and ambulances are called.

Whispers. Gasps. Tears.

Men of power fail to take charge, standing by in shock.

A gurney is wheeled in by a team of medics a few moments later. The crowd parts for them and I watch as they put President Magnus Troy onto the stretcher.

He is unconscious.

It worked.

I did it.

I turn on my heel, and I leave the ballroom through the southeast corner. Walking briskly, I make my way directly to Enzo and Eva. Two quick blocks later, I rap on the sliding door.

Enzo opens it and pulls me into his arms.

Where Hudson brings me a safety that feels like gentleness and comfort, Enzo's safety is menacing and unyielding. He'd burn down the world for those he loves.

Little by little, I think I might become one of those people.

He pulls back and takes in the calm, cool, and collected woman in front of him—no mask, no role—the real me. The *whole* me.

A small smile dances across his lips. "You did it," he whispers.

I simply smile back. I'm at a loss for words.

"Fuck, Pippa. How do you feel?" Eva asks from her seat farther inside the van.

I give Eva a huge smile. "Fucking amazing."

She approaches and pulls me in for a hug, too. I know she's glad this is over for me, too.

I take a deep breath. "That was definitely Junior. He clocked me."

"We know," Enzo replies. "We'll deal with that later."

"Are you sure you don't want—" I start.

"*I'm sure,*" Enzo replies. "Tonight isn't about him. It's about you."

The weight of a million memories, scars, and painful regrets are lifted. I feel…I feel ready.

Ready for a new chapter.

TWENTY-EIGHT

imminent

Hudson

Friday Morning, Day 37

By the time I badge into the Hoover Building the next morning, Troy is dead in every possible sense. Dead overnight. Dead on the news. Dead in the mouths of analysts who never met him and anchors polishing the word "legacy" like it doesn't make them choke.

The media repeatedly shows him carted out of the gala on a gurney, and I relish it, knowing he'd hate looking weak and vulnerable.

The lobby hums with urgency. Agents move faster than usual, voices clipped, eyes sharp. All hands on deck. The chaos brings my body to life, and I try to hide the smile that lives inside of my chest.

Last night, Enzo took Pippa back to her place after the gala and her victory. I joined them a few hours later when my official FBI duties were complete—duties that I want to be permanently complete someday soon.

We showered Pippa in effusive praise as we literally washed the night off our skin and collapsed into bed. Hugs, kisses, cuddling, talking. Nothing more, nothing less.

She shared a bit more about her past last night and that seeing him face to face sent her into a flashback. That gutted me. It's time for that bitch Sophie to pay her fucking penance.

It took everything in me to leave today for work. I didn't want to leave the comfort of Pippa and Enzo's bodies—didn't want her to be alone after such a huge takedown.

Enzo had to leave before me. His phone was blowing up after the world caught wind of Troy's death. His clients are freaking the fuck out. He wouldn't have left Pippa's bed for just anyone; Jonathan Vale wanted an in-person meeting. Pippa and I agreed we still needed access to him until Sophie resurfaced. Enzo was tasked with pressing Vale with some questions.

Eva is spending time processing the audio logs of Vale's bug to see what we can find on Sophie or "Michael Grant"—aka Junior.

Fuck, I really don't like the idea of Pippa home alone today. She insisted she was okay and she looked it. Relaxed, content, light. I just have to trust she wasn't lying, but I would much rather be with her right now.

My burner vibrates before I reach my desk. It's a thread Jules started this morning to ask whether Pippa was actually okay.

JULES

She really didn't want to go to the mansion?

LUNA

Can we force her?

ENZO

I tried.

EVA

I bribed her with food.

You all know Pippa can't be forced to do anything.

JULES

I know, but I don't want her alone.

ENZO

I have men stationed outside.

LUNA

It's not the outside world I'm worried about.

There is a pause in the chain. I look across the bull pen at Luna's desk, but she is not there. She got in earlier than I did. I can only imagine all the rooms she's being pulled into today.

ENZO

I can have Luca drive Eva over to Pippa's later.

We have to trust her. Pippa said she's okay. She wanted a day to rest and sleep and she's more than earned that. She'll reach out if she needs us.

I may be the temporary voice of reason, but it comforts me to know my girl has so many people that look out for her.

A few hours of emails, calls, and meetings pass. Luna and I shared glances across the room once, as she was passing from one meeting to the next, but nothing more, yet. I stand to go grab lunch when my phone rings. Director Marsden. I pick up right away.

"Director."

"Cross, I just spoke to Novak."

"Yeah?"

"His lead on Sophie Delacroix is getting hotter."

"That's great," I say. And I mean it.

"You'll never believe who he spotted at the gala last night."

I pause as I prepare to pretend like I don't know what he's about to say. There was a time when a Junior Volkov sighting would have been the biggest reveal to Enzo, Eva, and me. It would have halted everything until we had him. But now, there are more important things going on around us.

"Who, sir?" I ask.

"Konstantin Volkov—Junior."

"Wait. What? I was there last night. Is he sure?" *Seriously, I should have been an actor.*

"Yeah. He had a hunch and asked one of our contracted security members to put a tracker on him. The mark ended up at the Volkov estate."

"Well, shit. Why would he have been at the gala?" I ask, genuinely curious about his answer.

"I want to know the same thing. He was there with Lily Blackwell under the alias Michael Grant."

"Damn." I sigh.

"I have Steele running his alias and digging into Blackwell. I told Novak to bring you in just this morning. I want all my best on this—I want to be the team that finally brings Sophie Delacroix in. Understood?"

"Yes, sir."

"Good. Novak will swing by later today."

"Sounds good, sir."

This is a good development. I have a feeling that Luna, Jax, and me working together on-book—and Luna and I working with our team off-book—might finally lead us to finding her. I can feel it in my gut.

I walk toward the cafeteria, stomach grumbling, when Luna catches me in the hall by the elevators.

"Marsden ask you to join Novak's taskforce yet?" she asks.

I confirm that he did.

"I feel good about this." She seems on edge, but not in a good way.

"You okay?" I ask. I need to know where this energy is coming from.

She shakes her head yes, looks around, and simply says, "It's just a lot."

I agree. We stand there for a moment, letting it all settle.

"They're reporting services will be in two days," she says.

"That's what I heard."

"TruthDrop could be a bit more aggressive this time," she whispers.

This time I look around. I tell her to join me on the elevator. We manage to catch one just the two of us. I use my de-bugging app to quickly make sure there are no hot mics before telling her to spill.

"Eva and I were brainstorming, and we think we can not only drop the unredacted Whiteman files about Maribel Island—"

"You have those?"

She gives me an incredulous look. "I've had them the whole time."

I chuckle and shake my head. *This fucking girl.*

"Anyway, I think we can hack into the news outlets, too—TV, radio, social—make sure they don't air the funeral. We are working on video content we can play on a loop instead. One that shows the world the truth about Whiteman, Troy, McCarter, Malin, Sophie, Volkov—all of them."

Ping.

The elevator lands on the cafeteria level, but I'm in a bit of a daze at the magnitude of her suggestion.

Luna pulls me by the arm out of the elevator, toward the cafeteria.

I release a slow breath. "Wow. That's. Shit. Yeah. I like it."

"Me too." She smiles faintly. "They don't get to mourn a lie. If the cameras are on, the truth is on, too. And we'll keep the media override for at least seventy-two hours. Ignorance is a choice the public will no longer have."

A huge smile takes over my face. "It's fucking perfect. You and Eva came up with this?"

Her smile is confirmation. A swell of pride rises in my chest. I'm so proud of all of them—all of them. The three sisters who survived hell teamed up with my chosen family, doing the work people in power haven't had the courage to do.

I really fucking like it.

Jax rounds the corner, so quickly he almost doesn't notice us.

"Steele, there you are. I need you. That lead on Sophie just expanded, but I want confirmation before I run it up the chain."

Before they turn to leave Jax says, "Heard you might be joining the task force."

"Marsden said there's overlap," I say easily. "You spotted Volkov last night?"

"Yeah," Jax says, a bit of reluctance in his shoulders, "he looked familiar." The lie rolls off his tongue like honey. I know exactly who helped him track Junior and it's a rush. "I had to pull in Sinclair from Redline. Needed her tracker tech. It worked. Pinged back to the Volkov estate."

I nod and look impressed, like this is news I'm still digesting.

"There's more." He turns to Luna. "We picked up a conversation off a West Coast bug. This DeShawn Crown party next week —Sophie's name came up, which we knew—but they also mentioned a Michael, and Volkov's alias is 'Michael Grant.' Sounded like they're arriving *together*."

Shit, that's actually fucking wild.

"Any thoughts on how Volkov has been coming and going all these years undetected?" I ask, genuinely curious.

"Not, yet. But now that we have an alias, I'm going to lean on Steele here to do her magic."

"Well, she's the one for the job, that's for sure. The rest of my team and I will support your investigation however we can."

Jax nods, then walks off, already dialing someone.

Luna is fast on his heels. Ready to use her skills to finally find Sophie—a culmination of meticulous planning and execution. She and her sisters planned for her FBI access to lead her to this one day. Three masterminds who planned so far in advance, no one would ever see them coming.

Not for their own glory. Not only for revenge, either.

No. They've worked in the shadows for over a decade because no one was doing a damned thing to stop these predators in power. And they knew no one ever would.

And somewhere between grief and justice, they have ensured that the sins of these pedophiles are collected in full.

TWENTY-NINE

profess

Enzo

Friday Evening, Day 37

I spent the entire day itching to get back to Pippa. Meetings stretched longer than they needed, fires popped up out of nowhere that only I could put out. Each hour, another small irritation surfaced—another reminder I wasn't where I wanted to be.

As I enter Pippa's apartment, I breathe deeply. It smells like tea and clean laundry and something baked. Vanilla, maybe?

Comfort, distilled.

She is curled up on the couch in leggings and an oversized sweater, cozy socks, hair loose, cascading down her back. No armor. She's never looked so at ease.

Beautiful. *Bella*.

She gave Hudson and me the code to the building and a key each this morning before we left. It feels like coming home. She looks up from the couch, unfazed, a smile on her face.

I'm unable to wait another minute to have her in my arms.

After texting her entirely too many times today, I wasn't sure if she would be annoyed when I arrived, but she rises from the couch and embraces me as enthusiastically as I embrace her.

"You look great, *bella*."

"I *feel* great," she whispers.

I pull back and look down at her face. I take her face in my hands, rub my thumb across her cheek, staring into her eyes. She looks rested and content. She reaches up and gives me a soft kiss.

"I made cookies."

"What kind?"

"Italian lemon cookies," she says with a mischievous grin.

I groan. "Those are my favorite."

"I know." Her smile stretches. "Eva told me."

"She did?" I ask, surprised. "I'll have to thank her. I had no idea you baked."

"Oh, I don't." she laughs. "But I found a popular recipe online and it seemed simple enough. Baking and chemistry have a lot in common."

I chuckle. "I believe that."

"Don't worry, I tested a few and they're not poisonous."

"If you're telling me my little chemist mastered lemon cookies on your first go, I may put you to work in the kitchen with Marco." I squeeze her hips.

A key turns in the front door lock with a *click*.

Hudson drops his keys in the bowl by the door like he's done it a million times. I watch the casualness of the motion and feel something settle in my chest—belonging.

"How're you feeling?" Hudson crosses the room.

"Tired," she admits, "but okay."

I kiss her temple and then pass her to Hudson so they can embrace. She leans into him without thinking, like her body already knows this is safe. We fall into place easily. Hudson on one side, me on the other.

I tell Hudson that Pippa made lemon cookies. He's even more excited than me.

I plant a kiss on him, as well. His enthusiasm over these simple pleasures draws me to him like a moth to a flame.

"I quit today," Pippa says suddenly.

Hudson blinks. "You *what?*"

She huffs a laugh. "Cramden called, angry I wasn't at work. Said Jake complained to him about my 'behavior' last night. Apparently, I was rude and embarrassed him. Poor little guy."

My jaw tightens.

"I told Cramden exactly what kind of man Jake is. Then, I told him I wasn't going to work for someone who protects that kind of behavior. And I hung up."

Hudson exhales. "Good."

I echo him. "Good."

Pippa retrieves the cookies and we make ourselves drinks before moving to the larger couch together. Pippa is situated in the middle.

I take one bite of a cookie and moan loudly.

Hudson does the same, adding curses under his breath, very him.

"Boys. Those noises are doing things to me, stop." She laughs.

I stare at her with desire.

Pippa teasingly waves me off. She really is lighter.

I didn't know what I'd come home to today, but I didn't expect this. She looks happier than I've ever seen her—no mask, no armor, no pretense, no need for the fire or fight that I've come to expect from her.

"Do you plan to do more baking with your free time?" Hudson asks as he grabs his third cookie.

"Enzo thinks I should work with Marco," she reports.

We all laugh at Hudson's enthusiastic support of that idea.

"Eva and I were texting," she says.

Hudson and I exchange a glance at that. *My sister and my girl getting closer. I love it.*

"I think I want to go to medical school and work at a women's clinic, helping victims—something like that. Eva was helping me research programs and clinics. She was really supportive." Her smile is easy. A beat passes before she adds, "Or I *could* just rest—for, like, the first time in my life. But that kind of feels illegal."

Hudson smiles. "You've earned rest."

"I know." She glances between us. "I just don't know how yet."

"You'll learn," I say. "We'll help you rest. *And* we'll help you do whatever you want to do next. Not that you need our help…"

"I might not need your help, but I appreciate the support. Going back to school in my thirties seems like a bit much, but I was looking at the MCAT material this afternoon and I think it could be—" she trails off.

"Great! It'd be fucking amazing, Pippa," Hudson says, wrapping his arm around her and kissing her cheek.

"You'll make a *great* doctor," I add, kissing her other cheek.

She blushes at the praise. I lock that away. Not much makes Pippa Saint James blush, but something tells me she hasn't received nearly the praise in life she deserves. That changes today.

Hudson shifts and I sense a topic change. "Marsden officially put me on the task force with Jax. I'll be helping him and Luna find Sophie."

Pippa's eyes widen. "That's…*good*."

"It is," he says. "I don't want Luna running that alone—not with that asshole Volkov involved."

"Thank you," she says.

"Of course," he whispers.

"But I thought you wanted to quit soon," she says.

"I'll give my notice after that bitch Sophie is dead or behind bars."

I inform them about my meeting with Vale. He seemed antsy and frazzled at our meeting. Troy's death rattled him more than I expected for a man of his power and prestige. He mentioned California and two other clients called to tell me they'd be in California next week, too.

We all agree that something big will be going down in Hollywood in one week's time.

"I wonder if any of Jules's clients might be heading West, too."

Pippa furrows her brow, unsure. "We'll ask her tomorrow."

There's a pause. A quiet one that holds weight and takes up space.

We just closed one huge chapter for Pippa and her sisters, but we know threats still lurk around every corner. No matter how much we each want to step away, we have to stay in this until everyone we care about is safe.

"I talked to Eva," I begin again.

They both look at me expectantly.

"She's supportive. About—About my stepping away from the family business. She agreed Niko and Luca are ready," I continue. "They'll step up, take over, and still provide our family with protection. I'm going to talk to them tomorrow—once Niko's back from Virginia."

Hudson's eyes soften. "You sure?"

"I am." And I mean it. "I can't do this forever. I don't want to. Besides, I can keep the real estate holdings. They'll keep me plenty busy."

Pippa reaches for my hand and squeezes. "We'll help you. All of us."

"I know."

We talk logistics then—six months, maybe a year—but Sophie's demise comes first.

Hudson grabs Pippa's hand, pulling her closer to him on the couch.

She snuggles into him.

I lean back on the opposite arm of the couch, taking them both in. They are gorgeous.

Together, separately—just stunning. And I can't believe they're mine.

The thought comes fully formed, terrifying and simple: "Move in with me."

They both still.

"There's plenty of space. Room to breathe. Room to plan. It's safe. I know both of your apartments are safe, but I—I just—" I take a breath. "I want you both with me. All the time. I don't want to be apart more than when necessary."

Pippa swallows.

Hudson doesn't look away from me. His eyes are shimmering. "You're sure?"

"Yes."

A beat.

Pippa sits straighter. "I think that makes sense for the two of you. Definitely. I mean Hudson would probably already be living there if it weren't for his work at the FBI. And I appreciate you including me, but—"

"But what?" I challenge.

"It's…it's so, fast. I mean, Enzo, you and I were at each other's throats a week ago."

"I barely remember that," I say with a small smile.

Hudson grabs her hand again. "Pip, do you think Enzo and I aren't as committed to you as we are to each other?"

She looks at him for a long moment, then back to me. She takes a long, slow, inhale. "It's not that. Not really. I mean, maybe a little. I'll never have the shared history you two have. But that's not what bothers me."

"Then what is it?" I ask.

"I just never pictured myself…*settled.* Domestic? Me? It seems—"

Hudson laughs a deep, belly laugh. It causes me to laugh a little and even Pippa cracks a big smile.

"What's so funny?" she asks, clearly knowing the answer already.

"No one can domesticate you, baby, but I get it. If you would have asked me a few weeks ago if Enzo and I—" He starts laughing again. "*Fuck.* I was convinced my whole life that this would never happen." He gestures between him and me. "I've spent half my life pretending to be someone I'm not. I never considered I could…have any of this. You're not the only one feeling off kilter here." He throws a wide grin my way. "Things are definitely moving fast."

I'm worried he's going to say we should slow down, that we should take it one step at a time—something reasonable.

Instead, he says, "But it feels so fucking right. Doesn't it? I agree with Enzo. I want to spend as much time as I can with both of you."

I move closer to them both and place my hand on their already-clasped hands. "I love you, Hudson."

He reaches across Pippa with his other hand to touch my face. He tells me he loves me, too, and gives me a tender kiss.

I turn to Pippa. "I know it's soon, you're right, but I'm with Hudson on this. I'm done questioning myself, my feelings, my wants. I love you and I want you in my home, my bed. I want you to make my house a home."

"You…love me?" Pippa asks, voice barely above a whisper.

I swallow and nod yes. I do. I love her. "Pippa, I'll never be able to quit you. I need you and yes, I love you," I confess. Then I lean in and give her a soft, gentle kiss.

When I pull back, her cheeks are flushed and emotion swirls in her eyes.

Hudson turns her face slowly to his with one finger beneath her jaw. He touches his nose to hers. "Janey, you're impossible not to love."

Her breath hitches.

"Shit, I was obsessed with you before I truly knew you. And everything I've learned about you since has only made my addiction grow. You're strong. You're smart as hell. You protect the people you love without thinking twice. You care, even when it costs you. You fight. And you don't quit. What's not to love?"

A small tear rolls down her cheek as Hudson plants a tender kiss on her lips. I rub the tear away with my thumb. She turns to me and I plant another small kiss on her, too.

Yeah, my girl needs more praise.

"This is crazy," she whispers. "First, I don't cry." She wipes her other cheek. "Second, I'm not a big fan of men."

That makes us all laugh.

"I mean it," she says. "Men are the *worst*."

"You won't get an argument from us," Hudson says with that charming smile of his.

"Eva has always made sure we knew exactly how badly men have ruined everything. Don't worry, we are well aware."

"I knew I liked her," she chuckles. "Speaking of, should you talk to Eva about us moving in?"

I shake my head. "She'll be so excited. The house is too big for just us two. She's wanted Hudson there for years and she loves you. She'll be thrilled."

There is a moment of silence as I see the wheels turn in Pippa's brain.

"Okay," Pippa finally says.

My whole body lights up. "Okay?"

She smiles. "Yeah, let's do it."

We exchange celebratory kisses and a few laughs.

After a moment, Pippa gets serious again and takes our hands,

"I've never been in love. I never experienced love as a kid, but I know I'm capable of it because I love Jules and Luna fiercely—with all I have. The bond I've felt with you both these past couple weeks… After Hudson was shot"—she turns looks at him, then back to me— "and I thought you didn't want anything to do with me…it hurt. I felt the loss of you both and it nearly wrecked me." She sighs. "When we told you the truth, I just—I never thought we'd tell anyone those truths. I know that if I can trust you with that… If the truth didn't push you away, then, yeah…I can trust you enough to give you my heart.

"I've seen how you love. Your love and protectiveness for Eva, for each other. I recognize qualities I have and want in that. So—" She nods like she's made a decision. "Yeah, I love you both. I trust you, I care about you, I want you to be safe and happy, I want to protect you, I want to be protected by you…and that's what love means to me. I love you."

"*Thank fuck*," Hudson says, taking her mouth in a searing kiss. They chuckle as they break the kiss.

When it's my turn, I lean in and give her a slow, sensual kiss. When she deepens the kiss, the heat rises and she lets out a small moan.

I kiss down Pippa's neck and move my hand up Hudson's thigh. "Let's take this into the bedroom," I say in a low voice.

We are off the couch and moving to the bedroom, limbs touching, hands roaming until we're standing next to Pippa's bed. Mine and Hudson's shirts are unbuttoned; her sweater is removed. We are taking turns kissing, putting lips on mouths, necks, chests.

"Enzo, it's time," Hudson says. "I want you to fuck me."

My half-hard cock turns to steel in an instant. I take a deep breath. "Are you sure?"

"Fuck yeah. I can't wait any longer. Please, Enz." He pulls me into a deep kiss.

Pippa rubs our cocks over our pants. "I've been wanting to see this for days now. I'll get the lube."

"Fuck, I almost forgot—" I say, breaking our kiss. "I heard from Doc today. Results were clean on all of us." The night Pippa was drugged, she wanted STD tests run just in case. Hudson and I agreed to do the same.

"So, fuck, we can skip the condoms? I'm going to come just thinking about it," Hudson groans.

"Are you okay with that, Pippa?" I ask.

She tilts her head, seductive and assured, confirming that she is very okay with that.

Hudson undoes his pants, then mine. My eyes roam his body as I lick my lips.

"Pippa, take off your clothes and get on the bed," I command.

She complies like the sexy little vixen she is.

"Hudson, on your hands and knees in front of her. I want you to service our woman while I get your ass ready."

Hudson curses under his breath and moves into position. He and I have discussed our shared desire to explore every possible position together—I want to take him, he wants to take me, I want to be taken by him—I want to try it all. We are taking things one step at a time, enjoying the discovery of what works for us. I'm so ready to take this next step with him.

Pippa is in ecstasy as he feasts on her.

Hudson uses some lube so he can have his fingers in her cunt and her ass. Her moans and the sight of the two of them have me almost ready to explode.

I begin to explore his rim. I apply a generous amount of lube before my first finger enters him. He lets out a loud moan. I use my other hand to cup his balls and squeeze a bit—I've learned he likes this.

"Shit, fuck, I might come," he says.

He and Pippa are so responsive, it makes me feel like I've been at this for years. They've been building my confidence while I learn about their bodies and my own. I put a second finger inside and move my fingers in a circular motion to stretch and loosen him. He's so tight, I really don't know how I'll fit. Just the idea of squeezing me into his tight hole...*goddamn*, I'm leaking just thinking about it.

"You ready, pretty boy?" I grunt out.

He nods his head, saying he is very ready.

Pippa props herself up on her elbows to watch. One thing I've learned about my girl is that she really does love to watch us. It turns her on so much.

"Hudson, once I fit my cock into your tight ass, Pippa is going to get beneath you and you're going to take her. I want to feel you as you wreck our girl. You got it?"

They both moan their approval.

I position myself behind him on the bed and begin to enter him. When my head pushes past the resistance, we both cry out our pleasure. He feels so fucking good.

"Damn it, Hudson. You're so fucking tight. I—Fuck, this is not going to last long," I say, panting.

I work myself in and out slowly, gaining slow inches. We are both panting and sweating and cursing.

"You feel amazing, Enz...you're so big. Jesus Christ, I'm so fucking full. I can't—I'm not going to last long either."

Pippa is so turned on watching us. She's pulling at her breasts, licking her lips, ready.

"Then get inside our girl."

Pippa moves into position, using a pillow to raise her hips higher.

Once I'm fully buried inside him, Hudson positions her. He pushes her knees up to her chest, then he plunges inside her in one deep thrust. I feel every inch of his pleasure as his ass tightens around me like a vice.

A few stilted moves and several cuss words later, we find a rhythm and it feels *so fucking good.*

"Enzo, I can…fuck, I can feel every movement you make through Hudson. This feels—Fuck. His piercings. I'm going to come so fucking hard," Pippa says, breathing heavy.

"How does she feel bare?" I whisper into Hudson's ear.

"Fucking heaven," he grunts.

I have one arm wrapped around Hudson's chest as I ram into him. I use my other to reach down to rub Pippa's clit. A moment later, she screams in ecstasy. The sound causes me to explode inside Hudson. He follows me over the edge a moment later.

We collapse on either side of Pippa, spent, sated. Pippa showers us with kisses and praise and caresses.

I pull myself up to get warm washcloths for all of us. We clean up and climb under the covers, wrap ourselves around each other, tangled.

Sleep claims us quickly.

For the first time in a very long time, the future doesn't feel like something to survive.

It feels like something we get to choose.

Something we get to create.

Together.

THIRTY

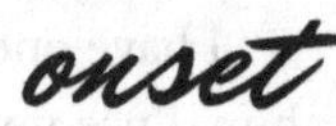

Pippa

Sunday Morning, Day 39

The weekend settles over the mansion like a deep exhale. Morning light pours through the tall windows of Enzo's bedroom, gilding everything it touches.

Or—I guess I should call this *our* bedroom now.

We moved fast. Literally and figuratively.

Hudson and I will still keep our properties in the city, but we packed the belongings we needed over the past few days and made it official.

We've moved in together in the quiet, intimate ways that matter most. Clothes migrating into shared drawers. Toothbrushes multiplying on the sink counter. Late nights tangled on the couch. Mornings waking wrapped in warmth and certainty.

I look over at the two of them as they sleep. Hudson's hand rests absentmindedly in the curve of Enzo's shoulder. My eyes sweep over to the beautiful and masculine arch of Hudson's neck as his head rests on my shoulder.

I take in a deep breath and I feel...*happy*. No longer alone in a world that seeks to destroy. Claimed by two men who love and protect as fiercely as I do.

Love—steady and unafraid.

I feel whole.

Hudson stirs. A few chaste kisses later, Enzo joins the morning wake up call. Kisses, I love yous, reverent touches, and daily plans discussed.

We've invited Luna and Jules over, and we agree to rise and get ready before things get carried away. I get out of bed and shoot off a quick message.

Looking forward to seeing you both today. 11 still work?

JULES

Yes. Wrapping up a few things at the office and leaving soon.

LUNA

Same.

I feel a little guilty. I stepped away from DC with a simple phone call, but they are still locked into everything that is going on with the mess of Troy's death, the media take over, and the lead on Sophie. We've kept each other up to speed the last couple of days about the plan for this upcoming party at DeShawn Crown's place. Eva, Enzo, and Niko have been helping out, even.

Meanwhile, I've been packing, unpacking, sleeping, baking, and having an extensive amount of sex. Actually, no. I don't feel bad at all.

If they need my help, they'll ask.

Luna and Jules have been nothing but happy for me. They are

glad I'm taking this time to recoup and nest. Everyone is supportive of our goals to all step away later this year.

I identified a local medical school and even talked to Doc. She was so great with me the night she treated me. She was very encouraging of my plan and even offered to let me shadow her and her team. I'm excited.

An hour later, Enzo is at the stove, sleeves rolled up, hair slightly damp from his shower. He felt like cooking today. I didn't even know he knew how to cook—I assumed Marco had been cooking for them since birth.

I like that our relationship is solid enough to all live together, but still new enough to discover each other. And I'm very drawn to this domestic side of Enzo.

Hudson sits at the island with his tablet, pretending to read something while watching Enzo with that soft, private look he never bothers hiding anymore.

We catch each other's gaze and exchange a knowing look. *Our man is fucking hot.*

Eva came to the kitchen around the same time we did. She's perched on a stool next to Hudson with a mug between her hands, hair pulled into a loose knot. She catches my eye and smiles. Real, unguarded. It still hits me how far we've come, from suspicion and fear to this new normal. She rolls her eyes and teases Hudson when she catches him ogling Enzo. It's sweet.

"Niko just texted, Jules is here," Enzo announces while flipping something that smells like heaven.

Jules steps into the kitchen, expression sharp and familiar and comforting all at once. Her gaze lands on me. "Look at you," she says softly. "You look...peaceful."

I smile because I am. The word fits so perfectly it almost makes my chest ache.

Hudson pours her a mug of coffee, and I steal a few minutes alone with her near the windows while Enzo finishes. Jules leans against the windowsill, arms crossed loosely, eyes studying me in that way she has since we were girls, like she's checking for cracks.

"I'm good," I tell her before she can ask. "Really good."

She nods, relief easing the tension around her mouth. "I can see it. I'm happy for you."

"Thanks, Jules. And you?" I ask gently. "You haven't shared much about Jax. How's it going working with him again?"

Her mouth doesn't quite form a smile. "Complicated," she answers honestly.

We share a quiet moment of understanding. Her calm, steady energy is great in a pinch or under pressure, but in moments like this, when she's contemplative and guarded, I want to push her. Force her to let me in. That's my nature, but I've learned over the years, it's not hers. She'll tell me when she's ready—she knows I'm here for her.

Enzo announces the food is ready and we all move to the dining room. Hudson slides into the seat beside me. Jules sits across from me. Enzo sets plates down and Eva moves to the table with a graceful confidence I have come to admire. Everyone settles in, and the hum of domestic normalcy wraps around us.

I love it. I love sharing normal, everyday things with the people I care about. It feels suspiciously like family. I never had that. I never thought I'd find it, but somehow it found me.

We are laughing and chatting for a few minutes when Eva says, "The heat is officially off me for TruthDrop."

"That's great news," I say. "How did that happen?"

"With the complete media takeover, they are now pointing fingers to an inside job. The general public believe TruthDrop must be a group of disgruntled government employees who have reach and access to do something at this scale.

"Ironic how when I *actually* join the effort and make a bigger splash, no one thinks I have the access to pull this off." She rolls her eyes in faux annoyance, but I know she feels relieved.

"I'm just glad you're not in danger anymore," Enzo says.

Eva scoffs, reminding him that any of us can be in danger at any time.

I chuckle at the sibling banter.

"I'm really impressed," Jules says. "You and Luna working together is…powerful. Troy's funeral came and went and not a single news outlet was able to cover it live and once they got back on air, the narrative shifted to TruthDrop, trafficking rings, and government failures. It's brilliant."

"That man didn't deserve fanfare and now the world knows it," Enzo says with finality.

I love that we can all talk shop around the table, easy and normal. Everyone an open book, no more secrets.

When I catch the time on the clock above the stove, I see more time has passed than I realized. It's strange that Luna isn't here yet. She's hardly late and always reaches out if she's running behind.

"Anyone hear from Luna?" I look around the table, then check my phone. Everyone shakes their head.

Eva shoots off a text. When Luna doesn't respond after a few minutes, the air grows heavy. This isn't like her.

Jules calls her, then reports, "She's not answering."

"Check her location," I instruct Eva. We've all been sharing our phone locations since the night of the gala.

"It has her at her house," Eva says slowly.

"Didn't she say she was at work?" Jules looks to me.

I nod.

"Why would she be at the office today?" Hudson asks.

"I don't know—I just assumed, but you and Jax aren't at the office today," she says. Hudson looks at his plate, deep in thought.

Eva tries calling Luna next, still no answer.

Hudson tries her work phone, since the rest of us are using the burner. He has no luck either.

"How did you guys find Pippa the night at the biker bar?" Eva finally asks.

"That's right," Enzo says. "You said it wasn't her phone, but we never came back to it."

Jules and I look at each other. "Sorry, guys. Yeah, it slipped our mind. It's not a secret." I look around the room, making eye contact with everyone, assuring them we aren't hiding anything. "I guess it just hasn't come up. When we started on this path and things grew increasingly dangerous, we needed a way to find each other that wasn't reliant on a phone or piece of tech," I explain. "The three of us have surgically implanted trackers at the base of our skulls, in our hairline. They are imperceptible, undetectable," I tell them, lifting my hair to show the spot mine is located.

"It's a GPS tracker that we can access from our devices or a browser," Jules says as she pulls out her phone to open the app Luna created for us.

"Okay, that's a little intense, but I get it. You three have always been so careful," Eva says. "So, what does hers say now? Where is she?"

Jules's face goes pale. She looks directly at me, her eyes wide.

My heart lurches. I stand immediately and go to Jules's side so I can see what our app says.

Eva, beginning to panic now, asks again, "Where is she?"

Everyone crowds around Jules's chair, looking at the phone.

"I'm not really sure," Jules says in a measured tone. "It's not HQ, it's not her place or the warehouse. She's on the outskirts. It looks like Embassy Row, maybe... *Shit...*"

Enzo's expression hardens. "That's the Volkov estate."

I look to him, then Hudson.

Hudson's gaze sharpens in recognition.

"Wh—Why would Luna be at the Volkov estate?" Eva asks.

"Jules and I are just as surprised as you, I promise."

Enzo and Hudson look nervous, but Eva is near panic.

Our phones vibrate at the same time. Jules and I both have a message from Luna.

Eva's pings a moment later.

My hands tremble as I open my phone to read it.

LUNA

I need to confront Junior. Alone. I found overlap in Malin's files and the bug we've been running on Vale. The Hollywood parties, Sophie…the FBI is looking in the wrong place. Please don't follow me. I need to do this on my own.

My heart seems to stop.

Jules gasps.

We lock eyes then look at Eva.

Her face crumbles as she reads her message. She sinks into the chair, tears welling, voice barely a whisper. "She says to please trust her."

Silence crashes around us.

Luna is gone. She's walking into the lion's den.

Alone.

She found something that she doesn't want us to know. Which can only mean that whatever she's walking into is bigger, darker, and far more dangerous than any of us were ready for.

We don't care what Luna says. She knows better than to think that we won't follow her into danger.

I take a deep breath. "Jules and I are going to Junior's."

TO BE CONTINUED…

sneak peak

WHAT TO EXPECT IN BOOK 2 OF THE INHERITED SIN SERIES... *RUIN.*

When the optimist breaks, the damage is catastrophic.

R*UIN* follows Luna, the heart of the sisters, as she confronts the cost of seeing the world as it is, not as she wishes it to be.

Her hacking uncovers an elite event unlike anything they've encountered before: a convergence of billionaire predators, all in one place. For the first time, Luna has the chance to take them all down at once.

As the plan takes shape, Luna is pulled in opposite directions. The boy she loved before everything fell apart reappears, reopening wounds she never fully healed. At the same time, her bond with Eva, a fellow hacker and the one person who truly sees her, deepens into something neither expected.

Book 2 explores love triangles, personal demons, and the

danger of hope. The stakes are higher, the consequences irreversible, and the fallout impossible to contain.

Because when the optimist breaks, she doesn't crack.

She ruins everything.

If Pippa, Hudson, and Enzo have permanently rewired your brain chemistry...*same.*

Before the bullets fly and the war begins, there's one explosive night inside the mansion you haven't seen yet. 🔥

Unlock exclusive bonus chapters featuring their first night living together. 👀

RoseVohs.com/bonus

author's note

I still can't quite believe I get to say this—but thank you for reading my debut novel. I'm deeply grateful you chose to spend your time in this world, with these characters who came to mean so much to me.

I wrote *RAGE* as an outlet for my own anger at the world. I grew up believing that if I did my part, if I voted, marched, volunteered, donated, spoke up, then good would eventually outweigh evil. I believed effort and intention were enough.

They aren't.

That lesson has been reinforced for me many times over the past decade, most painfully when I lost my mother to cancer in 2017. For two years, my family did everything "right." We believed that positivity, persistence, and hard work would be enough to save her. When it wasn't, I was forced to confront a truth I had managed to avoid for most of my life: The world is not fair and righteousness does not guarantee justice.

I don't have answers for how to fix that harsh truth. Instead, I created a fictional world where anger is not dismissed, where silence is not mistaken for consent, and where accountability exists even when the systems meant to provide it fail. This is ***not*** an endorsement of vigilante justice, but an exploration of the emotions that arise when justice feels unreachable.

More than anything, I hope this story offered you a sense of release. And I hope it reminded you that rage, especially when born of injustice, ***is not something to be ashamed of.***

I don't know the way forward, but I do believe this: Together, we are more powerful than we have ever been allowed to be. If we can find a way to harness that power, we can fix the systems that suppress us.

acknowledgments

RAGE started in January 2025 with my small but mighty writing group, alongside women who found each other on BookTok and wanted to start writing. Thank you Janene, Ashley, and Lauren for listening to my crazy ideas, supporting me when I had no idea what I was doing, and believing in me from the beginning.

Massive thanks to my alpha readers: Liana, Meagan, Janene, Erin. You've seen every iteration of this story—the good, the bad and the ugly! Your thoughts, insights, and feedback made it better every step of the way and I literally could not have done this without you.

Nicole, Nicole, Nicole. You're more than a cover artist or illustrator. You've become such a good friend. Thank you for reaching out to me and for believing in this story so much that you wanted to be a part of it. Thank you for putting up with my crazy long voice texts, indecision at times, and chaotic mess of a brain. You have been an absolute rock.

Lee!! You're basically a co-creator of the #vohsverse at this point. You care so much about this world, these characters, and my journey as an author. Thank you for the countless phone calls, texts, brainstorming sessions, and for listening to my middle-of-the-night rants. And we legit have you to blame for this new chapter in my life. If you don't introduce me to *Fourth Wing* in January of 2024, are we even here? No, no we're not. Thank you!!

Allison, Ashlyn, Claire, and the team at Golden Editorial... life savers. Literal life savers. Thank you. I was overwhelmed, confused, and often nervous. You held my hand and helped me along every step of this journey. You answered my hundreds of questions and guided me confidently through every element of publishing that I knew nothing about. I could not have done this without you!

I'm so blessed that my closest friends and family have been so supportive. Every time I shyly shared that I was writing a book, I was met with enthusiasm, curiosity, and unabashed support. Every interaction fueled me and helped me to keep going. There are too many of you to name, because I am truly that lucky...but you know who you are. I don't know how I got so lucky, but thank you from the bottom of my heart.

And to my husband, Anthony. When I told you I wanted to start writing, you were more excited and confident in me than I was in myself. You've been my biggest cheerleader and kept me sane when I was ready to give up. I wasn't sure I was going to tell our family and friends that I was writing a romance series... but you were! You told anyone who would listen. And without you, this journey wouldn't have been nearly as enjoyable. Thank you for always supporting my dreams.

And lastly, I wouldn't be who I am or where I am without my mom. Penny was my best friend and biggest supporter. It's hard to believe it's been nine years since she passed. I miss her every day. I know she'd be so proud of this new chapter in my life. My pen name and launch dates are in honor of her. Happy birthday in heaven, Mom, and thank you for everything you sacrificed so that I could be the strong woman I am today. As we always said—*miss you, love you.*

about the author

I consider myself an extroverted introvert. I love quality time with people I care about—I consider my friends to be my family—but need to rest for a week after most social interactions. I live in Upstate New York and I'm originally from Central Florida. I'm an eldest/only daughter, first-generation graduate, corporate girly, actor, writer, producer, entrepreneur, proud Aquarius, wife, and dog mom. I'm a bit chaotic, and I wouldn't have it any other way.

When I'm not writing, I'm probably devouring romance novels, posting bookish content on social media, watching true crime documentaries, baking something sweet, cuddling with my dogs, bantering with my hubby, or soaking in a long bath (because self-care is a core tenet of my life).

My life has been filled with adventure, risk, fun, love, loss, and every good and hard thing this world has to offer. I consider myself one lucky girl. Let's be book besties!

You can find me at rosevohs.com and on social media.

ROMANTIC SUSPENSE
where women don't run from danger—
they become it.

instagram.com/rosevohs
facebook.com/RoseVohsAuthor
tiktok.com/@rosevohs

www.ingramcontent.com/pod-product-compliance
Lightning Source LLC
LaVergne TN
LVHW031257150826
845672LV00009B/2516

* 9 7 9 8 9 9 5 6 8 8 2 0 4 *